YASMINE

GALENORN

D1565508

A SHADOW OF CROWS

A WILD HUNT
NOVEL

BOOK 4

A Nightqueen Enterprises LLC Publication

Published by Yasmine Galenorn
PO Box 2037, Kirkland WA 98083-2037
A SHADOW OF CROWS
A Wild Hunt Novel
Copyright © 2018 by Yasmine Galenorn
First Electronic Printing: 2018 Nightqueen Enter-
prises LLC
First Print Edition: 2018 Nightqueen Enterprises
Cover Art & Design: Ravven
Art Copyright: Yasmine Galenorn
Editor: Elizabeth Flynn

A Nightqueen Enterprises LLC Publication
Published in the United States of America

Acknowledgments

Welcome back into my world of the Wild Hunt. This series has taken full hold with me and the world is expanding in wonderful and mysterious ways. I'm envisioning more of Ember and Herne's world with each passing day and I'm so grateful that my readers have taken it into their hearts. I'm loving writing this like nothing else that I've written in a long, long time. I'm also planning to introduce a spinoff series, alongside the original, next year.

Thanks to my usual crew: Samwise, my husband, Andria and Jennifer—without their help, I'd be swamped. To the women who have helped me find my way in indie, you're all great, and to the Wild Hunt, which runs deep in my magick, as well as in my fiction.

Also, my love to my furbles, who keep me happy. And most reverent devotion to Mielikki, Tapio, Ukko, Rauni, and Brighid, my spiritual guardians and guides. And to the spirit of the Wild Hunt, Herne, and Cernunnos, who still rule the wild places of this world.

If you wish to reach me, you can find me through my website at Galenorn.com and be sure to sign up for my newsletter to keep updated on all my latest releases!

Brightest Blessings,
~The Painted Panther~
~Yasmine Galenorn~

Welcome to A Shadow of Crows

"We found him, yes. Viktor and I also found the three others who were missing." I wasn't sure how to tell her—or how much to tell her.

Raven stared at her hands, sitting still on the sofa. Her back was straight, so straight she looked like a statue. Her hands were on her knees, clutching at the velvet of her skirt. She sat frozen, barely breathing.

"He's dead, isn't he?"

I remembered that moment. That single moment when you know something is coming, and you know it's going to be bad, but it hasn't quite hit you yet. It's that moment when you prayed for something to interrupt, to turn the clock back ten minutes, or make time stop altogether, or for someone to wake you out of a nightmare. I had felt it when I found my parents' bodies. I felt it when I saw the back door was open and pushed it wide just enough to see the trail of blood. I had stood there, staring at the drops on the floor, wanting to step back outside, to return to five minutes before, when everything was normal.

I let her breathe another moment. I let her freeze time for just a little longer. Then I reached out and put my hand on top of hers.

"Yes, he's dead. Viktor and I found his body."

Chapter 1

I CROUCHED, ONE knee on the ground, as
I hid behind the huckleberry bush. As I waited
for Viktor's warning, I glanced up at the sky. The
clearing was open to the heavy cloud cover, and I
could smell the lightning as it churned overhead.
The storm hadn't broken yet, but I could feel it,
like a slow spiraling monster, waiting for the pre-
cise moment to let all hell break loose. We were
due for a big one—one of our November wind-
storms in September—but storm or not, we had
a job to do and Cernunnos had made it clear how
important it was.

I brought my focus back to the task at hand,
listening intently, trying to tune out the chanting
in the center of the clearing. A group of Light Fae
were there, surrounding a statue of Callan, one of
the ancient Fae warriors who had single-handedly
driven the Fomorians back during the first of the

Tuatha-Fomorian Wars, back in Annwn. Unfortunately, they weren't just here to honor him, but they were attempting to reach back through the mists of time to summon his spirit. And Cernunnos and Morgana had decided that would upset the balance, so we were here to stop it.

A low hooting of an owl echoed through the grove, then it called a second time, and a third.

Viktor's signal. It was time to move.

I slowly began to shift my weight, taking care not to make any noise. As the chanting grew to a crescendo, I darted around the huckleberry bushes. Directly opposite me, across the clearing, Herne appeared from behind a cedar. To my left, Yutani broke into the clearing, and to my right, Viktor appeared. We raced toward the group of Fae. The moment they saw us, they sprang into high gear, upping their pace as they desperately tried to finish their ritual. They knew who we were, so they didn't draw their weapons, but they *did* form a barrier between us and their priest.

I tackled the nearest one, rolling him to the ground. He put up a good fight, trying to keep me from breaking through. As I stared down into his face, he spit at me.

"*Tralaeth*," he said, sneering.

"Thanks, you just made this easier." I raised my fist and brought it down, smashing his nose. I felt a flicker of satisfaction as I felt the cartilage give way and break. As I pulled my hand away, he began to bleed heavily.

"Bitch."

"Aww, now you're sweet talking me? How lovely,

but sorry, snookums, I'm busy." I jumped up, giving him a not-so-gentle kick to roll him out of the way, and turned to the next one.

Viktor had already flung three of the Fae to the side—having a half-ogre on our side helped—and he was about to grab the next. Yutani had managed to take down two of them. Herne watched us, arching his eyebrows. Then, producing a scroll from his backpack, he held up the parchment, unrolling it. Once he had, he began to speak.

"By order of the Covenant, forged between Cernunnos, Lord of the Forest, Morgana, Goddess of the Fae, and the Dark and Light Courts of Fae, I order you to cease and desist your efforts. You are to stop, *now*." His voice echoed through the clearing.

The priest who was attempting to summon the spirit hesitated, looking like he might ignore the command, but when Herne took a step toward him, he stopped. Yutani grabbed the scroll out of the priest's hand and glanced at it.

"Almost through. We have to negate what he's done so far," the coyote shifter said. He frowned. "I'm not sure how. If we burn it, will it finish the spell or negate it?"

Herne clasped a hand on the priest's shoulder as the rest of the Light Fae moved to the side. "Tell us. *Now*."

The priest smiled, the corners of his lips turning up in a self-satisfied smug. "What if I don't?"

"Then I'll haul your ass in front of Névé and tell her you refused to cooperate with the Wild Hunt. You know how well that will go over, don't you?"

Herne's voice took on a gravelly edge and he glared at the man, looming over him.

The priest hesitated.

He'd better answer soon, I thought, *if he doesn't want the wrath of the gods on him.* When pushed, Herne was hell on hooves.

The priest stared at him for a moment, then cleared his throat. "Burn the scroll."

Herne motioned for Yutani to put the scroll on the center dais in front of the statue. As soon as Yutani had cleared out of the way, Herne stretched out his hand and wiggled his fingers. A flame flared from his hand, leaping to the scroll.

As the paper began to burn, the skies decided it was the perfect time to open up and drench us. But despite the downpour, the scroll continued to burn.

As the paper curled at the edges, I began to sense something that made me uneasy. The magick wasn't lessening. In fact, I felt it begin to grow stronger. I glanced over at the Fae whose nose I had bloodied and realized that he—and most of his companions—had edged out of the circle and they were taking off through the woods.

Viktor jerked around as the trees around us rustled and was about to go after them, but Herne shook his head.

"Let them go." He waited, staring at the scroll.

As it flared its last, there was a brilliant flash overhead as lightning forked through the sky, and thunder rolled along behind it. The next moment, the grove began to ripple with energy.

Crap, the fire hadn't cancelled the spell—it had

freed the magic to work!

"It finished the spell!"

But Herne seemed to realize what was happening at the same time as I had, because he lifted the priest in the air and slammed him to the ground.

"You fool! You dare to defy the edict of the Forest Lord?" Herne seemed to grow, though I realized it was his astral form taking shape, rising a good ten feet above his actual body. The priest suddenly seemed to realize what hell he had let himself in for and he fell to his knees in front of Herne.

"I'm sorry. Milord, please, forgive me—"

"Shut the fuck up." Herne raised his head, looking around the forest. "Where is the spirit now? What were you going to—" He paused as the statue at the back of the dais began to shift and morph.

As the rain drenched us, I gazed steadily at the statue, trying to pinpoint what was happening. Then I knew. The spell hadn't just summoned the spirit. It had given him form again. He was anchoring into the statue, which was shifting to life.

I darted forward, dagger raised, and Viktor and Yutani joined me. We couldn't allow the ancient Fae warrior to get free. Cernunnos had assured us that it would cause havoc in the world should the spirit be set free, leading to outright war between the Fomorian giants and the Fae, which would throw humans and everybody else right into the middle.

As the cloud of energy around statue began to swirl, I held my gaze steady. We had to return Callan to the past. I prayed that the bronze of the statue would shift into flesh. It was a lot easier to kill a creature of flesh and blood rather than a metal golem.

"Ember, are you ready?" Viktor asked.

"I hope so," I answered, holding my gaze firm. I was scared, yes, but Viktor was a half-ogre and he was strong. And Yutani was quick.

Herne slapped a pair of iron cuffs on the Fae priest, who began to scream from the pain, and tossed him to the ground, out of the way. "You'd better stay put, if you know what's good for you," he said to the man as he joined us.

As the energy swirled and finally settled, the statue—which was of a tall, lithe man who carried a massive sword—took on the color of flesh, the structure of bone and muscle. Another bolt of lightning flashed through the sky, illuminating the grove, and then as it died, the statue was suddenly a man, eyeing us keenly.

He said nothing, simply brought his sword to bear. I realized I was no match for him at this point. My dagger was for up close and personal encounters, not for jabbing at arm's length when a sword was holding me at bay. I broke off and darted to the side, intending to veer behind him, to attack from there.

Wielding a katana, Yutani froze in his stance, waiting. He was turned to the side, his back knee bent forward, and his front leg bracing his body, as he held the katana ready near his back hip, his gaze glued on Callan, the statue brought to life.

Viktor brought his sword up, easing toward the warrior.

Callan looked somewhat confused, but he prepared for attack.

Yutani began to circle around him as Viktor kept him engaged from the front. The tension as they jockeyed for position was so thick I could spread it like butter. But then, as Viktor took another step forward, the Fae warrior decided to meet him head on, and he swung his sword, engaging the half-ogre's blade.

They met, metal kissing metal, as the sound of their blades clashed through the clearing. Viktor was bigger and stronger than the warrior, but Callan was quick and sure-footed. Yutani moved in from the side, bringing his katana to bear. The blade swept through the warrior's side but Callan laughed.

I blinked. Yutani's bite had drawn no blood. So Callan wasn't fully flesh and blood, even though he looked like it.

Viktor drove hard, right to left to right again, forcing Callan back toward Yutani, but the warrior suddenly ducked to the side, darting away from both of them. He was headed my way.

Instinctively I brought my dagger up, but then realized Callan was sweeping his blade in front of him and I'd be caught in its trajectory. I dove to the side, coming up into a crouch on my heels as he passed. I was about to go after him when he reached the boundaries of the clearing and—with another laugh—he shimmered out of sight, vanishing as though he had never existed.

I glanced toward where the statue had been. It was gone.

"Where... So... Did he escape?" Viktor asked.

Back to his normal form and size, Herne hauled the priest to his feet. He was the only one of the Light Fae remaining in the grove.

"What happened to Callan? Where did he go?" He lifted the hapless man up off the ground, gripping him by his throat as he slammed him against a tree.

"I don't know. I only know that I was supposed to summon him." The priest squirmed, trying to free himself. "The iron burns."

"You do realize that I'm taking you before Cernunnos?" Herne once again tossed him to the ground. "My father's going to throw you in irons that will make these cuffs seem like a love tap. If you won't talk to us, you'll talk to him."

The priest whimpered but Herne had had enough. He motioned to the rest of us. "Come on. We have to get back to the office."

"We have to catch Callan—" Viktor started, but Herne waved him off.

He was angry, yes, but I knew that he was mostly angry with himself for believing the priest's story. Cernunnos wasn't going to let his son get off easy for this one. Herne was going to get his ass handed to him on a platter.

As we packed up our gear, I glanced back at the forest. A Fae warrior's spirit was now running around loose in Seattle. We had been told to prevent him from manifesting back into this world and we'd screwed that up royal. Cernunnos was going to light a fire under all of us for this one. And on top of everything, I felt cramps coming on.

Lovely—just what I needed on top of everything. My period.

ANGEL GLANCED UP as we dragged our butts into the office. The elevator opened into the reception area, and we slogged into the room like a pack of drowned rats. We were all soaked through to the skin. We had worn light jackets, given how much stealth had been required, and none of them measured up to the pouring rain that was now saturating the ground outside. Herne had taken the priest straight to Cernunnos's, so I had ridden back with Viktor and Yutani.

The Wild Hunt Agency was Herne's baby, but the company supported all of us. A cross between a divine law enforcement agency and a bounty hunter's squad, the Wild Hunt was one of many similar operations across the world.

Supervised by Herne's mother and father—Morgana, a demi-goddess of the Sea and of the Fae, and Cernunnos, Lord of the Forest—we were in charge of preventing wars between the Dark and Light Fae from spilling over into the mortal world. The two factions were both petty, belligerent, elitist, and too smart for their own good. And unfortunately, I was caught between the two. My mother had been born Light Fae, and my father came from the Dark side. *I* was rejected by both heritages.

"Hey, Ember." Angel stared at me as I dragged my sorry ass out of the elevator, into the waiting room. "I got a call from...oh good grief. You're *soaked*. You all are." Angel was my best friend and roommate. Human, she was an empath of significant degree. She frowned, pointing to the carpet. "You're tracking mud on the carpet. Take off your shoes, *all* of you."

I grumbled, but sat down in the waiting area to untie my sneakers. I should have worn boots. Boots kept my feet dry, but I thought I'd give my new silver-tone sneakers a chance. Now they were covered with mud and gunk, and they were wet both inside and out. So far, I wasn't impressed with them.

Viktor and Yutani quickly joined me. Over the past few months, as Angel and I both grew more confident with our places in the agency, she had blossomed out as the office administrator and now she bossed everyone around. Even Herne jumped to her commands.

She vanished into the back, then returned with a mat, which she placed on the other side of the waiting area. "Put your shoes on that until they're dry and you can brush off the mud. Here, I brought towels." She handed each of us a towel and we began to dry our faces and hair.

I shivered. Now that we had stopped running around, and were no longer in a warm car, I was starting to get chilled. But like the others, I had a change of clothing at the office. In our line of work, it made good sense.

"I'm going to change."

"Where's Herne? We have a client coming in at five-thirty and that's only an hour away." She headed back to her desk and I followed her.

"He'll be back in time. I hope." I leaned down as she returned to her seat and whispered, "Do you have a tampon?"

"Sister Red hit again, huh?" Angel reached into her desk drawer and handed me two of them. "I need to restock the bathroom tomorrow. Take two."

"Thanks. Do we have chocolate?" Cramps weren't the only symptom I was feeling.

"In the break room. Talia brought in a chocolate cake with raspberry filling this afternoon." Angel leaned back, eyeing me carefully. "So, nobody's cheering. The stakeout go okay?"

I shook my head. "You'll hear about it during the meeting. Until then, don't even get me started. It didn't go as planned and we're all going to have our asses in a sling over this one, especially poor Herne."

Cernunnos and Morgana held their son as accountable as they held us.

"*Uh oh*. That bad?"

"*That* bad. Okay, I'm going to go change clothes and wash my face." I headed toward the back, waving at Talia—our main researcher—as I passed her office. I had hoped we could quit early. I wanted to go home and curl up under a blanket with a bag of chips. But given everything that had shaken down with the priest, and the fact that we had a new client coming in, we were fated to stay through the early evening. With a sigh, I grabbed my spare jeans and sweater and headed into the bathroom before Viktor or Yutani could co-opt it first.

SO, I'M EMBER Kearney. As I said, I'm half Light Fae—Leannan Sidhe to be exact, and half Dark Fae—from the blood of the Autumn's Bane. And both sides reject me wholly. When I was fifteen, my grandparents killed my mother and father for daring to love one another, and they would have killed me too, if they had gotten the chance.

Earlier in the year, I had been a freelance investigator, putting a stop to sub-Fae who were bothering members of the SubCult. When Angel asked me to find her little brother, DJ, who had disappeared, everything went so far south that it tipped our lives upside down.

I found DJ, all right, but the fallout resulted in both Angel and me being recruited into the Wild Hunt. DJ now lived with a foster family for his safety and his best interests. I had recently bought a house and Angel had moved in with me.

Oh, and Herne? He's my lover. Loving a god— even a demi-god—is a mixed blessing. Sometimes, I think I've landed myself on a slippery slope and I'm not sure where it's headed. Other days, life seems wonderful. Either way, being Herne's lover is never boring.

And life as an agent of the Wild Hunt? Well, it's not a job for the faint-hearted. But I've never been one to back down, and as long as I don't get myself killed, I think it's one of the best jobs I could ever hope to have.

HERNE RETURNED SHORTLY before we were to meet the new client.

"Damn it, I was hoping to call a meeting now, but...we'll just have to wait to talk about what my father said until tomorrow morning." He glowered at Angel.

She plastered on a smile so fake I knew she had to be picking up on his moods. "Would you like me to reschedule the client's appointment?"

"Now? When she's due here in ten minutes? I don't think so," Herne barked so loud that Angel flinched. He paused, then let out a long sigh. "I'm sorry. I didn't mean to bite your head off. I just got my ass handed to me on a platter by my father and I'm not exactly happy about it, but that's no reason for me to take it out on you."

Angel nodded, accepting his apology. "I'll buzz you when she gets here."

Herne motioned to me. "Ember, I want you to sit in, as usual. Yutani, go tell Talia what happened and start researching to see if you can find any clue where Callan disappeared to. My father confirms he's still in this world, though he can't pinpoint where he is. Viktor, see to the weapons. Make certain everything is polished and ready to go." He turned back to Angel. "For now, take names and numbers if any other new clients call, and I'll see what our caseload looks like. With what happened today, we may be up to our ears trying to mop up this goddamn mess." He headed into his office.

Angel and I exchanged glances and she mouthed, "Wow, he's upset."

I nodded, whispering, "Yeah, and mostly at himself," before following Herne into his office.

I closed the door behind me, noting that he had changed clothes before returning to the office. I took a seat next to the desk and waited. Herne leaned over my shoulder to plant a light kiss on my cheek.

"I'm sorry for acting like an ass. I can't believe I let myself fall for that damned priest's trick. I didn't think he'd actually put his own ass on the line like that. He had to know it would land him in front of my father, but he went ahead and lied to me anyway."

"You have to let this go," I said. "We'll find Callan. Mistakes happen. Remember, though, the Fae are fanatical in their hatred for the Fomorians. Given what happened with the virus, I don't blame them for looking for a savior, to be honest. That plague could have killed *me*, as well. Never, ever discount how deep the hatred between the two factions runs. The giants have been out to eradicate the Fae since time began. I can't believe I'm defending my people, but there you have it."

"You're right. I shouldn't have let my self-confidence blindside me. I thought the priest would be so anxious to save his butt that he'd give in immediately." Herne snorted, shoving a file to the side of his desk.

His office was a tangle of plants. The walls were a pale robin's-egg blue, and the ceiling was white.

Herne's desk sat beneath a massive rack of antlers mounted to the wall. The desk was dark and solid, heavy walnut, with a black leather chair. There were two sets of wingchairs in the room, one pair in front of the desk, and another off to one side. A daybed covered with a plush velvet comforter sat against the wall to one corner, and weapons cases lined the walls with daggers, crossbows, and other weaponry inside.

Herne dropped into his chair and leaned back. "I was so stupid."

"Will you stop beating yourself up? You got tripped up this time. It happens." I winced as a cramp hit me, and pressed my hand against my stomach.

"You okay?" Herne asked, noticing.

"Yeah. Just started my period. At least I'm not pregnant." I laughed, shaking my head. "One thing we have to be thankful for."

"True." Herne nodded. "Well, I guess we'd better get ready to meet our new client. I wonder who the cat dragged in this time."

He rolled his eyes. We had been scraping the bottom of the barrel with the last few clients. Meaning: they had been sloppy, drunk, prone to lying, and one—a sprite with a penchant for chewing snuff—had been married to a goblin. The goblin was female, as far as we could tell, and she had offered herself to Herne as part payment for services rendered. The offer had gone over like a lead balloon, and the sprite had been so offended on his wife's behalf that he stomped out, refusing to pay anything beyond the retainer even though we had solved his case.

Herne had instituted a new rule at that point—no goblins allowed in the office. Which made sense, given goblins were off-limits within the boundaries of the city.

"She's here," Angel's voice echoed over the intercom.

"Bring her in, please." Herne straightened up and put on a professional smile. I did the same, tucking in the hem of my sweater.

But when the door opened, we were both in for a shock. Angel escorted our client in, handing Herne a file folder.

One look told me that—whoever she was—she was about as human as me. As she entered the room, I could swear we were facing one of Ante-Fae.

Chapter 2

ANGEL CLEARED HER throat. "Raven Bone-Talker, here to see you."

I blinked. The woman standing in front of us was breathtaking, although I wasn't sure if *beautiful* was the right word to describe her.

On the plump side, Raven BoneTalker was buxom and curvy, with an hourglass figure, and her hair was coffee colored, streaked with plum, but it didn't look dyed. It flowed down her shoulders in a cascade of waves to her waist. Her eyes were the brown of rich soil, and her skin was pale, almost alabaster. She wore a long black skirt, with a silver overbust corset embellished with black embroidery, and lace-up granny boots. She practically crackled with magic, and I found myself magnetized, unable to look away.

Herne leaned across the desk as she approached and extended his hand. "Welcome to the Wild

Hunt, Ms. BoneTalker." He glanced at the file, then back at the client as Angel withdrew, shutting the door behind her. "Please sit down."

Raven took the chair nearest me, opposite Herne's desk. I was sitting to his side, taking my own notes. We had developed the system over the past few months, which allowed me to notice things he might not, and vice versa. He asked for facts, I watched the nuances of body language.

"I'm Herne, and this is Ember Kearney. So, what brings you to the agency? What can we do for you?" Herne sounded unnerved. I wondered if he knew who she was. The Ante-Fae were to the Fae what the titans were to the Greek gods.

She paused for a moment, glancing at me, then back at Herne. I swallowed hard. The energy around her sizzled. If I poked her arm, would I get shocked?

"I have a problem, and I heard that you're good at solving problems," she said after a moment. Her voice was low and smooth. She tilted her head to one side, still staring at us.

Herne opened the file and glanced at it. "You're looking for your fiancé? He's gone missing?"

"Yes." She frowned. "Ulstair vanished about ten days ago, maybe a few more. There have been times when he's been gone this long on business trips, and he's taken a few road trips with a buddy or two that have lasted this long, but this time, something feels different. I'm worried, and the spirits seem restless. They tell me something's wrong, but they won't tell me what. I've checked all of his usual haunts, but no one has seen him. And the cops won't look into it."

"So you reported it?" I asked.

She nodded. "Yes, I did, three days ago. They let me file a missing person's report, but they barely paid any attention to what I was saying, and they haven't come up with anything. I called to ask if they've made any progress and they said no, that he's probably just on an extended trip. For some reason, they've been stonewalling me." The intensity of her eyes shifted, replaced by the look of a worried lover. She suddenly seemed more human.

Herne let out a soft breath. "I'm going to ask you a number of questions and some of them may sound personal. Are you up to answering them, and do you mind if I record your answers? Ember will also be taking notes."

"That's fine. Ask away," she said.

Herne motioned to me and I got ready.

"What's your fiancé's name, and is he human or part of the SubCult? We need a description of him." Herne added, "Also, do you happen to have a picture we can keep?"

Raven opened her purse—a big leather handbag weighed down with studs, chains, and a massive amount of hardware bling—and sorted through it, producing a photograph that looked like it had been printed out from a digital photo.

"Here, this is Ulstair, and it was taken about a month ago, so it's recent. He's Dark Fae." She handed the picture to me. "Ulstair Forrester."

I glanced at the paper. The man did, indeed, look Fae. He was handsome, with red hair caught back in a ponytail and dancing blue eyes. He was wearing what looked like a V-neck sweater over a pair of jeans, and he was sitting on a large rock, laughing. A bright gold tooth stood out in place of one of his canine teeth. He had a scruff of a beard, and was holding a ferret.

"Is that real gold? And do the two of you live together?" I asked.

Raven shook her head. "Yes it is, and no, we like having our own spaces. We've been engaged for about fifty years, but neither one of us is ready to get married yet." She gave us a little smile. "Ulstair and I both have commitment issues. I did give him a ring about ten years ago, though. So we're making progress."

"Who's the ferret?" I asked.

"That's Templeton. He's mine. I have three of them right now." She sighed, leaning back in the chair. "Honestly, Ulstair *never* vanishes without a word. Even when he takes off for his business trips, he always calls me while he's away, and he always lets me know how long he's going to be gone."

"What does he do?" Herne asked.

"He's a software engineer with CTN—CalTecNology. They develop video games. I went over to his apartment to look for a note. His suitcases are still in his closet, and there was a sink full of dishes. Ulstair never leaves a mess. He always cleans up every night. If he left on a trip, he would have taken at least one of his suitcases with him." She leaned forward, her brow crinkling. "I know something's happened to him. Can you please find him for me?"

Herne glanced at me, and I nodded.

"We can try," Herne said. Then, more slowly, he added, "Do you know if Ulstair has any enemies? Anybody who might want to hurt him?"

This was always a sticky question. It usually brought on a shower of tears because when we dealt with most missing-person cases, the person bringing us the case usually hadn't even considered foul play. They usually assumed there had been an accident, or their partner ran off with somebody else.

Raven slumped back against the chair, then shook her head. "I don't know. Ulstair never mentioned anybody, if there is. I do know that in the computer industry, there's a lot of competition. He was good at what he did. There was a lot of nit-picking and infighting at work, from what he said. But he never hinted that it might be anything more than just a bunch of bitch-slapping."

I saw the tear at the corner of her eye and handed her a box of tissues.

She took one and dabbed the tear away, then gave us a bleak look. "I've asked the spirits to help. They whisper that something's wrong, but their voices aren't clear to me on this."

"What do you do? Are you a medium? I can tell... You're Ante-Fae, aren't you?" I finally got up the courage to ask. In what little I had to do with the Ante-Fae, they had left me both impressed and intimidated.

"Yes, I'm Ante-Fae. I'm called Raven, the Daughter of Bones, by my own people. I use BoneTalker as a last name, since the current society seems to insist on surnames. My mother is Phasmoria, one of the Bean Sidhe, and my father is Curikan, the Black Dog of Hanging Hills." She paused, then added, "I'm a bone witch and a nec-romancer. The spirits whisper their secrets to me, and I work with the magic of the dead."

I blinked. The Ante-Fae were certainly a tidy group of peculiar mixes.

"Hanging Hills?" I asked.

"In Connecticut. That's where I was born. I made my way here about a hundred years back and shortly after that, I met Ulstair. I'm a baby, as far as the Ante-Fae are concerned. The Fae, as well. I was born on November 1, 1900. My mother was bringing a death-message to one of the Scottish families in the area when she met my father. He had shifted into his human form, and she didn't know right away that he was one of the Black Dogs."

The Black Dogs were a group of Ante-Fae found mostly in the UK—but apparently America, too— who were Dark Fae of dubious natures. They usually carried trouble in on their paws. The Bean Sidhe were harbingers of death. The resulting mix of blood had to be shadowy, at best. No wonder Raven was a bone witch.

"And the spirits won't tell you what happened?" Herne asked.

Raven shook her head. "No. They talk to me about the troubles of others, but for me...it's as though I'm blinded to the knowledge. I'm also a fortune teller and a tarot reader, but I cannot read for myself. I suppose it's one of the pitfalls of my particular heritage." She rubbed her forehead. "Do you think you can help?"

"We can certainly try," Herne said, and I found myself glad he was taking the case. The more Raven talked, the more intrigued I was. Whatever else she might be, I felt she was genuine and sincere. I wondered what Angel had picked up.

"Herne, do you mind if I step out for a moment?" I closed my notepad and set it on the table. I used my tablet for a lot of things, but I preferred taking notes the old-fashioned way.

He shrugged. "That's fine. I'll just get some names and addresses from Ms. BoneTalker—"

"Raven, please," she said.

"Fine, then, I'll get some information from Raven and send her out to Angel with the invoice." He motioned for me to leave and I gave him a quiet wink, slipping out the door.

Angel glanced over her shoulder as I approached her desk. "Hey, you guys done?"

"Almost. I came out early. I wanted to ask what you thought of Raven?"

"I actually like her energy," Angel said. "She's scary-strong with some shadow stuff, but...it's clear even though it's dark, if you know what I mean. Why?"

"Because I feel the same way. I was just curious what you had picked up on her."

Angel was an excellent judge of character and I trusted her hunches and intuition.

"Is she Dark or Light Fae?"

"Neither. She's Ante-Fae." I waited.

One beat. Two beats. And then...

"*Ante-Fae*? We have one of the Ante-Fae in our office?" Angel's jaw dropped. She had heard us talking about the Ante-Fae before, especially when we had gone up against Blackthorn, the King of Thorns. But Angel had never met one of them.

"Apparently so. She's a bone witch, whatever that is." I paused as the elevator opened and Yutani got off. He had changed and his hair looked freshly washed and braided.

"Dude, did you go home?" I asked. "Don't you keep a fresh set of clothes at the office?"

He snorted. "No, I didn't go home. I went down to the dance studio to use their shower. They don't mind if there isn't a class going on. Or rather, they wouldn't mind, I like to think."

"You mean, they don't know you're doing that?" I asked, suppressing a laugh.

"That's none of their concern, Tweedle-Dum." He wrinkled his nose at me. "When the cat's out of town, the mice will party down."

"You're calling yourself a mouse now?" I liked needling him. We got on just fine, though I still picked on him for thinking that I wasn't capable of handling the job when Angel and I first joined the agency.

"Scat, and take Tweedle-Dee with you," he countered, jabbing his thumb at Angel. But he suddenly froze as his phone rang. He pulled it out and I recognized that it was his work phone. We all had the same brand for work, as well as our personal phones. "Uh oh. Excuse me, but don't go anywhere. This may be important." He darted off to the side to take the call.

I let out a long breath. "Today seems all out of sorts. We really fucked up on the case today. Although, technically, it was Herne who messed up. I'm thinking his father probably ripped him a new one. We let Callan get away and that was a major gaffe."

Angel nodded. "Yeah, so I heard. Viktor told me all about it while you were in there with Raven. What's your next step?"

"I don't know. Herne will have to figure that out. We don't even know what his father told him yet." I paused as the door opened and Raven came out, Herne following her.

She moved like she looked—with a sinuous edge, graceful and fluid. She was carrying a paper—the invoice for our retainer.

"Thank you, both of you," she said, glancing from Herne to me. "Please, let me know the minute you find out anything."

"It will take us a few days to sort out everything, but we'll be in touch. You'll get a call by Friday whether we've found anything or not. Meanwhile, if you hear anything new that could relate to the case, please let us know." Herne motioned to Angel. "Go ahead and take her retainer, and also, let the others know we're meeting first thing tomorrow morning in the break room. Eight o'clock, sharp on the dot. Then, you can close up and go home."

I gave a little wave to Raven. "I hope we can help you," I said, receiving a smile in return. To Angel, I added, "I'll be out in a few. Just saying good night to Herne."

She gave me an absent nod, already inputting Raven's information and payment.

I returned to Herne's office and shut the door behind me. As I crept up behind him, he turned from where he was examining the fronds on one of the ferns.

"Come here," he said, holding out his arms.

I pressed my face against his chest, bringing in deeply the scents of autumn and crisp leaves and cinnamon apples. "You smell so good."

"All thanks to the hellacious new deodorant I bought," he murmured, pressing his lips against the top of my head. "It's been a day, I'll say that."

"Angel likes our new client. She thinks Raven is genuine. I like her too." I kept my eyes closed as I swam in the warmth of his embrace. "Mmm, don't move. You feel good." I wanted to walk him over to the daybed, but I sensed he needed to talk more than to fuck. "What's up?"

Herne lingered for a moment, his lips still against my hair. Finally, he let out a soft sigh. "You can always tell, can't you?"

"Yes, I can." I nodded, disentangling myself from his embrace. I took his hand and led him over to the daybed, where I curled on it and patted the seat next to me. "Sit down. Talk."

He paused for a moment, then silently slid onto the cushion beside me and leaned back, resting his head against the wall as he closed his eyes.

"Father was...not happy."

"How not happy?" I had met his father. Cernunnos was intimidating and, when he wanted to be, he was downright scary.

"He chewed me out. I 'fessed up. I told him I had been the one to burn the scroll. Let's just say that some of his remarks might have contained the words 'stupid' and 'idiotic' and 'pathetic.' And I deserve them. I can't believe that I accepted the priest's word about the scroll." Herne slapped his thigh, staring at the floor.

I leaned over to stroke his face, bringing his chin to bear so that he was looking at me. "Listen to me. Any one of us could have made the same mistake. You have no reason to think the priest was going to be that stupid."

"I suppose." Herne shrugged, the frown still plastered on his face.

"What will happen to him? What did Cernunnos do?" I wasn't sure I wanted to know, but if it helped Herne to talk about it, so much the better.

He ducked his head. "Well, I doubt if he'll see the outside of a jail cell for any time soon. My father threw him in the dungeons for disrespect and there he'll sit until Cernunnos gets over his miff. Or until the priest begs for forgiveness. I have no idea who will break first. But I can tell you this— some prisoners have been there several hundred years and I doubt my father even remembers why he sent them down to the dungeons in the first place."

I nodded. "What are you doing tonight? I'm cramping, so I think I just want to crawl into bed with a heating pad and a movie."

Herne laughed. "That time of month, is it? At least we know the Queen's Root is working."

Queen's Root was the name of an herbal mixture

that Ferosyn, Cernunnos's main healer, had given me to prevent me from getting pregnant. He had pointed out that condoms weren't likely to withstand the ardor of a god, and if I didn't want little godlings running around, I'd better religiously down the mix. Once a month, on the same day every month, I was to stir two teaspoons of the Queen's Root into a cup of hot water and drink it. This was the first month I had been using it, and my period was right on schedule.

"Thank gods for small favors. Or rather, thank Ferosyn." I grinned as he flashed me a curious look. "Come on, don't tell me you want me to—" I stopped at a knock on the door.

"Who is it?" Herne called.

The door opened and Angel peeked in. "Pardon me. I don't want to interrupt you, but there's someone here to see you, Herne." The look on her face was unreadable, but there was a quiver in her voice that put me on alert.

Herne frowned. "Who is it? Another client? Ask them to come back tomorrow, would you?"

"I don't think she's a client." Angel shifted, an uncomfortable look in her eye. "You'd better talk to her. She seems to know you."

Still frowning, Herne and I followed Angel out into the waiting area.

There, standing by Angel's desk, was a statuesque woman. At first I thought she was Fae of some sort, but then I realized that wasn't the case. Taller than Herne, she didn't exactly look human, either. I wondered if she could be a demi-god. She was wearing a gray pinstriped pantsuit and her long blond hair was pulled back into a neat French braid. With a pair of sunglasses in one hand, and a Louis Vuitton handbag draped over the other arm, she looked every inch chic and pulled together.

She swept past me without a glance, coming to stand in front of Herne. As Angel and I watched, the woman reached out to stroke his face. Herne quickly glanced from her to me, then back to her again, and took a hasty step back.

"Herne, what's this? You're not *happy* to see me? It's been a long time, hasn't it?" She didn't sound pleased, and she was so solidly planted on the floor that I doubted Viktor could have moved her if he tried. She glanced around at the room. "So, this is your office, is it? Hmm, smaller than I would have thought fitting for a demigod."

Herne tugged at his collar. He was wearing a turtleneck sweater with black jeans, and his hair was gathered back in a braid. He also looked guilty as sin, though I wasn't sure what he had to be guilty about.

"Myrna, I..." He seemed at a loss for words.

Wondering what the hell was going on—the tension was incredibly thick—I cleared my throat. "Hello, I'm—"

"Did I *ask* who you are?" she said, interrupting me without even looking my way. "I'm here to talk to Herne. You may leave us. I have something to discuss with the Lord of the Hunt."

I swung around to stare at her. I'd had just about enough with the hoity-toity attitude. "Excuse me, but—"

"Ember, please. It's better if you just let me talk

YASMINE GALENORN

to her in private. Everything will be all right. You and Angel go home and I'll call you later." Herne gave me his *do-as-I-ask* look, then his gaze flickered back to Myrna and he gave her a slight shake of the head.

She straightened her shoulders, still studiously ignoring Angel and me. A swell of anger welling up, I clenched my fists and turned to Angel. If Herne was going to stand here and let her talk to me like that, then I wasn't going to stick around to take it.

"Come on, Angel." I gave Angel a quick shake of the head when she started to say something, and she gathered her purse. "I'll get my things and meet you downstairs." Without a word to Herne or to his visitor, I spun on my heel and marched into my office. By the time I gathered my jacket and purse and returned to the waiting area, Angel was the only one there. I looked around. "Where are they?" I asked, lowering my voice to a whisper.

She nodded to his office. I thought about creeping up to the door to listen in, but then decided that I was better than that. As we headed toward the elevator, though, I could hear raised voices behind the door. To my grim satisfaction, neither one of them sounded happy.

I WAS TOO angry to speak, and Angel let me stew as she drove us home. We had come in her car today, and so I jammed myself back against the seat, staring out the window. I might be quiet on the outside, but inside, my mind was whirling.

Who the hell was the woman and why had Herne let her talk to me like that? Where did he know her from? More important, *when* had he met her? And if she was an old friend of his, why had he never mentioned her? The thoughts swirled in my head till I couldn't stand it. We were about a block from home when I slammed my hand on the dashboard.

"Who the hell did she think she was, talking to me like that?"

Angel snorted. "Apparently, she's someone named Myrna."

"*Myrna schmyrna*. That doesn't tell me who the hell she is." I crossed my arms and slumped back in the seat. "Do you think she's his lover?"

"*You're* his lover. You know Herne's a good egg." Angel eased the car into the parking spot in front of our house.

"He's also gorgeous and hot and a demigod and...and..."

"And he treats you like his own private goddess. Herne isn't stepping out on you." She paused before opening the door. "At least, I don't *think* he'd do that."

I jammed the door open and slid out of the passenger seat. "I know," I said. "But damn it, you don't let people walk all over your partner—man or woman. When somebody treats them like shit, you speak out. You tell them to knock it off. You tell them to shut the fuck up."

"There are probably circumstances that you

know nothing about. But," she added, grinning fiercely at me, "if there aren't, I'll help you whip that godly ass of his. And I promise not to enjoy it."

I stared at her for a moment, then sputtered, laughing. "I love you, you know that?"

"I do, but it's nice to hear it now and then," she said.

Still laughing, I looped my arm through hers as we sashayed through the front gate and up the sidewalk to our home.

Chapter 3

BY THE NEXT morning, the worst of my cramps were over and I had managed to shake off most of my anger, thanks to Angel and Mr. Rumblebutt—my Norwegian Forest cat, who was as black as night. His fur was so long that he looked like a powder puff on legs.

Although if I was forced to admit it, some of my anger had morphed into fear.

Herne hadn't even *called* me, and I was reduced to playing out a dozen scenarios in my mind, at least half of which ended up with him and Myrna rolling around on the floor of his office, all naked and sweaty. I tried not to go there, but combining hormones, along with the knowledge that Cernunnos was pissed at us, and then throwing Myrna into the mix, I couldn't help but let myself dwell in What-If-ville.

"How did you sleep?" Angel asked as we lingered

over coffee the next morning.

We had both woken early, for a change, and Angel had fixed breakfast. Bacon, eggs, and her incredible French toast. The woman could put a world-class chef to shame with her cooking.

She brushed a strand of hair back from her face. Angel was modelesque—tall and slender, with rich brown skin, and hair that coiled tightly down to her shoulders. She was as beautiful inside as she was out, and we had been BFFs—best friends forever—since we were eight years old. When we met on the playground, Angel had pushed me into a mud puddle. I had dragged her in with me. We came out of the fight united in friendship.

"Like a log, actually. No dreams, no nightmares, just uninterrupted blissful sleep. Mr. Rumblebutt woke me up once for not petting him, but ten minutes of chin scritches later, he was good and I was back asleep." I lifted my coffee cup, saluting her. "Fantastic breakfast."

"It's easy to cook here."

The kitchen was so different than the one in my condo. That had been cramped and tiny. The kitchen in our house might not be a gourmet kitchen, but it was spacious and updated and had just about every gadget that Angel could hope for.

Angel paused, then said, "I got a text from DJ this morning."

DJ was her little brother. He was currently being fostered by a shifter family. DJ was actually Angel's half-brother, and he was a wolf shifter. His father had abandoned Mama J. early on, just like Angel's father had. When Mama J. died in a car accident, Angel had taken over caring for DJ.

"How is he?"

"Doing good. He's maintaining straight As, and he sounds happy." She looked anything but over-joyed.

"So what's wrong?" I *knew* Angel. She wasn't the only one who could sense when something was wrong.

She pushed her plate back. "I miss him. I miss having him around. He's my little brother and he's growing up without me. Don't get me wrong, I know that Cooper and his family are doing a great job of taking care of him, and keeping his nose out of trouble, but I feel like..."

"Like he won't need you anymore?"

She ducked her head and nodded. "Yeah. I feel like he doesn't need me *at all.*"

"Do you think that if he didn't need you, if he was forgetting about you, he'd go to the trouble to text you about his grades? He wants you to be proud of him. He adores you, Angel. You mean the world to him. But he's really in the best care right now. It would be dangerous for him here, with our line of work. And right now, he needs to learn about his shifter side as he approaches puberty."

She squared her shoulders. "You're right, of course. I know you're right. DJ loves me. He texts me good night every night before he goes to bed, and he texts me every morning to remind me to be careful. I guess I'm just feeling a little lonely. He's the only family I have. Well, besides you."

I didn't take offense. I had a feeling I knew what was going on, beyond her feelings about DJ. "I'm your soul sister, but I have Herne and I'm busy a lot with him. Right?"

Blushing, she stared at me, then finally nodded. "Right. I'm happy for you. You guys make a great couple, but..."

"Kipa has asked you out five times," I reminded her.

She snorted, then, the tears gone. "Kipa is gorgeous and sexy and funny, and he's just about the worst boyfriend material ever. Nope. Not even going there." She gathered up our plates. "You're doing dishes tonight."

"The dishwasher is doing them, technically, but yes, I'll rinse and stack when we get home. And I think you could do a lot worse than Kipa. At least he'd be fun to practice with." I took the plates from her and carried them over to the sink where I rinsed them to keep the syrup from hardening up. Then I fed Mr. Rumblebutt, who had hopped up on the counter, and made certain the trash was firmly tucked away under the sink, out of his reach.

"I could do a lot *better*, too," she said.

With that, we headed to the office, opting to take both our cars. I had the feeling Herne and I were going to be having a long talk that evening.

THE WILD HUNT Agency was in downtown Seattle. During the day, the area was a cluster of humanity, home to the *streeps*—the street people—and the disenfranchised. Old Town, as the area was called, was in the Pioneer Square area, an unending array of private offices, restaurants, thrift stores, neighborhood markets, and boutique brothels where you could order anything from a spanking to a lap dance to hardcore deep and dirty sex. Prostitution had long been legalized, and the revenue alone helped pay for a number of the street repairs. But not much could spruce up Old Town, and it labored under the weather and the wear-and-tear.

The Wild Hunt was in a five-story brick walkup, with an elevator that was on the blink about as often as it worked. The entry was a long flight of stairs off the street. The front door on the street entered into a lobby, which housed an indigent urgent care clinic. The second floor belonged to a daycare and preschool for the low-income mothers in the area. A yoga and dance studio shared the third floor, and the fourth floor was ours. The fifth floor was still empty. The building itself was old, but the landlord kept it up. The neighborhood streeps kept an eye out for people who didn't belong, because they knew we did our best to keep an eye out for them.

In the elevator, I found my anxiety growing. I had managed to push what had happened the previous day to the side, but now I was going to have to go in there and face Herne, and either he was going to answer some questions, or we had a serious problem on our hands. But when Angel and I entered the office, we found that only Viktor had arrived.

"Talia and Yutani are on the way. Herne hasn't

checked in yet." He glanced at me, a question in his eyes.

I brushed it away, heading for my office. As I entered the room, I shut the door behind me and pulled out my personal phone, staring at it.

Should I call? Shouldn't I? I debated the options—there were only two. Well, I could text him, too. That might actually be easier.

yo. where are you? we thought you said eight sharp. viktor and Angel and i are here. what do you want us to do until you get here?

The latter wasn't really necessary. We all had work to do, but I wanted some sort of response out of him.

I waited for a couple minutes. No response. Debating on whether to try again or to call, I quashed both ideas. I wasn't going to chase Herne around. I shoved my phone back in my pocket and picked up one of the files that I still needed to enter into the computer. While Angel set up all our electronic files, we were responsible for updating them with notes throughout the case, and after it was closed.

Sighing, I shoved aside my purse and rubbed my head. I didn't want to work, I didn't want to do anything except sulk until Herne came up with some answers, but keeping busy was preferable to sitting around whining, even if I was whining with my mouth shut.

I logged into my laptop and brought up the company-sharing network, then opened the case file that I was updating. As I began to enter the missing information, I narrowed my focus, trying to lose myself in the work. It didn't take long before I was engrossed in logging my notes on the case, and had forgotten that Herne hadn't arrived yet. So it was no surprise that when a rap sounded on my office door, I jumped.

"Holy shit, you scared me," I said, glancing over my shoulder to see Angel.

"Herne's here. Meeting in the break room. And before you ask, he looks good but not in the *I-just-had-sex* way. No afterglow."

"That's for *women*," I shot back.

"Is it, really? Think about it for a moment," she said, then vanished around the door.

I gathered up my tablet, a steno pad, a couple pens, and a coffee mug that needed to go back to the break room. As I entered, I caught sight of Herne. He was staring at his tablet. He glanced up to catch my gaze, but I quickly pulled my attention away and forced myself to stare at the counter for a moment, before depositing the mug in the sink. I found a clean one, poured myself a big cup of coffee, and added milk and sugar. Then and only then did I head over to the table.

I sat in a chair a few seats away from Herne to put some distance between us, but snuck a peek at him. He looked about the same as last night, though he looked tired and ready to take a nap. I wasn't sure whether to chalk that up to extracurricular activities, but given the fact that he was a god and didn't need as much sleep as we did, there must have been something mighty special about whatever it was he did.

"Late night, huh?" I asked, keeping my tone light.

He snorted. "You might say that." But he didn't look me in the eye, and right then, I knew something was up.

"What's going on?" I mouthed.

He shook his head, mouthing back, "Later."

Clearing his throat, he called the meeting to order. "All right, we have a lot to cover. Not only do we have a new case, but we have to deal with the fallout from yesterday's failed attempt to keep the Light Fae from bringing Callan into the present. I had a talk with Cernunnos and Morgana yesterday. Let's just say they weren't pleased."

"Should we put Raven's case to the side and focus on Callan, then?" I asked, forcing myself to slide into work-mode.

He shook his head. "No, she's so worried that I don't want to sit on this. I have a feeling we aren't just facing a case of a lover gone AWOL. Yutani, I'd like you to dig up whatever you can about where Callan may have disappeared to. We know the Light Fae have him. I'm going to ask my parents if we can demand extradition, should the Fae be harboring him. Which we know they have to be."

Yutani nodded, staring at his laptop. "They could be hiding him anywhere. Do you really think they'll just hand him over if you ask?"

"Nope. Which is why I'll talk to Cernunnos and ask for a formal writ of demand. If they refuse then, they'll be breaking the covenant." He frowned. "This wouldn't be happening if Elatha hadn't returned. Speaking of Elatha and the Fomorians, there's yet another issue that ties into this. I guarantee you, this is going to cause waves through the entire Fae nation. Both Courts and we're going to end up with fallout to clean up."

"Wonderful," Talia said. "Just what we need. More complications."

I took a long sip of my coffee, wishing I had added some chocolate. It was good, but I really wanted sweets right now. Thank the hormone goddess for that, as well. I spied a box of cookies on the counter and retrieved it, grateful to whoever had first envisioned blending chocolate with peanut butter. As I bit into the cookie, the sweet taste bled onto my tongue and I let out a long sigh as the sugar went to work on my nerves.

"What's going down?" Angel asked, a grave look on her face. "Do you think it will affect the agency?"

Herne gave her a grim nod. "Oh, yes, it's going to affect *everything*. Apparently, the United Coalition has been a busy bee the past month or so. They announced this morning they will be adding a fifth member to their ranks."

That was a shock. The United Coalition governed the country through four organizations—the Fae Courts, the Human League, the Shifter Alliance, and the Vampire Nation. That they were adding a new member was unprecedented. Or at least, it hadn't happened in a long, long time.

Herne's voice was as grim as his expression. "Apparently, the Cryptozoid Association silently filed a lawsuit, demanding representation. This morning the courts ruled in their favor, saying they haven't been adequately represented by the Shifter Alliance, the Vampire Nation, the Fae Courts, or the Human League. They're right, of course, but this is going to go over like a lead balloon."

I froze, my cookie halfway to my mouth. "The Cryptozoid Association? I've never heard of them. Who are they? Not *goblins*?"

"No, not goblins," Herne said. "They're a group of giants, ogres, and a few other oddball Cryptos who have banded together." He let his words settle for a moment.

I thought furiously, but Viktor beat me to it.

"*Giants*. Elatha and the Fomorians are behind this, aren't they? I hate to say it, but most of my kin—on my ogre side—aren't the brightest bulbs in the socket. They'll pretty much do what they're told by anybody bigger and stronger." Viktor was half-ogre, half human. His father, an ogre, had turned his back on him when he was a baby, but his mother had brought him up to appreciate the finer things in life, and Viktor was as smart as they came, in addition to being a wall of sheer brawn.

"Damn." I set my coffee mug down a little too hard, cracking it, and jumped up to grab a roll of paper towels as the liquid began to spread. As I wiped it up and carried my mug to the sink, I said, "Saílle and Névé are going to be livid."

"Ya think?" Yutani said, tapping the table with his fingers. "They had to already know about this already, which is the reason they summoned Callan. They *knew* the Fomorians were making a bid for power and they wanted to be prepared."

"Bingo, you win!" Herne said, snapping his

fingers. "Saílle and Névé knew, and you know how they are. Both Fae Queens are spitting furious that Elatha returned in the first place, and I can't say I blame them. After all, he did try to poison the entire Fae race. So they have summoned someone they trust to lead them to victory."

"Callan actually did that?" Talia asked.

Herne nodded. "Yeah, once. Long ago, back in Annwn, during the Tuatha-Fomorian Wars, Callan managed to drive Elatha and the other Fomorians back into the mountains for a long time. Hundreds of the Fomorians were killed, along with a number of the Bocanach and the Fachans. Callan's charge destroyed the enemy's stranglehold on one of the strategic passes high in the Éirín Mountain Range. He ended a war that had been raging for over one hundred years between the Tuatha and the Fomorians."

The Tuatha were another name for the Fae, mostly used back in Annwn now—the home of the Celtic gods. The Fomorians were the sworn enemy of every Fae alive, even me. I had witnessed firsthand what Elatha had almost managed to do. He had been out for genocide, and if we hadn't managed to find a cure for the iron plague, he would have quite possibly managed it.

"So, there's no stopping the Cryptozoid Association from taking a seat on the United Coalition?" I asked.

Herne shook his head. "No. It was approved this morning, in a raging debate down in Washington, DC. The Fae Courts aren't about to pull out because of it—that would give the giants too much power, but I have a feeling we're going to be kept a lot busier now. The formal induction takes place in early November."

"This bodes trouble, for certain," Talia said. "All right, so you're setting Yutani on Callan. I think it's a waste of time, but I suppose we have to pay lip service to this mess. Where's that leave us?"

Herne motioned to Angel. "Did you send out the files on Raven?"

She nodded. "This morning, before the meeting. Everyone should have a file in your email box on Raven BoneTalker."

"Raven's boyfriend vanished about a week ago, but nothing seems to be missing from his apartment. They're engaged, and although he has to go out of town for his job, he always lets her know ahead of time. The spirits have told her that something's wrong, but they won't tell her what." Herne paused. "One other thing. Raven's one of the Ante-Fae."

Yutani jerked his head up. "We're taking a case for one of the Ante-Fae?"

"Isn't that a little problematic?" Talia asked.

Herne shrugged. "I suppose it could be, but Raven seems to be a good sort. She's a bone witch—a necromancer of sorts. And she's young enough to still be concerned about others. She's the daughter of a Bean Sidhe and one of the Black Dogs."

"Lovely," Talia muttered under her breath. "That means she's worse than I ever was when I had my full powers."

"I liked her," Angel said. "She's genuine, and she's truly worried."

"I liked her too, from what I saw of her. Anyway, she's a paying customer, so let's give her the benefit of the doubt, all right?" I was feeling particularly touchy, and it occurred to me that so many others had said the same thing about me over the years. Being half-Dark and half-Light Fae landed me an outcast. The caste system was alive and well among the Fae Courts, and I was firmly on the outside of it, snubbed for my mixed blood.

"All right, where do we start?" Talia asked.

"I want you to check on Ulstair's credit cards and his phone. See if they've been used during the past week. If so, where? Also check on the hospitals and healers around the area, see if he's been admitted—or anybody looking like him," Herne said, as Talia jotted down his instructions.

"What about me?" Yutani asked.

"For now, you stick with Callan. We'll pull you onto Raven's case if we need to. Ember, I want you to go over to Raven's. Ask her to let you into Ulstair's apartment. Go through it with her to see if there's anything she missed."

"Check," I said.

"Viktor, depending on what Ember and Talia find, be ready to roll out to check out things. Meanwhile, maybe you could give your buddy on the force a call, see if she has anything on Ulstair that Raven didn't tell us. He's one of the Dark Fae."

Viktor nodded. "Erica's a good sort. She'll be straight with me."

Herne looked around the table. "I guess that's it for now. Let's get busy. I'm going to talk to my mother again and see if there's anything she can do to defuse the situation between the Fae and Fomorians. It's a long shot, but you never know."

With that, he stood and, after a quick nod, headed for his office. I started to follow, wanting to talk to him, but he turned at the door.

"I'm sorry, but we need to hustle. We'll talk a little later, okay?" He leaned in to give me a kiss, but I turned my face and his lips landed on my cheek. Looking concerned, he whispered, "I love you, Ember. Please, just give me some time. We'll talk tonight." And without waiting for an answer, he headed into his office and shut the door.

I stared at the closed door for a moment, then turned and strode back to my office. If he needed time, I'd give it to him. Once again irritable, but not wanting to ruin the rest of the day, I gave Raven a call. She was home and said I could come over whenever I wanted.

"You live on the Eastside? I'll be there in thirty minutes to an hour, depending on traffic." And with that, I grabbed my jacket and headed out of the office, still angry.

A WIDE SWATH of metropolitan area mixed with forest on the east side of Lake Washington, which divided the Eastside from Seattle, the "East-side" had once been a sprawling metropolis. When the Fae Courts had bought up thousands of acres and pretty much taken over, building their cities of TirNaNog and Navane, the area became a haven for magical folks and various Cryptos.

The Shifter Alliance held sway to the north in areas like Bothell, and to the south in the Renton-Kent-Federal Way jurisdictions. The vampires pretty much stuck to Underground Seattle, and they stayed within the city proper. The vamps were eyeball deep in controlling a vast financial interest in the country. They pretty much ruled Wall Street, while the Fae had crept their fingers into influencing the cops and judges. The shifters and the humans were more upfront than either the vamps or the Fae, but all in all, everybody had their fingers in the pie.

Now, I thought, the Fomorians would try to take part of that pie for themselves. I really didn't want to consider the snarl that was bound to happen. Whatever form it took, one thing I already knew: it wouldn't be pretty.

Raven's house was near where Angel had lived with her brother, in the UnderLake District. The entire subdivision was haunted, abandoned except for a number of lower-income families from all walks of life. UnderLake Park was a huge copse, thick with trees, a thicket that held as many hidden ravines as it did secrets. And its secrets were dark and sinister. A good share of the grounds of the park had once belonged to an order of monks, who were long gone. The monastery remained, filled with ghosts and memories better left in the past.

Yet another fifty acres had been donated by the Castle family, and the old Castle Hall estate still stood, though it was crumbling like the monastery. The owners had been presumed to be brutally murdered, but no bodies were ever found. But so much blood had been found that the medical examiner had stated that there was no chance the Castles could be alive. The boundaries of the park touched a number of neighborhoods, including the one in which Raven lived.

As I eased down 61st Place NE, I realized that she lived at the very edge of the park, in the last house on a cul-de-sac. The cul-de-sac ended right at the edge of the park, and she was on the left side. I eased into the driveway, making certain not to block the Toyota sedan parked in the driveway. It was probably Raven's, but until I found out, I didn't want to trap somebody in.

The house had once been nice, from the looks of it. It was a one-story ranch with a dark gray roof and eggshell siding. The trim was a dark blue, and a slate stone walkway led up to the house. The walkway was shrouded by overgrown vegetation.

There was a tangible energy running through the air—so strong I could almost touch it. It wasn't water energy, that much I knew, but it was magic, all right: dark like the night, and mildly foreboding.

I made my way up to the door, stepping cautiously to avoid the breaks in the stone walkway, when I heard something to my right. I froze, not certain what was there, but I could feel it watching me. I slowly pivoted, staring into the undergrowth.

There, with glowing green eyes, was a gargoyle the size of a large dog. And it was creeping toward me, its gray leathery haunches quivering ever so slightly in the breeze.

Chapter 4

THE GARGOYLE WAS breathing slowly, his gaze locked on me. He tilted his head to one side in a curious lean. After a moment, he crept out from beneath the bushes that blocked the pathway from the lawn and street. He lumbered along like a dog crossed with an orangutan, walking on his knuckles and feet. When he reached my side, he plopped down on the sidewalk and stared up at me.

I had never met a gargoyle before, though I knew enough about them to be both wary and intrigued. They were usually bound to someone, like a witch, and they acted as both guardians and sentinels. Sometimes the huge ones acted as full-on bodyguards. And when a grown gargoyle hit, it hit hard. They were so thickly muscled that even this one had to be a good eighty to ninety pounds. They usually had wings, though, and I didn't see any on this guy.

I was still a few steps from the door, not close enough to ring the bell, but the next moment, Raven popped her head out. She snorted.

"Raj, back off."

The gargoyle let out a grunt, then backed away, still staring at me.

"Will he bite?" *Or hit, maul, or tear me to pieces*?

"Hold on." Raven emerged from the house, wearing a gauzy black skirt with a purple tunic over the top that laced in front like a corset. Her hair was pulled back in a braid that draped across her back and over her shoulder, hanging down almost to her waist. She swiftly crossed to where I was standing, then knelt and held out her hand to the gargoyle.

"Come on, Raj. Come meet Ember."

Raj slowly lumbered forward again, giving me another curious look.

"She won't hurt you. Ember's a friend. She's okay-people." Raven stroked Raj's head and he sighed happily, then looked at me again and held out one hand. "Go ahead, shake. He won't hurt you now that I've told him you're safe."

Gingerly, I leaned down and held out my hand. Raj took it and shook it, one firm handshake. His skin felt leathery and crinkled, but the grip was intensely strong and he could have broken my hand with one squeeze, if he had wanted to.

"Hi Raj. I'm Ember. Nice to meet you." I wasn't sure what to do next, but he let go and waddled back off into the undergrowth, sniffing his hand.

"He knows your scent now, so next time you

come here, he'll remember. Come on in." Raven led me into the house.

As cluttered with plants as the outside was, the inside was almost minimalist. The decor was nice, but neat and uncluttered, and I couldn't see any plants at all in the place. The living room was spacious—open concept in the best way. The floor was a checkerboard tile in black and white. The walls were pale gray, and the drapes over the window, a filmy set of lilac sheers.

The furniture looked comfortably worn but, again, neat. A black sofa, a set of black and white nautically striped armchairs, and several end tables painted in a frosted pearl completed the decor. The living room led directly into the kitchen, which was again, done in black and white with shades of pearl and gray. An eat-in nook overlooked a sliding glass door that led out into the back yard. To the left, a hall led to what I assumed were bedrooms and a bath. To the right was a door that I guessed led into the garage.

But as minimal and tidy as the house was, the walls were alive with art. All of it worked together, but it was a kaleidoscope of color and shape and form.

"You have quite the collection," I said, staring at one painting in particular of crows overlooking a harvest field. The moon was high in the sky, and the shadows made it look as though the painting were in black and white, instead of the gentle washes of color that crept in around the edges.

"Thank you. Please, sit down." She motioned to the table. "Would you like some coffee or sparkling water or juice?"

I shook my head. "If I have any more coffee, I'll be up all night." It wasn't exactly true, but I was already on edge and didn't want to give myself a reason to be any more shaky. "So, where are your ferrets?"

She smiled. "They're in one of the back rooms, asleep. Ferrets are a lot like cats, only more crafty. I'd introduce you but I don't want them up and running around just yet. If they're happy to sleep, I let them."

"I understand. I have a cat—Mr. Rumblebutt. He's a Norwegian Forest cat and he's a handful on his own. So," I said, leaning back in my chair. "I suppose you wonder what I'm doing here."

"I assume it's about Ulstair?" She filled a tumbler with ice from the refrigerator and poured sparkling water over it, adding a twist of lemon. It looked so good that I found myself thirsty.

"If the offer still stands, I'd love to have what you're drinking."

She smiled, setting the glass in front of me. Then, pouring herself another, she joined me when she was finished. "What do you need?"

My smile vanished. "I was hoping you could take me to Ulstair's apartment. Herne wants me to walk through it with you, to see if we can find anything out of the ordinary."

Raven let out a soft murmur. "I expected this. I don't mind telling you, it's all I can do to sit here and not go running amok in the streets, trying to track him down like a lost cat." She paused, leaning back as she sipped her water. "I know you probably hear this a lot, but Ulstair wouldn't just up and leave. I know something's happened to him. I just hope he's still alive."

I paused for a moment, watching her. Any drama was purely a part of her nature, not put on for show.

"You said you're a bone witch. Pardon me, I haven't had much to do with the Ante-Fae, but... what is it that you do? I work with the water element. I'm pledged to Morgana."

Raven contemplated my words for a moment, then nodded. "I work with the dead. I actually enjoy it. I bring a lot of comfort to people, though not all of my dealings with the dead end happily. I communicate with the spirits for people who have need, cleanse houses of unwanted ghosts, and so on."

"I would think that one of the Ante-Fae wouldn't have much to do with humans. Are you saying you take human clients?"

She shrugged. "I don't really care about who my clients are, only that they can pay and that they have a need. I've worked for humans, the Fae, even a few shifters have come to me, but most of them wouldn't trust me. I may be one of the Ante-Fae, but I feel more attuned to the world in front of me than the world as it has been." She motioned for me to stand. "Come, I'll take you to Ulstair's apartment."

On the way out the door, she swept up her keys and purse, and whistled for Raj to come inside. She locked the door behind her, and we headed to our cars.

ULSTAIR LIVED IN an apartment about half a mile from Raven's house. It was a four-story house that had been converted into four separate apartments, each with an outside entrance. Ulstair lived on the second floor.

Raven darted up the steps, and I followed her. The neighborhood here was seedy, run down and a pall of resignation hung heavy in the air. I glanced around, making certain nobody was following us. It was that kind of neighborhood—the kind where you hunched forward, pulling your coat tightly around you and sped up if you were out too late.

"You have a key?"

She nodded. "I have a key to his place, and he has a key to mine."

We stepped off the landing at the front door. She fit the key in the lock and the door swung open as she turned the knob. She reached inside and flipped a switch, and a bright light flickered on in what appeared to be the main room. "He essentially has a large one-bedroom. A living room with a kitchenette, a bedroom, and a bath. This used to be an old Victorian until the owner flipped it and turned it into what he calls townhouses."

So this is what they were calling townhouses now, I thought. Then, feeling uncharitable—after all, I had lived in a condo not much bigger than this for years—I brushed the thought aside.

"Why does he live here? I thought CalTecNology

was over in Seattle." It also occurred to me that we should check Ulstair's financials in depth. He was a software developer but lived far under what his salary probably could cover.

"CTN is over in Seattle, but the rest of Ulstair's family lives out in TirNaNog. His mother is one of the ancients, and she's close to passing through the veil. He likes to keep as close as he can, just in case he needs to rush over there. As far as why he lives in this dump...well, it was the only apartment available close to my house when he moved in. He actually likes it, though. His neighbors are cool, and they all watch out for one another."

She looked around the room. It was tidy, though not as spotless as her house, and I saw clean dishes in the dish drainer on the counter. "Did you do the dishes?"

"Yeah, I found a sink full of dishes. He usually does them before bed, so I figure he disappeared some time during the day. I didn't want them to attract gnats or flies, so I washed them. Otherwise, I checked on his suitcases and they were all here." She ducked her head. "His car's down on the street, so I know he didn't take it. As I said, I called the police but they blew me off. I think Ulstair's made a few enemies over the years in TirNaNog, and a number of the cops in this district come from there."

"Yeah, that can make a big difference in whether they listen to you, all right." I glanced around the apartment. Most of it looked tidy and in order. "He's a software developer. What about his computer?"

She led me over to a desk in the corner. "He's got both a laptop and a tower. And they're both here."

"Can you get into them? If so, we can check to see if he's had any unsettling emails."

"The desktop, yes. The laptop no, because that's his computer from work and he's not allowed to let anybody else have access to it. His password on the desktop is *3945olive#*." A smile flickered across her face. "He loves olives."

I sat down and tapped away at the machine. "Have you checked his messages?"

"He doesn't have a landline, so I couldn't. I should call his work again, though. They know who I am. I called them a few days ago." She moved to the side and pulled out her phone while I concentrated on the computer.

I booted up the computer. It looked top of the line, and he had a four-monitor system rigged up. I brought up the log-in screen. His name, "Ulstair," was already listed, and I typed in the password. A moment later, I was staring at his desktop. There must have been over eighty icons there, and I scanned through them, looking for his email program. That would be the first thing to check. When I found it, I double-clicked it and waited.

Raven returned, looking grave. "They said they've tried to call him several times a day to find out where he was, but there's been no answer. I forgot to leave them my number last time, and Ulstair neglected to give them an emergency contact. They thought perhaps his mother died, since they knew she was sick. I told them I've called the cops and contacted you. They have both my number and your agency's number now."

"So he hasn't shown up at work, and there wasn't any planned leave?"

She shook her head. "He had time off scheduled for next month. We were going to take a vacation."

I glanced back at the email program. It had downloaded about two dozen messages, most requesting him to get in touch with people. "You recognize any of these names?"

Raven glanced over the list of contacts. "Yeah. Most are from work, I think. That one there is one of his best buddies."

I glanced through the backlog of messages he had already read. Nothing sparked off any alarms. No arguments. No debates or threats. After a few minutes, I pushed back the keyboard. "This is getting us nowhere fast. Let's go through the apartment. See if you can spot anything that appears to be missing. Anything at all."

We started over at his closet. All his suitcases were there. Raven began sorting through his clothes and shoes. She suddenly stopped.

"Wait. There *is* something missing. Look under the bed to see if you can find a pair of sneakers. They're fancy, with light-up racing stripes on the sides."

I glanced under the bed. Nothing. Not even a dust bunny. "Nope."

We scoured the apartment and turned up empty.

"Okay, so if the sneakers aren't here, he was probably wearing them, you think?"

She nodded. "He goes running several times a

week. I remember the shoes because I laughed at them when he bought them. He thought they were cool, and he said they're the most comfortable running shoes he's ever worn. So chances are, he went out for a run. Let me look for his hoodie that he wears over his sweats when he runs on cool days." She checked in the closet again, then went over and rifled through his dresser. "All right, his running hoodie and his blue sweats are missing. He has three pair of sweats—gray, blue, and black. The blue ones aren't in the dresser, and they aren't in the laundry basket."

"Where does he go running?" At least we had a point to start looking now.

"He runs through UnderLake Park." Raven gave me a look that told me she knew exactly how dangerous that could be.

"Do you know the route that he usually takes?"

She nodded. "He almost always takes the Bird Trackers path. About a block down the street is the entrance. He runs about a half mile on that path, then crosses to the Beach Trail, runs along the shore till he reaches the Grotto Trail, then loops back. It's about a five-mile run. He usually runs about three times a week."

"Do you ever go with him?" I asked, sitting back down at the computer. I pulled up a map of Under-Lake Park and began studying the route.

"Do I *look* like I run?" Raven shook her head. "I'm Ante-Fae, yes, and I'm strong, but I don't jog. I don't run. And I don't sweat. Well, I try not to." She twisted her lip. "I did go with him once. We walked the route, since I had no intention on jogging. It was beautiful, but eerie. There are so many spirits in that park and they're all clamoring for someone to listen to them. The overload almost did me in. I begged off ever going again. At times, I've had to visit the park for ingredients for my spells, or for people who have come seeking answers, but I'm uncomfortable with the amount of psychic energy there."

I nodded. "It's definitely not a place for the sensitive or those who are magically open."

"I don't like it, but if you want me to go with you, I will," she said. "I might be able to pick up on something. My powers mostly lie with communicating and working with the dead, but with Ulstair missing, I feel like I need to do anything that might possibly help."

I thought about it for a moment, then shook my head. "I'll call Viktor and he can go with me. If we find something you might be able to help with, then we can call you out."

She pressed her lips together, but a stray tear trailed down her face. "I know the Ante-Fae are seen as dangerous, but though all of us can be deadly, not all of us are heartless. I love Ulstair and I'll do whatever I need to in order to find him."

I turned off the computer and looped my arm through hers. "Come on. You go back to your place and rest. I'll call Viktor and he and I'll go look through the park. Don't give up hope. Sometimes, that's all that keeps us going."

VIKTOR MET ME at the edge of the park. I filled
him in on the route, and what we thought Ulstair
was probably wearing and he handed me a flashlight and a backpack, which I shrugged into. It had
basic supplies in it, and I usually kept it in my car
but I had forgotten to bring it.

As we stepped off the sidewalk, onto the Bird
Trackers Path, an immediate hush descended
around us. Oh, there were still sounds—the birds
were singing their rain songs, and the bushes rustled with the sounds of small animals, but it was
as though everything outside the park had become
muffled.

UnderLake Park was riddled with ravines, and
the path we were on was wide enough for two to go
abreast, but directly to our left, a ravine led down
into a deeper section of the park. The slope was
filled with blackberries and brambles and stinging
nettle, all painful deterrents to straying from the
path. About halfway down the slope, it looked as
though the vegetation changed over to vine maple
and waist-high ferns. The trees were thick, mostly
tall fir covered with moss, but there were also birch
and cottonwood and cedar and a few tall maple
trees tucked in among the rest. Their branches
were covered with brilliant leaves—the rusts and
reds and golds of autumn were in full array.

"It's beautiful here," Viktor said as we began our
hike. We were going at a slow to moderate pace
so we could look for anything that might point to
Ulstair still being in the park.

"Beautiful but deadly." I stopped, raising my

head to catch whatever scents I could. If we were near a water elemental, I might be able to coax it to talk to us, but I didn't have that same connection with the land. At least, not as much. But there was something on the wind, something that felt like it was coaxing me on.

"Something's stirring. Can you feel it?"

He paused, then shook his head. "No, but I don't carry much magic in me. What do you think it is?"

I closed my eyes, reaching out with my inner senses. There were whispers all around us—probably the ghosts Raven had talked about. And there were other creatures lurking in the woods. Startled, I realized I was able to sense them much stronger than ever before. I knew, absolutely knew, that we were being tracked by something. It felt old and shadowy, hidden under layers of molding leaves and decaying bark. Whatever it was, it was covered with mushrooms and mildew and it smelled... I wrinkled my nose. I could smell it now. It was pungent, like freshly turned earth in the autumn. It seemed to sense me and reached out, stretching a long, gnarled hand toward me, the knobby fingers long with sharpened nails on their tips.

Startled, I jerked back as I opened my eyes. Viktor steadied me.

"You all right?"

"Yeah, I think so, but I'm much more in touch with the forest than before. I think I may have just stumbled onto the heart of the park. Or something close to it."

Every forest, every body of water, had its heart.

Everything possessed a spirit of some sort, a consciousness that existed on one level or another. Some were sentient, others rudimentary, but consciousness was universal, and a web of energy connected everyone and everything. What happened a thousand miles away, even on the smallest scale, had an effect the world over. Theorists spoke of the butterfly effect, witches and psychics talked about how any action would alter reality. Whatever the case, I had long learned that the universe was inherently chaotic, that the world did not run on a clockwork system.

"What do you think is causing it?" Viktor glanced around us, looking nervous. "Is something here attacking you?"

I shook my head. "I don't think so. This feels..." And then I froze, as I knew—*absolutely knew*—what was happening. "My father's blood. It's rising."

Autumn's Bane, or the Autumn Stalkers as they were called, were part of the Dark Fae, and they were a band of raiders, now mostly located in Annwn. But their descendants lived here, and I was one of them, along with the Leannan Sidhe side from my mother. The Autumn Stalkers excelled in hunting and tracking and reading the forests. I was approaching the ritual when I would formally "meet" this side of myself, which was necessary before the Cruharach. My father's blood was starting to make itself known in me.

The Cruharach was the time in every Fae's life when the aging process drastically slowed down, and at that point, whatever powers they inherited from their parents came to full force. If the proper rituals weren't observed, the Cruharach could bring about madness, or even death. Nervous now, for I wasn't sure just how strong that side of me was going to be and the last place I needed for it to unleash itself was out in UnderLake Park, I cleared my throat and turned to Viktor.

"Keep an eye on me. If I start acting weird, call Herne and ask him to contact Marilee."

He nodded. "All right, but I assume you mean oddball weird, and not your normal self." He stuck his tongue out at me as I smacked him on the arm.

"Dork. Come on, let's get a move on. We've got a long hike in front of us."

We started off again, heading down the path as it began to descend deeper into the park. We had gone about half a mile before we found the turn-off onto the Beach Trail, and that looked like a steeper hike than the trail we were on. Going down wouldn't be the problem, but going up? Quite another matter.

"The fact that Ulstair can jog this path gives me an instant respect for the man," Viktor said. He was sure-footed and steady on steep slopes, given his half-ogre blood, but he was also the first to give credit where he felt it warranted. And though this trail was easy-peasy for him, he wasn't the type to diss others who weren't so athletically inclined.

"Yeah, I wish I had brought a walking stick for balance. I'm no slouch, but I can tell you this—I wouldn't try running this trail. Walking is plenty difficult as it is." I stared at the five-foot drop in front of me. It was almost perpendicular. I finally just jumped, landing firmly at the bottom. The gradient was still steep, but not as bad as that last scramble.

"I can get you one, if you like."

I shook my head. "No, I don't think I want to carry anything that comes from—"

I paused. A stray shaft of sunlight broke through the clouds, temporarily blinding me. I covered my eyes, squinting. Then as the clouds rolled in, the sun faded just as quickly as it had arrived, but before the last glint of it vanished, I caught sight of something shining in the bushes to the right side of the road.

"What's that?" I pointed to the object.

Viktor picked his way through the brambles. He froze, then pulled out a vinyl glove and put it on before picking up what was a phone. "It's got blood on it, Ember."

I held my breath as he hit the "emergency open" button and checked out the recent calls. "A dozen calls at least in the past week. All from Raven BoneTalker."

My stomach lurched. We had found Ulstair's phone, but there was no Ulstair in sight, and given the blood on the phone, I had the feeling that we were now looking for a corpse rather than a missing person.

Chapter 5

WE BEGAN TO comb through the nearby tangle of brambles and briars, but the phone was the only thing we found. I was relieved that we hadn't found a body, but that just left us with more questions. Finally, with the light waning, we headed back up the trail to the car. By the time we got to the parking lot, the afternoon was slipping toward dusk.

"Do you think I should tell Raven we found Ulstair's phone?" I stared at the device, which Viktor had bagged. We probably wouldn't pull any usable fingerprints off of it, but it was worth a shot. Not unless whoever had tossed it in the bushes had been human. Most Cryptos weren't fingerprinted.

"No, not yet. Let's see what we can find out first. If you tell her now, she'll just think the worst and that's not something she needs to do until we know for sure whether he's dead." Viktor paused as we approached our cars. "Ember, is something going on between you and Herne? You both seemed out of sorts this morning."

"Why don't you ask *Herne*?" I paused, shaking my head. "I know something's up, but he's apparently decided that I don't need to know whatever it is." My words came out more harshly than I had planned, and I immediately regretted it. I gave a frustrated shrug. "Don't mind me. I'm just... I'm not used to being in a relationship, especially one that's lasted this long, and I've never dated a god before. Sometimes things just feel a little surreal."

"Not a problem, Ember," the half-ogre said. "But if you need to talk, I'm here." He tossed me a two-fingered salute. "See you back at the office."

I slowly got in my car and with a whirl of thoughts in my head, followed him back to the agency.

YUTANI WAS BUSY on the Callan case, so Talia took Ulstair's phone and started work on it. She carried it into the back room to run some analyses on it, shutting the door behind her so nobody bothered her.

I slumped down in a chair beside Angel. Herne didn't seem to be around, but right now, I wasn't even sure if I wanted to talk to him.

"So, I haven't told Raven about the phone yet. Viktor thinks we should sit on the news until we know more." I wasn't happy about keeping her in the dark, but Viktor was right. If we contacted her with the information now, we'd just worry her.

"I like her," Angel said.

"So do I. She's got the cutest gargoyle. He's a guardian, I think. His name is Raj. He's about the size of a Rottweiler. I don't know how young he is, but he seems to be a sweetheart. She's also got ferrets but they were asleep and she didn't want to wake them." I paused, then said, "I wouldn't mind asking her over for dinner some time, if you're game."

"Sounds good to me—" Angel stopped, glancing up as Herne exited his office and, catching sight of Angel and me, he made a beeline for us.

"Hey," he said, looking strained. Possibly more strained than I ever remembered seeing him. "Ember, can you come over to my place tonight?" He paused, looking uncomfortable, then tugged at the collar of his T-shirt. It was a "Save the Forests" shirt, with a picture of a massive oak tree on it.

I glanced back at Angel, tempted to blow him off. We'd see how he liked being treated like he had treated me. But then, I decided that was childish and it wouldn't get us anywhere.

"Sure, for a while. When?"

He glanced up at the clock. "Now? It's almost five. We aren't going to get much else done today. Did you find anything out about Ulstair?"

I nodded. "Yeah, Viktor and I found his phone. Apparently, it looks like he was on a jog through UnderLake Park when he vanished. Talia's working on it right now. Meanwhile, I've got a pretty good bead on Raven. She's someone that I think I could be friends with. Ante-Fae or not, she's pretty cool."

"Just be cautious," Herne said. "The Ante-Fae are always more than what they seem."

I nodded, glancing at Angel, who shrugged and shook her head. "So you'll be late for dinner?" she asked.

I turned back to Herne. "Will I be home in time for dinner?"

He just muttered noncommittally and held up his keys. "Do you want to ride with me, or drive over on your own?"

I had the feeling I might be glad to have my own wheels. "I'll drive, especially since Angel and I both brought our cars today." Turning to her, I lowered my voice. "Go ahead and eat, but...you know, leave me some binge food in case I come home with mascara stains on my face."

She nodded, squeezing my hand. "You always know I've got your back."

"Yeah, I do. And sometimes, I think you're the only one."

HERNE LIVED IN a spacious house that bordered the North Meadow Carkeek Park, off of 119th Street. He rented it, though I had the feeling the owner was someone he knew. I hadn't ever bothered asking, though. The house was gorgeous, open concept with one giant "great room" that housed the living room, dining room, and kitchen.

There were three bedrooms and two baths off to the left, and a sunroom off the right. While Herne stayed at my house a lot, every now and then I'd sleep at his place. We would wake up early and head out back, onto a trail into the park. He would turn into a stag and I would ride him down the edge of the water where we would follow the train tracks to a patch of sandy shoals in another part of the park.

All the way over to Herne's, I dreaded what he was going to say. Was he tired of me? Was he angry? I couldn't imagine what had happened, but whatever it was, it seemed to have sent him into a slump. I wondered if Myrna had reminded him of some promise he made her and now he had to find a way to tell me we were done.

Gripping the steering wheel tighter, I tried to focus on driving. I reached Herne's house shortly after he did and as I walked up to the door, I wasn't sure whether to just walk in—like I usually did—or knock. I opted for ringing the bell.

He opened the door, looking confused. "Why didn't you just come in?"

I slowly entered the foyer. Tiled with shale rock, it was beautiful. The ceiling was a good twenty feet, stretching to the second floor. The second story housed a library and a workout room. Both had been bedrooms, but Herne preferred sleeping downstairs.

"I wasn't sure if I was welcome." I paused in the hall, not certain whether I should kiss him or not. He answered the question by slowly pulling me to him and pressing his lips to mine for a long, quiet kiss. As I broke away, I felt my eyes stinging and tried to blink back the tears that had been threatening every time I wondered what was wrong.

"All right, tell me. What happened between yesterday and today? What's going on?" I stepped back, wanting to know whatever the truth was. "You've been so quiet and aloof that I'm worried you want out of the relationship. If so, please, just tell me now and get it over with."

He blinked, but didn't look surprised. "I knew you thought that, but I needed a little time to process how to tell you what I've just found out. First, *no*, I don't want out of the relationship. I love you, Ember."

I breathed a little easier. "Then, what's going on? What happened? Does it have to do with Myrna, whoever she is?" I hated feeling jealous, but the fact was that I did.

He sighed. "Come sit down. We need to talk about this. Something has happened—something I wasn't prepared for, and that I still don't know quite how to deal with. But deal with it, I must." Herne led me into the living room and poured us each a goblet of mead. "You're going to need this. I did."

Frowning, I curled up on the leather sofa that stretched out facing the back windows, which were floor to ceiling. They overlooked the park, and I liked sitting here with my coffee, musing over my thoughts. Sipping my mead, I waited until he sat down beside me. He leaned forward, setting his goblet on a coaster, on the long wooden slab of log that he had turned into a coffee table.

"Okay, first, you have to understand that I used to be a bit wild. Nothing like Kipa, mind you, but after he broke up my engagement to Nya, I went through a bad patch. I sowed my oats...well...quite happily. And Myrna was one of my last good-time girlfriends before I began to settle down again. This was about sixty years ago."

"Okay," I said. So Myrna *was* an old girlfriend. But it sounded like they had never been serious. "We all go through that phase."

"Yeah, but...I never knew. Please believe me, nobody ever even hinted about this." He looked so hangdog that I wanted to wrap my arms around him, but I held myself back, waiting.

"What is it? Just tell me. We'll work through it." I held out my hands as he reached for them, setting my goblet next to his. "What's going on?"

He heaved a long sigh and let it out slowly. "Myrna has *just* seen fit to tell me that I have a daughter. *Her* daughter. The girl is sixty years old, which sounds older than it is, given the fact that I'm a demigod and Myrna is an Amazon. But apparently Danielle wants to get to know me, and Myrna has decided that it's time we met. Myrna wants Danielle to stay with me for a while."

I stared at him. *A daughter*? Herne was *a father*? Unable to process how I felt, I tried to search for the right words. On one hand, he wasn't leaving me. On the other, my lover and boyfriend just had dropped the bomb on me that he had a daughter who was older than I was. Clearing my throat, I reached for my glass and downed the rest of the mead in one slug. Then, I sat back, letting out a sigh of my own.

"Ember? *Love*? Say something. Please." Herne looked like he was going through hell.

I finally found my voice. "I'm not sure *what* to say. I mean...this isn't exactly like telling me that you adopted a dog or that you bought a new motorcycle. You have a *child*, Herne. Granted, she may be grown up—is she?" I paused, wondering just how old the girl was, emotionally speaking.

"Think teenager, given her parentage."

"Lovely. You have a teenager, whom you've never met, and your ex-girlfriend wants you to take the girl in. I mean, I get it—I truly do, but why did Myrna wait until now to tell you? Why not tell you when she found out that she was pregnant?" I was beginning to feel a little testy. Finding out my boyfriend was a father was a little more than I'd been prepared for.

"Myrna didn't think I'd man up back then. I'm sad to say, she was probably right. I was pissed off and angry. I don't know if I would have done what I needed to do." He waited for a beat, but there wasn't much I could say. I had a million questions, but none of them were well thought out, and I was aware enough to know that I needed to calm down before verbalizing anything that I might regret saying later on.

"Ember? Honey? Say something."

I stared at him, trying to think of what *to* say. Finally, I asked, "So Danielle—that's the girl's name?" He nodded. "So, Danielle is coming to live with you for a while. What about Myrna? Is she moving in, too?"

He shook his head. "No. I promise you, there's nothing between us. But she will be moving to the general area for a while, in case Danielle needs her."

I stared at my hands, then picked up my goblet and refilled it, slamming the mead back. After wiping my mouth, I finally worked up the nerve to ask, "So tell me. How do you feel about this?"

"I don't know, to be honest." He blinked, then tugged at his collar. "Obviously, I'm going to do what's necessary for the girl. She's my daughter and I have to take responsibility. But..."

"But what? By the way, how do you know Myrna is telling you the truth? Is there some divine paternity test you can ask for?" It hadn't escaped my thoughts that this might just be a ruse for Myrna to worm her way back into Herne's life.

He nodded. "Yeah. I'm waiting for the results. Last night, Danielle and I went to Cernunnos's palace and Ferosyn did the tests. We'll know in—" He paused as his phone beeped. He glanced at the screen. "My father, probably with the results."

He answered while I poured myself another glass of mead. At least I knew why Herne had been acting so oddly. And at least I wasn't the cause.

Herne pocketed his phone and turned back to me, a bleak look on his face. "Yeah, I'm her father. I've got myself a baby Amazon, it seems."

I set my glass down, clearing my throat. "Well, we know it's for real."

"Very much so. My father and mother are clear that I'm to make things right. Danielle will be moving in tomorrow morning. I have no real clue what to say to make this better. Ember," he slowly leaned toward me, looking as though he feared I might run away. "*I love you.* Please believe me. I'll do whatever I can to make this as easy as possible for all of us. But I can't push her away. I can't deny my own flesh and blood."

"I don't remember asking you to," I said, trying to control my own emotions. As upset as I was, I couldn't imagine being in Herne's position. And I couldn't even be angry at Myrna, given the fact that she had been knocked up by a god who then danced off to go party elsewhere. I let out a long breath. "So, Papa, how do you feel?"

He stared at me for a moment, and when I smiled, his shoulders sagged and he let out a sigh of relief. "Scared as fuck. I never expected to be a father this young. Some of the gods don't give a shit about where they sow their seed, but I've never been that type. Not really. Myrna was there during a bad time in my life. I'm afraid she paid for my heartbreak. I didn't exactly cut and run, but things were going fairly well, and I got scared. I decided I couldn't chance another broken heart, so I ended things abruptly. I guess she must have been pregnant when that happened. I do remember her saying that she had something to tell me, but I dumped her before she got around to it. I feel like I burned her, you know?"

He opened his arms to me, and I slid into his embrace, closing my eyes.

"Yeah, I suppose so." I paused, then asked, "Did you love her? Were you *in love* with her?" I had to know, because all it would take was something like this to rekindle old feelings. Herne might say he loved me, but I knew all too well how the past could infect the present.

He kissed my forehead, then the top of my head as he held me close, swaying gently. "No, love. I didn't *love* Myrna. I liked her. She was fun to be with, but I was still so angry at Nya for fucking Kipa and flaunting it in front of my face that I was numb."

Herne had been engaged to a dryad named Nya. Kipa, Herne's distant relation and spirit of the wolves, had bedded her. When Herne caught them, they invited him to join them and that had ended any friendship between the cousins. Nya had been lucky—she made it out with her skin intact.

"So, Myrna was a rebound fling."

"Yes. She and several others. I just hope to the gods none of the other women I was with show up with a paternity order. I was always careful, but mistakes happen." He froze, then looked at me. "You're using that concoction Ferosyn put together for you, right?"

I pulled back, almost insulted. I didn't want a child, but neither did I care for the tone Herne had used. "Yeah, I'm on my period, remember? I guess you'll be luckier with me than you were with Myrna." There was a bitter tone to my voice that I couldn't rein in.

Herne groaned and dropped to the sofa. "I didn't mean it *that way*. Oh hell, I'm just making a mess of everything. I'm sorry. Please forgive me. I can't bear it if you're angry with me right now."

I stewed, but finally let him draw me down to

the sofa again. "Listen, I know you're flummoxed over this, but dude, you have to let me have my *own* feelings. This isn't an easy tidbit to accept. All of a sudden, you have a family and you have responsibilities to them. I understand that. I do. But I feel like I'm on precarious ground. You have to bear with *me* a little bit, too."

I paused, realizing we were just going around in circles.

"Okay, I'm going home for the night. You're going to get an early night's sleep so you can meet Danielle tomorrow. We have a lot to do at the office, so we just go through the motions and deal with whatever comes our way until the shock wears off."

He looked ready to protest, but finally acquiesced. "You're right. You're absolutely right."

I bit my lip, wondering whether to ask the last question on my mind for the night. "Does Myrna know about me? Are you going to tell Danielle about me?"

He nodded, still looking bleak. "Trust me, I didn't keep our relationship secret. But I think you'd better wait before coming over to visit. I need to see where I stand with...my daughter. Give me a little time with her before I introduce you. But I've already told Myrna I'm in love with you." He hesitated, then asked, "You believe me, right?"

I studied his face. Herne was a gorgeous man, with long silken hair and eyes that shimmered with magic. And right now, all those eyes were saying to me was that he was telling the truth. I had two choices: I could believe him, or not. I chose the former.

"I believe you. I trust you, even though I'm nervous. But I believe you love me."

"Thank you," he whispered, pulling me in for a long, warm kiss. The fire of his lips against mine stirred my hunger for him, but I thought it might be too soon. There was too much at stake right now. Sex could so easily muddy the whole evening. I kissed him long and hard, though, before gently disentangling myself.

"I'd better go, I guess."

"Stay? I need you." The panic in his voice told me he wasn't faking it. The man was scared out of his wits. "I don't know how to be a father. I don't know if I even want to be, but that option's off the table. Ember, how am I going to do this? What do I tell her when she asks why I wasn't there for her?"

I pressed my fingers to his lips. "Shush. I can't answer that. You'll know what to do when the time comes. Meanwhile..." I straddled his lap. Muddy or not, maybe this was what we needed. I reached down and clasped his belt buckle, slowly unbuckling it. He said nothing as I unzipped his jeans.

Herne fumbled with my top, pulling it off me as I undid my bra and dropped it to the side. He leaned forward and nuzzled my breasts, then took my right nipple in his lips and began to suck, licking till it was hard and stiff. His arms were around my waist, and I rose on my knees, leaning forward as I pressed against him. Herne began to unzip my jeans, and between me kicking and him pulling, I was free of them.

"I'm on my period," I whispered.

"I don't care," he whispered back.

"I'll be right back." I jumped up, padding into the powder room to get ready for him.

When I returned, he was naked, laying on the sofa. A family of deer were staring in the window at him. The vision of my lover, the King Stag of the Woodland, watching the doe and her fawns was too perfect, too beautiful. I caught my breath as a last shaft of sunlight broke through the heavy clouds and shone into the room, illuminating Herne.

Caught by the light, he closed his eyes, leaning his head back, and I slowly moved to stand over him. He was aroused—his cock fully erect, and he looked every inch the god he was. I slowly straddled him, lowering myself onto him, feeling him spread me wide with his girth. As I moaned, cupping my breasts, he took hold of my hips and guided me down.

We made love, slow and hard and deep, in silence—unusual for both of us—with only the deer watching us. The evening wore on, and we rested for a bit, then made love again and it felt like we were the only two people in the universe. We didn't speak, just rested in each other's arms, drinking mead as we kissed and cuddled until near midnight.

Finally, I dressed as he watched.

"You aren't going to leave me, are you?" he asked, a plaintive note in his voice.

I stared at him. "If I were going to leave you, I wouldn't be here with you, naked. But you—you won't forget me, will you?"

He shook his head. "Never. The moment I met you, I couldn't get you off my mind. I still can't. I think about you day and night, Ember."

A sudden chill ran up my spine. *Now that you've met me, you'll never forget me.* That was part of my Leannan Sidhe heritage. Had I managed to bewitch a god? But I left that thought unspoken. We had more than enough to deal with for now, and I didn't want to add to the worry.

I kissed him again, then headed out the door. As I started my car, I wondered just how this was going to play out. More than a little afraid to find out, I drove the distance home in silence, not even wanting to hear myself think.

Chapter 6

ANGEL WAS ASLEEP by the time I got home, so I tiptoed past her bedroom to my own and curled up with Mr. Rumblebutt. Mr. R. seemed to recognize that I needed him because he purred me to sleep. He was still stretched out beside me when I woke up.

I slowly got out of bed, groaning from too much mead the night before, and the aftereffects of the emotional hangover I had developed. I crossed to the window, opening it and leaning on the sill as I stared out at the overcast day. The screen was covered with raindrops, and a striped orb weaver spider had spun its web in the upper right corner outside of the window screen.

The abundant rain of the autumn had turned our yard into a brilliant jungle. My house sat on two lots, half of which was given over to feral gardens that we were in the process of taming. Angel rented from me, and the arrangement moved like clockwork.

Shivering, I pulled my robe tighter around me. The temperature had dropped into the low forties during the night and the chill felt good against my skin. It also did wonders in waking me up. I breathed in a long, slow breath, then frowned. I felt tight, and realized that I hadn't gotten to the gym enough lately. Most of my time was spent at work and with Herne. I glanced at the clock and made the decision to pencil in more workouts. Then, shutting the window so Mr. R. couldn't claw his way through the screen, I headed downstairs.

Angel was in the kitchen, still in her robe, making breakfast. Bacon sizzled in a pan, and she was scrambling eggs in the small skillet. I smelled cinnamon buns heating in the oven. Angel made batches of buns and rolls and froze them, popping them into the oven to bake when we needed them. There was fresh-squeezed orange juice on the table and what looked like a super-strong latte, along with a vase of freshly picked mums from our tangled garden.

"You have bad news for me?" I asked, staring at the spread.

"No, but just in case your evening went south, I thought I'd greet you with a good breakfast," she said, dividing the eggs and bacon on the plates, and handed them to me. I carried them over to the table as she took the cinnamon rolls out of the oven and transferred them to a plate.

As we settled in to eat, she said, "Well, was it as bad as you were worried about?"

"Yes and no. In a way, this has nothing to do with me. But who am I kidding? This is going to affect my relationship with Herne. There's no two ways about it." I paused, taking a bite of bacon to fortify myself. "Herne just found out he's a father. Of an Amazon, no less."

Angel's jaw dropped. She quickly shook her head, blinking. "*Father*? He has a child? Is she a baby? Has he been two-timing you?"

"No, nothing like that. She's the equivalent of a teenager, apparently. She's twice my age, but apparently the gods age on a different scale. With Herne as her father, Danielle's going to age far more slowly than I will." I paused, not wanting to dwell on age. Angel was human, and unless we found a way to prevent it, her lifetime would be a blink of the eye compared to mine.

"How do you feel about that?" Angel asked, forking a mouthful of eggs.

I shrugged. "How am I *supposed* to feel? I'm not overjoyed, I'll tell you that. Truth is, I don't know how I feel. Except his daughter is coming to live with him for a few weeks, starting today, and that complicates matters even more."

Angel stared at me for a moment, then motioned to my latte. "Drink up."

I did, letting myself linger over the steaming mug of joy juice. After a few minutes, I let out a long sigh. "How can I be mad at him? He didn't know. And I can't justify being angry at Myrna. She just wants her daughter to know her father. I feel like I'm caught between a rock and a hard place, Angel. *My* feelings don't matter when it comes to this situation, but my feelings matter to *me*. I guess I'll just have to see how this plays out. Meanwhile, I've decided to call in sick today. I can't face going to the office right now."

"You want company? I'll ditch work, too." Angel grinned. "It will be good for them to realize just how important we are. I've revamped that damned filing system until it finally works, I've upgraded all of the forms, and I know where the bodies are hid."

At that, I laughed. "Angel, you're the glue that holds it all together. You know what? Yeah, take the day off. Talia can call us if an emergency comes up. I'll buzz her and give her the heads up. Let Herne deal with Myrna and Danielle. Without me there, it will be less awkward if Myrna decides to drop off the girl at the office."

Angel pushed the plate of cinnamon rolls toward me. "Eat. We'll go shopping. The rain's supposed to break today. If the sun decides to show its face, we can work in the garden this afternoon."

Feeling a little better, I finished my breakfast and latte, and then called Talia to tell her that, barring emergencies, not to expect either Angel or me.

Talia was silent for a moment, then said, "It's because of Myrna, isn't it? Herne told me what happened when he came in this morning."

"He's already there?" Usually he arrived at the office a few minutes before the rest of us, but we still had an hour before we were supposed to be there. "Why are you there so early?"

"I'm attempting to pinpoint Ulstair's financial transactions the past week. I'm getting some flack from my usual sources, but I'll make them talk. Anyway, Herne was here when I arrived. He's leaving around three. He told me all about Danielle and how she's staying with him for a while. How are you doing, sugar?" Talia wasn't a coddler, but when a friend of hers was upset, she definitely held out her shoulder.

I wasn't sure what to tell her. "I'm not exactly sure. I think I need to take the day and just relax and let the news settle."

"That's probably a good idea. Viktor can watch the front desk for Angel—I assume she's going to hang out with you and keep you from stewing?"

"Yeah. Thanks, Talia. I know I'm letting my personal life interfere with my business but…"

"But how can you help it when you're dating the boss? Don't sweat it. Go shopping. Watch a movie. Pamper yourself. We'll see you tomorrow."

I set my phone down, looking over at Angel. "She knows, so everybody will know. At least I don't have to deal with a lot of concerned looks and questions today. And Herne can handle his business with Myrna without me around to complicate matters."

I still wasn't happy, but the relief of not having to go into work settled in and I picked up a feather toy and began playing with Mr. Rumblebutt, who had finished his breakfast. He looked at me, then at Angel, almost suspiciously. We weren't supposed to be around during the day.

"So, what do you want to do today?" Angel asked, clearing the table. I followed her, carrying the leftover cinnamon rolls, and rinsed the dishes while she stacked them in the dishwasher.

"You mentioned shopping. Why don't we go hunting for a new table and chairs? This one's too small to throw any really good dinner parties. It fit in my condo, but not here." I poked at the utilitarian table, frowning.

"I can get behind that. Let's go dress and plan out our day. The shops won't open for another hour or so." Angel gave me a little shove toward the stairs. "Come on. Get dolled up. We might as well look our best if we're going to gallivant around the town."

Laughing, I followed her up the stairs.

WE STARTED AT the Tandy Court Mall, named after the original developer, Robert Tandy, who was a werewolf. He had wanted a place where both humans and Cryptos would feel welcome, and there was a wide mix of shops there, everything from Full Moon Magic, a witchcraft shop, to McBride's Clothes for Shifters, which had easy-on and off clothing, to Filbert's Stationery, an office supply store, to Treadwell's Furnishings.

Angel and I headed straight to the furniture store. We had slowly been replacing some of our furniture, and filling out gaps. All my furniture had been condo size—small condo size at that—while Angel's belongings had burned up in a fire.

"What about this?" Angel motioned to a highly polished light oak table and chair set. The table legs were rounded, and they looked hand-turned, though I knew they weren't. But the grain of the wood showed through the stain in a gorgeous pattern of swirls and rings. The chairs were ladder-back, with black microsuede seats. I settled myself at the table to get the feel for it.

"This is nice, and at least Mr. Rumblebutt's fur won't show up too much. Black cat, black seats." I glanced around the shop. There were a lot of beautiful sets here, and I realized that I had no clue what kind of style I wanted my house to be. Right now, it was an eclectic mishmash of ragtag finds I had pulled together over the years.

"You look confused." Angel set her purse on the table. "What's wrong?"

"I just realized I have no clue, other than the colors we painted the house, what I want my home to look like. This is a pretty table, but I'll be replacing a lot of furniture over the next year or so and I don't want to end up with another throw-together decorating scheme." I paused, looking around at the other table and chair sets. "What should I do?"

"Well, before you buy anything, let's walk around the store and get an idea for what else you like. Maybe a theme will come through." Angel motioned for me to stand up. "Come on. We'll figure it out."

An hour later, I had seen more furnishings than I ever wanted to. I had a better idea, though, of what I liked, and Angel and I agreed to hold off on buying anything while I let everything settle in my mind.

"Whatever you keep coming back to will tell

us what you like. We can go to other stores, too. There are a lot of furniture stores in Seattle," Angel said.

"Maybe this weekend. Meanwhile, let's actually buy something. I need new boots for the autumn." I stared down at my feet. My boots were still good, but they were looking a little worn.

"You do not *need* new boots. You *want* new boots. At least be honest about it," Angel said, with a laugh. "And I want new shoes, too. Let's go shopping."

The shoe venture turned out to be a lot more successful than our table excursion. I came away with three pairs of boots and a pair of slippers, and Angel walked out of the store with two pairs of boots, a new pair of sneakers, and some kitten heel pumps. We stopped in at the Fountain, an old-fashioned soda fountain, for root beer floats, before heading out to the car.

"What do you want to do next?" Angel asked.

"I thought I might work out in the garden. The sun is starting to break through." I pointed to the clouds, which were thinning out. "This afternoon, maybe we can watch a movie."

"That sounds like a good plan. Let's stop on the way home and grab a couple pizzas for dinner." Angel looped her arm through mine as we sauntered toward the door.

"I'll have to eat early," I said. "I have my meeting with Marilee tonight at eight."

Marilee was guiding me through the Cruharach, introducing me to both of my heritages. I had encountered the Leannan Sidhe side of me, inherited from my mother. And tonight, I was scheduled to face the Autumn Stalker side—my father's heritage. I had to embrace both before I could integrate their powers during the Cruharach. Marilee couldn't tell me exactly how they would blend, given the two sides were at war with one another, though how much of that was genetic and how much was societal, I wasn't sure.

"Do you think you should go through with this, right on top of Herne's news?" Angel asked, settling into the passenger seat, since I had driven.

I shrugged, fastening my seat belt. "I don't think I have a choice. I'm into the Cruharach already, and nothing's going to stop it—not even my boyfriend finding out he's a father." As I pulled out of the parking lot, easing onto the street, Angel darted a look in the rearview mirror.

"Do you see the car following us? Whoever it is, they were parked a few spots over at the mall. I noticed because the car has a dent in its front bumper that looks pretty bad."

I glanced up at the mirror. Sure enough, there was a car keeping pace with us. It was a red Camaro, and there was one person in it, but I couldn't make out whether it was a man or a woman. "Maybe they're just going in the same direction."

We were coming up on Pizza-Paparazzi, our favorite pizza joint.

"We'll find out if they're following us or not." I flicked on the turn signal. Then, checking to make sure the way was clear, I made a left turn into the mini-mall and parked in front of the pizza place. I waited for a moment. The red Camaro turned into the lot and parked at another store. I frowned.

"I'll go get the pizzas and then, I might just head over in their direction. Watch to see if the driver goes into that dry cleaning shop. If so, it's probably just coincidence." I unbuckled my seat belt and headed into the store. After I picked up two ready-to-bake pizzas—one with pepperoni and extra cheese, the other a Hawaiian pizza—I wandered back to the car and set them in the backseat next to our packages.

"Did the driver get out of the car?"

"No, whoever it is is still sitting there." Angel shook her head. "I have an uncomfortable feeling that this isn't going to be good."

"I'm going over there."

"Be careful."

Nodding, I shut the door and then, noncha-lantly turned and headed down the narrow strip of sidewalk in front of the strip mall of stores. As I approached the red car, I realized that the driver looked all too familiar.

"Damn you, Ray Fontaine!" I broke into a run, aiming directly at the front of his car.

Ray jumped out, holding up his hands. "Ember, please, I had to see you!"

I skidded to a halt, my temper flaring. "You idiot. You get the fuck away from me and stay away. I told you to stop. I've sicced Herne on you. What the hell do I have to do in order to get you to leave me alone?"

I wasn't being entirely fair. Ray was hooked on me because he was human, and he had fallen under the glamour of my Leannan Sidhe side. But that didn't mean he could stalk me, harass me, and threaten me. I had told him numerous times to back the fuck off, but he wouldn't listen. Herne had tossed him down the stairs at work once, but still he wouldn't listen. I hadn't heard from him in a couple of weeks, though, and had hoped that he finally might be moving on.

Ray was a tall man, with dark hair and the stubble of a beard. He was also athletic. He had been almost killed by a goblin when he insisted on trying to help me, back when I was a freelance bounty hunter. I had broken off our relationship for his own safety—I had a bad track record when it came to prior boyfriends dying on me—but he wouldn't leave me alone.

"*I love you*. Ember, please, listen to me. I love you and I want to marry you—" He reached out, trying to grab my hands.

I shoved him back. "What is so hard to understand about the word *NO*? *I'm not interested in you*. I'm dating Herne. I'm not getting back together with you, I'm not going to sleep with you, and I'm sure as hell not going to marry you. Get that through your goddamned head, Ray."

I pivoted, swiveling on my heel, and began to stomp across the parking lot to our car.

Ray called out behind me and I realized he was following me. I turned around, intending on slapping him silly, when an SUV abruptly came barreling into the parking lot, headed right toward Ray. The driver was holding a phone to her ear. She tried to stop—I could see the terror on her face—but even though she put on the brakes, in an ear-splitting screech of tires, her SUV rammed directly into Ray.

The car slammed into him at a good thirty to thirty-five miles an hour. I lunged out of the way as the driver swerved to the side. Ray went bouncing off the hood and landed on the pavement as the SUV came to a halt. The driver threw open her door, still screaming, as she leaped out of the driver's seat.

I raced forward, kneeling by Ray. He tried to say something but I shushed him.

"I'm calling for the medics," I said.

Once again, he tried to speak, but he couldn't get the words out. I pulled out my phone and called 911, reporting the injury.

The driver of the SUV was on her knees, flailing around like an idiot.

"I didn't know he was there," she said. "I didn't see him."

"You didn't slow down, either, and you were on your phone. What the hell were you doing, screeching into the parking lot like a bat out of hell?" I glanced at her, *so* not wanting to be involved in this.

Angel joined us, kneeling by Ray's side. He wasn't moving, and when I glanced at his legs, I could see blood had already saturated the material on his right leg. His knee appeared to be wrenched in a way no knee ever should be.

He reached for my hand, moaning. I didn't want to take it, but I couldn't refuse—not with him lying there, all mangled.

Angel tapped me on the shoulder and I looked

at her. "He's fading in and out. I can feel his consciousness slipping."

"It would probably be a blessing if he fainted," I said. "The pain must be incredible."

The woman who had hit him sat down on the concrete, her cheeks stained with mascara smears. "I'm so sorry. I—" She paused as a medic unit and a police car pulled into the parking lot. The medics were out and jogging over with their equipment almost before the emergency response unit had pulled to a stop.

I let go of Ray's hand and moved out of the way. Angel joined me. The police glanced at the three of us, then at Ray's body.

"First, anybody know his name?" one of the officers asked. He was Fae, that much I could tell, but he didn't even give me a second glance. His nametag read, "Wish Dearborn."

"Ray Fontaine. He's an acquaintance of mine."

"And you are?"

"Ember Kearney. And this is Angel Jackson." I pointed to Angel.

"What's your name, ma'am?" Officer Dearborn asked.

The woman sniffed back her tears. "Renata Taylor."

"All right, who can tell me what happened?"

I spoke up before Renata could open her mouth again. "Ray and I were having an argument—he's been stalking me—and then she—" I pointed to Renata—"came barreling into the parking lot. She was on her cell phone. I heard her brakes screech but I guess she couldn't stop, and she hit Ray, sending him flying."

The cop turned a grave eye on her. "Well? Is this true?"

Renata looked conflicted, then her shoulders slumped. "Yeah, it's my fault."

"Were you on the phone?"

"No..." she paused, then let out a loud sigh. "Yes, I was. My husband called me and I know I shouldn't have answered while I was driving, but if I don't, he gets pissy on me. I needed to stop at the dry cleaners, and he was bitching asking why I wasn't home yet, and I just...I took the turn too fast, and I couldn't stop in time." She frowned, staring at Ray. "I didn't mean to hit him. I really didn't. Is he going to be all right?"

"We'll find out, ma'am," one of the medics said. He motioned to his partner. "Get the stretcher. I'll stay with him."

"How is he?" I asked.

"He's in serious condition. From what I can tell, one leg appears to be shattered, and he has a broken pelvis. He's unconscious right now, but he's breathing on his own." The EMT glanced up at me. "Did you say he's stalking you?"

I nodded. "We dated for a short time, and then I broke it off. He's been harassing me ever since. I'm seeing somebody new and he's really not happy about it."

"Well, he's not going to be following you around any time soon, that much I'll say." The EMTs slid Ray onto a backboard, then stabilized his leg and pelvis and lifted him onto the gurney. They began to wheel him toward the medic unit.

"That's his car, by the way. The red Camaro." I pointed to the car. The door was still open.

The officers took some more information from Angel and me, then let us go while they continued to talk to Renata. As we eased out of the parking lot behind the medic unit, they were still talking to her, but I didn't see if they arrested her.

"Well," Angel said as we headed back to the house. "That was unexpected."

"And unwelcome. That he was following me pisses me off, but man, that woman—she didn't even slow down when she turned into the parking lot."

"Are you going to check on how he's doing?"

I shook my head. "I feel sorry for Ray, but not bad enough to go visit him. The fact is, he's still a stalker and he has been harassing me for months. I don't think that warrants a whole lot of empathy from me. I wish he'd just move out of the state."

"I hear you. I was just asking," Angel said as I pulled into the driveway. "Come on, let's go get into gardening clothes and then do some work out in the rose garden. We should get it ready for winter and the work will calm us down."

Grateful for something to take my mind off what had just happened, I followed her into the house with the pizzas.

Chapter 7

WE MANAGED TO weed the entire rose garden, including pruning back the bushes, and we
worked our way through the jumble that had once
been an herb garden. Angel recognized a number
of the overgrown culinary herbs, and we saved
those, trimming them back to a reasonable size
and shape. There were plenty that we didn't recognize, so I decided to wait on pulling the rest of the
weeds because there were a number of established
plants there that we might want. The vegetable
garden was easier. It hadn't been used in a long
time, though we found a couple volunteer veggies,
but the season was over so we simply tilled the
dirt.

"Are you going to want a vegetable garden?" I
asked.

Angel leaned on her shovel, wiping her brow
with her sleeve. "I think so. I enjoy puttering

around in the garden, and fresh always tastes better than what you can get at the supermarket. I think probably just a kitchen garden. Though, it might be fun to grow our own pumpkins. And squash. And..." She stopped, laughing. "Apparently, I want a garden. I'll decide this winter just how much time I want to put into it. I'm thinking we should do raised beds, though. It's much easier to tend and the output tends to be higher."

I glanced at the sky. "What time is it?"

Angel glanced at her watch. "Two-thirty."

"Let's give it another half hour and then go wash up and watch a movie and eat pizza. That will give me time to get ready for tonight." I paused, fumbling with my hoe. My hands were too small in the massive gardening gloves, but we had forgotten to buy new ones. "You know, I haven't been thinking about Herne all afternoon. Working out here, getting busy with my hands, I think it's just what I needed."

"Good," Angel said, then pointed to the ground. "Now, if we get back to it, we can have the vegetable garden finished in about fifteen minutes."

I wrinkled my nose at her, then laughed. "Okay, boss. I'm getting to work."

And we went back to focusing on the garden.

BY SEVEN O'CLOCK, we had taken showers, eaten our fill of pizza, watched one of a half-dozen movies we dubbed our "go-to-smile movies," and I had done a yoga workout, readying myself for the meeting with Marilee.

"You going to be okay here alone tonight?" I asked as I gathered my things.

Angel held up her plate. She had attacked the leftover pizza. "Yep. I'm going to binge watch *My Favorite Werewolf*, which is DJ's favorite show right now. It will give us something to talk about. I've got pizza, cola, and for emergencies—a stash of chocolate ice cream."

I snorted. "You'll be fine. I hope to be home before eleven. I guess we have to go in to work tomorrow. I'd love to take another day off, but we have work to do."

"You think you'll be okay?"

"Yeah. I'll deal with it. Having today off helped." My phone rang and I pulled it out, glancing at the number. It was the hospital. "What the fuck?" I answered.

"Ms. Kearney? This is Nurse Ranger at the Lake Sammamish Hospital. Ray Fontaine listed you as his emergency number and asked that we get in touch with you about his condition."

"One moment, please." I pushed the mute button. "Fuck. Fuckity, fuck, fuck."

"What is it?" Angel asked.

"Ray put me down as his emergency number. What should I do?"

"Tell them to take you off his chart." She frowned. "We really have to put a stop to this."

"Pardon me for making you wait," I went back to the call. "I'm sorry, but I don't know why Mr. Fontaine listed me as his emergency contact. I'm really not his friend or family or anything."

There was a pause. "He said you were his girl-friend."

"No. Not under any circumstances. Mr. Fontaine wishes I was his girlfriend but it's not going to happen." I hesitated, then asked, "But while I have you on the phone, did he pull through the accident?"

Nurse Ranger sounded confused. "Yes, he did, but he's in serious condition."

"Thank you. Now please take me off his chart. I don't want to be his emergency number, I'm not his girlfriend, and I don't know how to get in touch with his family." Before she could answer, I hung up. Then, shrugging at Angel, I turned to leave. "Ray's still alive but in serious condition. I'm going to ask Marilee for a spell to counter his obsession tonight."

And with that, I headed out the door.

I ARRIVED AT Marilee's shortly before eight. Marilee Caulder lived near the sprawling arbo-retum, on Boyer Avenue. Her house overlooked the two hundred acre plus sanctuary, and we had spent several of our meetings walking through the trails there, examining the incredible array of both endemic and exotic plants and trees.

She was waiting for me by the door, leaning against one of the posts on her porch. Merilee was barely five-four, and she was trim and strong. Her hair hung to her mid-back, and she almost always wore it in a braid. The silver strands practically glowed, setting off the pale blue of her eyes. She was wearing her regalia, an indigo off-the-shoulder gown with a silver belt, and a silver circlet around her head. In the center of the circlet was a crescent moon, tines reaching toward the ceiling, and in the center of the moon was a sapphire cabochon.

As I darted up the porch steps, I stopped to give her a quick hug, and she led me inside. "It's chilly tonight. I can feel the crows riding on the wind."

I blinked. "Crows?"

"Autumn's harbingers. Their talk turns to all things dark and shadowed this time of year, when the magic begins to rise with the fog." She took one look at me and stopped. "What's going on? You feel agitated. What happened today?"

"It isn't what happened today per se." I dropped into one of her kitchen chairs and glanced around. Her house had a very Zen feel to it, and the energy flowed uninterrupted through her home. I broke down and told her everything. It was only fair, given she had to deal with the sides of me that weren't very nice at times.

Marilee listened, not interrupting until I was done. "I can see why you're upset. But you have to set it aside. Today's work is vital, and we can't afford for you to be scattered."

"I'm trying, trust me. But I'm not sure I know how. I've been keeping myself busy all day so that I didn't have to think about Herne and his daughter, but then with what happened with Ray, I think my 'sit tight on reality so I don't have to think about it' approach isn't going to work anymore." I paused, then barged ahead. "Marilee, Morgana said something when she first told me about my Leannan Sidhe side."

"Oh? What was it?"

"She said that the watchwords of the Leannan Sidhe were *Once you have met me, you'll never forget me.* I'm wondering...could that be what's keeping Ray tied to me? And if so, is there a way to break his obsession?"

Marilee held my gaze, and I could practically see the wheels turning in her head. After a moment, she motioned for me to follow her back into her ritual room. The room reverberated with magic, the energy rippling through the air like waves. There were crystals everywhere, on shelves and on the four altars spaced around the room to honor the directions. A round table sat in the center of the room with a black and silver cloth draped across it.

"Sit. Let me get my tarot cards." She crossed to a chest on one side of the room and withdrew a velvet bag. From the bag, she shook out a deck of cards and then returned to sit opposite me. The deck was large, and I had never seen another like it. Adeptly, she divided the cards and began shuffling them. She gave them a good ruffle five times over, then handed the deck to me. "Eight times. Then cut the cards once."

I shuffled the cards, feeling a little embarrassed by how difficult I found to hold them. But Marilee had smaller hands than me and she managed to shuffle without any problems, so I assumed it was a matter of practice. I handed them back to her and she tapped once on the back of the deck, then again before laying out an eight-card spread in the shape of a circle. As she turned them over, I felt a wavering in the pit of my stomach.

She stared at them for a moment, holding her hands over them, then pointed to the first card. "The Eight of Cups. He's developed an unhealthy obsession with you, as we know. It goes deeper. He feels stronger with you around. I think he's sourcing energy off of you. That goes hand in hand with the Leannan Sidhe tactic—and the word *tactic* relates to those who know what they're doing—of feeding their victims for a while before beginning to siphon their energy. The Leannan Sidhe get people hooked on them, before then leeching energy."

"I'd *never* do that—"

"No," Marilee interrupted. "*You* wouldn't, not consciously. But your very nature sets you up for unintended consequences. Ray fell into the glamour that emanates from you. I don't think it's at full strength, and whether you ever develop the full power remains to be seen. But for some reason, Ray fell under the spell of what you do have, and he responded to it."

She paused, then pointed to another card. "This is the reason. Right here. The Seven of Cups. Ray has an addictive nature. He's prone to get hooked on anything he can possibly get addicted to. If it wasn't you, he'd pick up another vice. Drinking, smoking, drugs...gambling. Whatever makes him feel like he matters, because my sense is that, deep inside, he sees himself as insignificant."

I stared at the cards. "I think you're right. He so wanted to play the hero for me, and that's how he almost got killed when the goblin caught him. I broke off the relationship to save his life. So, what can I do about this?"

She tapped another card. "Three of Wands, stay true to what you know. It's not healthy for him, or safe for you, to have him hanging around. Combined with the Magician and the High Priestess that flank that card, I'd say that we can figure out a magical solution to this. The Four of Swords tells me that we should focus on a spell that breaks his love for you. Since his love isn't from the heart, we need to break the illusion. And the Chariot tells me we should resolve this now, because his obsession will only grow stronger if we don't. The last card, the Queen of Swords, is an indicator that you don't play the victim and you don't work well with those who do. Time to quit feeling sorry for him, and assess every step you can take to make him back off."

"I told the cops he was stalking me when they arrived with the medic unit." I stared at the layout for another moment, then said, "All right. I need a spell that shatters the effect my glamour has on him." I snorted. "I'm so not a glamour girl, so it feels weird to talk about this."

"You may not think you are, but there's a difference between creating glamour and wearing it like a second skin." Marilee swept up the cards and put the deck back into the velvet bag. "I'll work on a spell tomorrow for this. If we can cast it before he gets out of the hospital, so much the better."

A weight fell off my shoulders as I forced a smile

to my lips. "Well, that's one problem down. Now, my next question regarding my Leannan Sidhe side is one that makes me cringe. Do you think that Herne was caught by my...*glamour* as well? Do you think that he's in love with me because of it? He says he can't forget me. That he thinks about me all the time."

Marilee reached across the table and patted my hand. "No, dear one. Herne can't be affected by glamour like that. He's a demigod and they're immune to most charms, except the charm that grows in the heart when you *truly* fall in love with someone."

I stared at her for a moment, then burst into tears. "Thank the gods for that."

She handed me a tissue. "Here, blow your nose. I'll get you some water and a little something to eat. I know you ate before you came, but the emotional toll of what you've been dealing with the past couple days saps a lot of energy. You need to be strong for tonight." She vanished out of the ritual room, returning in a moment with a bowl of fruit salad, a piece of cheese, and a bottle of cold water.

Feeling coddled—and grateful for it—I ate the fruit and cheese and drank the entire bottle. When I finished, I sat back.

"I suppose there's no getting away from it. I'm almost afraid to meet my father's blood. When I was out in the forest with Viktor yesterday, I noticed something different. I felt hyper-alert, as though I could hear and sense things differently. I wonder if that's part of the Cruharach?"

"Most likely, given your bloodline. Let me draw the circle. Go to the bathroom if you need to now, while I prepare for the ritual."

I obeyed, heading to the bathroom. Something was lurking on the outskirts of my consciousness. The Cruharach, no doubt, approaching.

I stared at my reflection. "Who will I be when this is all said and done with?" But I had no answer, only more questions. Finally, I returned to the ritual room where Marilee was waiting.

She had drawn a circle on the floor in salt, but this time there was no bowl of water on the table, no Veni-noir to taste my blood.

"What do I do?"

"Since we've already been through the first part of the ritual, this time you lay down in that circle and I simply give you the compound to send you deep into your subconscious. You've already met the Leannan Sidhe, and she's integrating into your psyche with each passing day. Today, the Autumn Stalker side will arise. I honestly don't expect as much difficulty as we had from the Leannan Sidhe. Members of Autumn's Bane might be ruthless, but they're generally more reasonable and they don't usually attack unless they've already decided on a raiding party." She held up a bottle that I recognized.

"Should I stick out my tongue, or get into the Circle first?"

"Get inside the Circle so I can seal it, please."

I handed over my phone. Electronics didn't fare well inside the Circle. Then, lying down, I spread my arms and legs wide to form the five points of the pentacle. She waited till I was ready, then sprinkled a ring of frankincense atop the circle of salt, and then a ring of powdered iron that made my body tingle and pulse. The iron would keep me within the circle, and would keep her safe should the Autumn Stalker blood prove too strong. As she whispered an incantation, I felt the barrier strengthen and the pulsing grew stronger. If I tried to leave the circle now, I'd be severely burned.

"Stick out your tongue," she said, placing the bowls on the table and returning with the tincture.

I obeyed. At least this time I knew what to expect. As three drops of the sweet, spicy liquid hit my tongue, I felt a sudden wash of energy roll through me.

"I think it's acting quicker than the first time."

"Yes, that's not surprising. This time probably won't be as hard on you, given you've already been through it once, but it's difficult to predict. Just take a deep breath and let it out slow and close your eyes."

Her voice was reassuring, and she was right. This time I was better prepared for what was about to happen, and I didn't feel as much apprehension. I wasn't expecting it to be a walk in the park, but somehow, this felt different. I felt like I had a little more control over the situation, and even if that was an illusion, it gave me confidence.

I closed my eyes, waiting for the tincture to take hold. A moment later, everything around me began to pulse and I realized that it was working. This time, I didn't try to talk or sit up, and when my tongue felt odd and thick, I didn't panic. I was breathing fine, drifting on a sea of sensation.

As the energy began to thicken, instead of feeling swept out into the ocean, this time I was walking in a forest, deeper and deeper into woodland. The trees seemed to tower hundreds of feet over my head, and all around me, I could hear and sense the motion of the woodland. Here—a fox racing beneath the undergrowth. Over there—the lazy drone of a bumblebee, out on a last late autumn hunt for pollen. The scurry of beetles beneath the bark of a tree caught my attention, and the sounds of a spider spinning her web from branch to branch in a cedar echoed through my mind. Everywhere I turned, the scents and sounds of the living forest were overwhelming.

Pungent earth, veined with mildew from the molding leaves that carpeted the ground...the astringent smell of rainwater dripping from fir needles, plummeting down to the earth, drop by drop...the smells of chimney smoke caught on the wind...that charred electrical smell that filled the air before a thunderstorm...

I was assailed from all sides by the perfume of autumn and it overwhelmed me, sending me reeling. As I tried to steady myself, the cawing of crows echoed overhead, then all around me as the great birds landed in the trees, watching me closely. I stared up at them, both afraid and yet pulled to them. Their glittering eyes followed me as I took a step along the path, and then I saw that they lined the trail, like spectators at a parade. They were waiting for me to pass through them, a crackling tension echoing in the sound of their caws.

I caught my breath, suddenly afraid they might swoop down and peck out my eyes. Or rip at my skin.

Then, as I started along the trail, I saw someone walking toward me and I realized that it was my father's bloodline, the part of myself that echoed the Dark Fae. Just as I had faced my Leannan Sidhe self, I had to face the Autumn Stalker within. Taking a deep breath, I began to pass through the line of crows guarding the way.

As I approached the woman I could see that she, too, looked just like me, except she was silent, making almost no sound as she walked. Her hair was pulled back in a long braid, and she wore an outfit that blended into the forest—woodland camouflage. She had a bow over one shoulder, and a long dagger by her side. She stopped, holding out her hands.

"You've been here before," she said.

I nodded. "Only with my mother's blood."

"Are you willing to brave the forest? Are you willing to run with the Hunt?" She was daring me, taunting me.

I felt a pull toward her that was stronger than the pull had been from my Leannan Sidhe nature. Reaching out, I grabbed her hand, holding tight. She laughed, then turned and—still holding my hand—began to run through the forest. Exhilarated, I let her drag me along.

We raced at a speed that defied my ability to run, but the blood pumped in my veins and I felt compelled to follow. We headed off path, and she led me up an embankment, and at the top of the ravine, I realized we were on the edge of a clearing, but I couldn't see what was ahead for the fog had risen thick around us and the path was obscured.

She turned to me, shoving me forward. "Walk into the mist."

I studied the roiling plumes of white vapor. They curled and coiled, beckoning me to enter. There was something in there, I could feel it, huge and terrifying. Yet I longed to find out what it was. I glanced back at my companion, hesitating.

"Will you come with me?"

"Every time you enter the woodland, I'm there. Every time you plunge into the mist, I'm shadowing your back." She reached out her hand toward me. "Do you choose to enter the fog with me?"

Hesitating, I stared at her hand. If I accepted her offer, I would be letting her in.

Slowly, I placed my fingers in hers, and we walked toward the wall of fog. As we approached the coiling plumes, she turned to me and then, without a word, she pulled me toward her. I closed my eyes as she engulfed me in her embrace.

Our energies began to merge, our bodies superimposed one over one another. Her essence entered my heart to mingle with my own nature. But she didn't feel alien or "other." She felt like *me*, and right then, I realized that I knew her. I had *always* known her. She had saved me on more than one occasion, guiding me with her intuition, her drive, and her knowledge. I let go of resistance and closed my eyes. And she became me, and I became her, as I finally acknowledged her existence.

THE AUTUMN LEAVES crunched under my feet. I could feel the tang of the season biting deep as I breathed in a deep lungful of air. All around me, the noises of the forest set up a racket, and before long, a symphony of grunts and clicks and whistles and low growls reverberated in the background. I was alone, unable to see through the wall of mist that surrounded me, but with every footstep, I knew that this was a side of me that I couldn't deny—that I needed. Strength flowed through my veins, and the desire rose to hunt and seek, to pounce and claim for my own.

Ahead, the mists began to thin as the darkened shadows of the wood took hold. Something was coming my way on the trail and I darted out of sight, hiding behind a nearby tree. I fumbled with my bow, nocking an arrow as I waited. An unusual patience flowed through my veins, and even as I fought against it—wanting to jump out to see what was coming—I forced myself to wait, silent and unseen. The quarry would come to *me*, I would not go to the quarry.

After a time, instinct bade me to peek out from the tree. There, on the path, was the most beautiful deer I had ever seen. Beautiful and statuesque, he had a rack that spanned ten tines. Instinctively, I brought up my bow and then stared at my hands, horrified. An inner voice whispered, "Shoot. You must complete the hunt."

I can't kill this magnificent creature.

*You must. You're hungry, and you must feed
your family. If you don't, they will starve.*

But he's too lovely. He's too alive and vibrant.

*Either take him down, or go home and watch
your children starve.*

I warred with myself as I waited...as the stag
waited. I knew where my food came from, I had
never denied that. But I had never killed a beast
that meant me no harm, that was just wandering
by, minding his own business.

Then, the stag caught sight of me. He stared into
my eyes and I gazed back. And within his gaze, I
saw the life cycle complete itself—the chain that
wove through every layer of life on the planet. Regardless of what we ate, we killed to survive. Every
creature did this. Every creature hungered and
sought food to assuage the pangs of its belly. Every
creature ate to survive, and in doing so, something
else had to die. Even the lowest one-celled creature
fed on something that had once been alive.

Trees absorbed nutrients out of the soil, but
those nutrients had to come from somewhere. And
they came from decomposing material that the
Mother absorbed back into herself. So the trees
ate from the death of both plants and animals. We
ate the fruit of those trees, and the flesh of animals. Animals fed on other animals, or on berries
or leaves. It was one grand magnificent chain—an
orgy of killing to feast, and then dying to feed others.

All of this synergistic wonder filled my heart
as I watched the stag. He waited as I raised my
bow, aiming true. The arrow flew, singing its way

through the air to land in the stag's heart and I cheered as he bellowed out, then went down. I ran forward, crying and laughing as I knelt beside him. Our gazes met again, and this time, I felt deeply humbled. I had taken his life. I owed it to him to honor his remains. To eat of his flesh, to make certain his death wasn't wasted.

As I pressed my head to his chest, listening to his last gasps, standing witness to the transition from life to death, I felt a warmth on my face. I realized I was crying. I was crying for the stag, and I was crying for all those who had died from starvation, from the breakdown of the cycle. Another moment, and the stag was dead, and I was back in the room with Marilee.

Chapter 8

MARILEE WAS WATCHING me as I sat up. Last time, I had tried to threaten her, but this time, I just felt an odd sense of calm washing over me. I didn't feel like something had taken over my body, and I didn't feel like I was fighting for control. I glanced up at my teacher.

"Is that all?" I asked.

"*Is that all*? What more do you want? A marching band?" Her eyes were sparkling and she looked delighted.

"I'm not sure what you're talking about." I felt a little crotchety. Her response wasn't the one I had been expecting. "Shouldn't there be...a struggle or something? Last time, my Leannan Sidhe side tried to jump out of the Circle at you."

"Last time was last time. This time is different. I told you, the Autumn Stalkers are more reasonable to deal with than the Leannan Sidhe, even if they're ruthless when they're on the hunt. How do you feel?"

I frowned, searching for exactly what I was feeling. I bit my lip, trying to decide if everything was okay or if I was still under the effects of the tincture. But there seemed to be no division—the image of my hunter self felt very much a part of me. And, when I reached for the Leannan Sidhe, she too seemed to be quietly resting, a part of myself who was waiting for me to lead.

"I'm confused. I've felt in a turmoil since the last ritual but now I feel so calm. It's like…"

"Like you're one person instead of three?"

I nodded. "Yeah, I guess that's the way to put it. I feel like I've settled down. Is this *it*?" I asked, suddenly hopeful. "Did I just pass through the Cruharach?"

Marilee laughed then, and fetched the broom to sweep a gate in the Circle so I could pass through without getting hurt. "Not at all. But now you are *ready* to face the Cruharach. You've met both sides of your bloodline and they seem to be integrating into you. It's like…you can't take the test without processing the homework. These rituals have been your homework. There will be more to come, but facing your heritage and allowing it to take its rightful place? That's vital to pass through the Cruharach without dying."

"Oh." My hope deflated. I had hoped perhaps this was it, *boom*—everything was good to go. "So, when do I go through the final phase?"

"One step at a time. I need to assess which side of your heritage is dominant. Cernunnos and

Morgana will want that information. They'll be the ones leading you through the final ritual. Morgana told me that last time she contacted me." At my petulant frown, Marilee laughed and shook her head. "Students. No matter how advanced they are, no matter how much props you give them, they always want more. Or at least, hope for it. You're doing fine, Ember. I'm pleased with your progress."

Trying to put aside my disappointment, I rubbed my head as I stood up, dusting myself off. I stepped outside the Circle and sat down in one of the chairs by the table.

"So, can we find that out tonight? Which side of me will be the more dominant?"

Marilee nodded. "It will take a little time to be certain, but I can venture a guess. The side that integrates more seamlessly is almost always the side that takes dominance. And that has everything to do with the nature you were born with. I'm going to say that your Autumn Stalker side will come out on top. That doesn't mean you're rejecting your mother's blood, but that your father's blood matches your own personality better than your mother's."

I thought about it for a moment. "Then, if that does turn out to be true, I'm relieved. As much as I loved my mother, her nature frightens me more."

"I think you're both wise, and lucky," Marilee said.

NEXT MORNING, I was up before the sun. Even though I had dropped exhausted into bed after my meeting with Marilee, I slept like the dead and woke at five-thirty. Usually, Angel and I got up at seven, to get to work by eight. I sat up, yawning, rubbing my eyes. Mr. R. gave me a lazy look from the bottom of the bed, eyeing me accusatorily.

"Yes, I woke you up, you giant furball. Go back to sleep if you want. I'm not going to make you move." I hopped out of bed, yawning again, and slid my feet into my new slippers. I padded over to the window and opened it, feeling the blast of chill air race in through the screen. Shivering, I grabbed on my robe and closed my eyes, filling my lungs with the scents of early morning mist and dew. After a moment, I closed the window and headed downstairs.

By the back door, I stopped to change into a pair of boat shoes, then headed out into the side yard, aiming for the gardens. The second lot that came with my house was separated from the house by a gate, and the lot was completely fenced in. Yutani and Viktor had built a matching fence around the rest of the property for us.

As I wandered into the gardens, trying to avoid the mud puddles, I saw a crow ahead on a post and the crow necklace I never took off vibrated against my throat. It had been a gift from Morgana, a symbol that I belonged to her. I reached up, touching the silver pendant, and slowly walked toward the crow. Crows and ravens weren't the same, but they were related, that much I knew. And this crow was eying me cautiously.

"Hey there," I said, my voice low. "Who are you?"

The crow stared at me, then let out a long caw, squawking at me loudly. I felt like it was trying to tell me something, but I wasn't sure what.

I reached out to the bird, and it eyed my hand, as if debating on what to do next. Finally, it let out another long caw and rose up, circling over my head before winging away to the north. I watched it go, wondering what that had been all about.

Padding back into the house, I took a quick shower, then dressed. As I slipped into a pair of black jeans and found a blue turtleneck, I thought about the night before. The Cruharach was coming closer, but after meeting my father's bloodline, I wasn't as nervous as I had been. The Autumn Stalkers could be dangerous, but they were also reasonable. The Leannan Sidhe, not so much. But together, the mix could be both powerful and yet workable. And my mother had managed to keep a hold on her own nature—she hadn't gone around leeching energy off others. I could manage this. I could do this, and make it work to my benefit. Once again, I was grateful to Morgana for sending me to Merilee.

I finished dressing and did my makeup. Then, brushing my hair back into a ponytail, I added a pair of sapphire studs to my ears, and eyed myself in the mirror. Today I'd have to deal with Herne, but I felt a peace that I hadn't expected. We would manage through this mess, and find a way to make it work. It wasn't like he was in love with Myrna.

I decided to surprise Angel. She wouldn't be up for a little while, so I rummaged through the cupboards till I found a skillet, and then brought out the eggs and bread. As I began making toast, I heard her coming down the stairs.

"Are you cooking?" she asked, peeking in the kitchen with a sleepy yawn.

"Hey, I made my own meals when I lived on my own. Yes, they were simple, and yes, I enjoyed eating more than I did the cooking. But I managed. I was up early, so decided to make us scrambled eggs and toast. You want grated cheese in your eggs?"

She nodded. "Always. I'll start your coffee. Can you put the tea kettle on for me?"

We worked in comfortable silence. She opened the cat food for Mr. Rumblebutt, who came running at the sound of the can opener, and we slid into our chairs at the table with our plates. The eggs and toast were simple, but they were hot and tasty. As I passed the raspberry jam to Angel, she scratched her nose and yawned again.

"I waited up for a while, but you came in late. How did the session with Marilee go?"

I licked a drop of butter off my fingers. "Good, actually. I met the Autumn Stalker part of my bloodline. Marilee thinks that my father's blood will be dominant. Even though I detest my grandfather, I'm actually relieved. Believe it or not, *that* blood is more reasonable than my mother's. I think I can do this."

Angel nodded. "You can. You're strong and you're determined. You can make it through this transition." She paused, then asked, "What about Herne? You going to go to work today?"

"Yeah. I needed yesterday off, but I'll go today. The shock's worn off a bit. So what if he has a child? She's an adult—technically—so it's not like she's going to need him to diaper her. And everybody comes with some sort of baggage in their lives. Ex-husbands, stalker boyfriends, kids from a short-term relationship...it happens. Maybe she and I will hit it off and we'll all end up one big, happy, extended family." I could almost let myself believe that, even though beneath the surface, the jaded side of me was whispering, "Oh sure...it's going to be *that* easy."

Angel ducked her head, laughing. "Hold onto that for when the going gets rough. One thing I've learned about kids from taking care of DJ, smooth sailing never lasts for long. But at least Danielle's on her way to adulthood. You just about ready?"

I nodded. "Yeah. Let's head out."

We arrived at work at quarter to eight. Viktor was there, hanging around the desk. He looked relieved when he saw us exit the elevator.

"Thank gods you're here today." He quickly slipped out of Angel's chair. "I can answer the phones but you've managed to organize things to the point of where I can't figure out where anything is." He laughed, though. "Seriously, Angel, you're priceless. Don't you dare quit."

"Is Herne here yet?" I asked.

Viktor shook his head. "He'll be in a little late. Staff meeting at ten in the break room to discuss Raven's case. I found out a bunch of stuff yesterday that may shed some light. Also, Charlie's due to start work soon."

"That's right—I had forgotten about that with all the crap going on." I glanced around. "Has he got a key to unlock the elevator?"

"Yeah, he does. Herne made sure. He'll work from home during the day, then come in for an hour after sunset to input his notes." Viktor grinned. "He's cleaned up quite well."

"Oh?" I laughed.

When we first met Charlie, we had been looking for his roommate, a human who ended up being part of a hate group. Charlie Darren was the quintessential nerd/outcast. He was also a vampire, turned just a year or so back when he was nineteen. He had been a math major putting himself through college while working in a doughnut bakery. His sire had been a rogue vamp. The Vampire Nation saw to it that the vamp never took another life, meaning they staked him. Charlie had hoped to move up in vampire society, but the lack of a sire to stand by him, and the lack of money and experience were big drawbacks. Charlie was also lonely, and he and Viktor had struck up a friendship of sorts.

It had occurred to Herne that having a vampire on staff might actually benefit us. Charlie could get into places we couldn't, and having that connection with the Vampire Nation might be a good thing when we needed their cooperation. So he offered Charlie a job and Charlie decided to take it. It beat cranking out doughnuts during the wee hours of the night.

"Yeah, his vampire glamour has taken hold, and I got him out of those empty eye-glass frames he was still wearing and convinced him to ditch the oversize jeans for ones that fit. He exchanged the ripped T-shirts for sweaters. He looks pretty snazzy now." Viktor sounded like a proud papa.

"Well, I'm glad he's joining us," Angel said. "He seemed way too lonely at the Labor Day party you threw."

"He just wants to fit in somewhere. And right now, he's not doing so hot on that count with other vampires. His family disowned him. So..." He stopped as Angel took her seat and began looking through the messages.

"Is Talia in?" I asked.

"Yeah, she's in her office, searching through the bank records that came in last night. Yutani's due in any minute. His aunt's with him. She's up here visiting."

"It's family week around here, isn't it?" I caught myself before I sounded too harsh. I really didn't want to go down that road.

"You'll like her. Celia's a firebrand. She comes up every year to visit him, since he's no longer allowed in the village." Viktor stopped as the elevator opened and Herne strode in, accompanied by Yutani and a very short, large woman. She was pretty, with dark eyes and long hair caught back in a gray ponytail. She crackled with energy and I could feel the shifter vibe coming off her in waves.

"Hey," Herne said. "Look who I found in the elevator." He wrapped his arm around the woman's shoulders and squeezed. "Yutani brought Celia with him!"

"Celia—it's so good to see you," Viktor said, stepping in for a big hug. At that moment Talia entered the waiting room and she, too, launched herself at the coyote shifter. After everybody was done, Yutani escorted Celia over to the desk.

"This is my aunt Celia. Celia, meet Ember—she's Herne's girlfriend, as well as a coworker, and this is Angel, our receptionist and all-around miracle-worker."

As I shook Celia's hand, a spark crackled.

I laughed. "You trying to electrify me?"

"Oh, girl, if I was, you'd know it." Celia winked, then said hello to Angel. "Don't mind me, I know you have a meeting to attend to. I'm going to do some shopping around the neighborhood and I'll be back around lunch time to take Yutani out for our traditional fish-and-chips fiesta." She waved and—before anybody could answer—slipped back into the elevator.

Yutani smiled fondly at the closed doors. "Celia came early this year." He turned around, glancing at Angel and me. "She usually comes up for Thanksgiving, but this year she's going on a cruise, so she planned her trip early."

"All right, let's get on with the meeting. Angel, lock the elevator and join us, please. You can take notes for Raven's case file." Herne paused as he started past me. He gave me a long look. "Are you all right? I missed you yesterday."

I shrugged. "I just needed some time to process all this."

"I understand," he said, softly pressing his hand

against my shoulder. "But please, talk with me about anything that concerns you. I don't want us to stop communicating. I don't want you to walk away from me."

"Speaking of walking away from, Ray's in the hospital," I said as we joined the others in the break room. I told them what had happened.

"So he's out of commission for a while?"

"Yeah, though I don't know how long. I'm hoping that Marilee will have a counter spell to break the obsession before he's released from the hospital. That would be a relief and much easier than trying to put him in jail or whatever we're going to have to do."

"Yeah, it would. Well, keep us informed," Herne said, sitting down with his tablet and a file folder. "Okay, let's get to work. Yesterday was a haphazard day due to many reasons, mostly my issues. You all should know that Danielle is settled in with me for a while. She's not exactly thrilled about it, but her mother has a business trip to Japan coming up, and while Danielle lives on her own, for the most part, she's used to Myrna being nearby."

Nobody said much, but then again, I doubted any of us knew exactly what to say, given the situation.

Talia cleared her throat. "Well, I ran through Ulstair's bank records. Nothing—no withdrawals, no activity on his credit cards since the day he disappeared. And I took a look at his phone. No usable fingerprints, and not much to go on. Raven called him twenty-five times, and his work called him every day. The messages were unread, so he didn't get any of them."

Viktor nodded. "That doesn't surprise me. But this may go deeper. I went to the station and talked to Erica. She dove into the files for me. There have been three other recent reports on missing persons from people who frequented the same trail in UnderLake Park. The cops did a couple sweeps of the area without finding any results, but they aren't touching the cases otherwise. All three were younger Fae men, who seem to bear an uncanny resemblance to Ulstair. Or maybe he resembles them—who knows? But whoever is kidnapping them seems to have a special type in mind."

He laid out four pictures, one of them Ulstair's, and I had to agree that he was right. All four men looked relatively young—for being Fae—and they were light haired, dark eyed, and seemed to be of a similar build. Toned, with a runner's physique.

"Does this mean we're following a serial killer? Or kidnapper? When did these men go missing?" Talia asked, leaning forward to study the pictures. "They're all Fae?"

"Yeah, all Dark Fae. Two of them disappeared in August, around two weeks apart. One in early September. And now Ulstair in mid-September. I asked Liu if he could look back further for any similar cases but he couldn't seem to find any that seemed to match up. At least not around Under-Lake."

"So, no activity on the credit cards, and there have been three other men who look like him who have disappeared. And the cops aren't taking steps on any of this. I have a bad feeling about this,"

Herne said. "I think we need to concentrate on Raven's case for now, at least until we find out what happens when I follow Morgana's instructions and carry word to Névé that anybody found harboring Callan will be hauled in before her and Cernunnos. Ember, you and I are meeting Saílle and Névé at Ginty's to discuss this today."

I groaned. "Another parley?"

"You know it's the only way that Saílle and Névé will enter the same room. Come on, we need to head out now. We're due there by eleven and traffic might be a bitch."

"What should we do about Raven's case while you're gone?" Talia asked.

"Since there have been three other cases like Ulstair's, look into the backgrounds of the other men. See what you can find out about them. There has to be some sort of connection. Or maybe that's just a hope, but whatever, Talia, you and Yutani spend the rest of the morning gathering all the details you can about them." Herne yawned, stretching. I caught my breath, reveling in the sight. Yeah, I had to make it work with Herne. There was too much between us—too much that I still wanted to explore with him.

We headed out after I grabbed my purse and he, his backpack. He tossed it in the back seat of his Ford Expedition and motioned for me to get in. I really didn't want to go hang out with the Fae Queens again, but I grudgingly climbed in the passenger seat.

Névé and Saílle might be from opposite courts, but they were cut from the same cloth and it wasn't exactly a pretty one. Oh, both queens were gorgeous, but their beauty stopped right below the surface. I had spent my entire life keeping as far away from my people—both sides—as possible, and now, once again, I was going to parade in front of them and rub their noses in the fact that I existed.

While both appeared to be superficially pleasant, they were actually unpleasant, petty, and both far too arrogant for their own good. I thought about the possibility of pointing that out, but decided that discretion was the better part of valor. And it took valor to even just meet them face to face.

Herne waited till he had pulled out of the parking garage before swinging to me. "Seriously, how are you doing?"

I blinked. "I told you, I'm all right. So, just what's on the topic for parley today?"

He paused for a moment, waiting, and when I didn't say anything else, he snorted. "Handing over Callan to us."

"Good luck with that one." I figured we'd be wasting our time, but it wasn't my call. If Morgana wanted us to face them down, we'd face them down.

"I thought maybe you might like to come over and meet Danielle." He said it so nonchalantly that I almost didn't hear what he said, but then his words registered.

I blinked and turned toward him. "Seriously? You want me to meet her?"

"Of course. You're an important part of my life. She's not exactly a child, although she would be considered a teenager in terms of the gods. The Amazons age quickly compared to the Fae, but even so, they're exceptionally long lived for humans. But my blood gives Danielle close to an immortal lifespan." He paused, then added, "I can't promise she'll be happy to meet you, but this has to happen sometime and we might as well do it now."

I wasn't sure what to say, but then cleared my throat. "What about Saturday?" I wasn't procrastinating, but I wanted to have some time to mentally prepare myself.

"Saturday morning it is, then. Come over for brunch, around eleven." He stared at the road, easing over into the right lane as we curved around the ramp, merging onto the 520 freeway. We were headed out across the floating bridge when he spoke next. "It's so weird. Danielle and I are jockeying for some sort of common ground. She resents me, I can tell that much. And she seems to feel that I resent her."

"Don't you? I'm not saying you're a bad person, Herne. But this was a bombshell dropped in your lap, long after your relationship with Myrna ended. I suppose I understand why she wanted to wait to tell you—or maybe I don't, but the fact is, you were presented with a fully grown daughter and you're suddenly expected to create some sort of relationship with her. You've never been in her life, maybe her mother never told her who her father was until now, and then—she's expected to cozy up with you and call you Daddy? Danielle probably resents the hell out of you, and maybe her mother, too. And it seems like it would be normal for you to resent her."

Herne let out a long sigh. "Yeah, I have to admit that I keep wondering why the hell Myrna didn't come to me when she found out she was pregnant. I wouldn't have married her, but, although I was an arrogant snot at the time, and pissed off, I really hope I would have done the right thing and made sure she and Danielle were provided for."

"Do you *want* a relationship with the girl?" I wasn't asking out of spite. I was genuinely curious. I knew how I felt when my grandfather had contacted me—I hadn't wanted a damned thing to do with him, and with good reason. He was a toxic person and a toxic force, and I wanted nothing to do with him.

After a moment's hesitation, Herne said, "I don't know, to be honest. I do—I suppose. I'm *supposed* to want this. There's a part of me who feels like I already let her down by not being there for her mother and her. I owe this to her. I owe it to her to help out, to forge some sort of amenable relationship with her. But so far, I can't say that I'm finding it easy. Danielle's spoiled, and Myrna brought her up to be a snob, an attitude I find spectacularly unattractive."

I stared out the window and Herne fell back into silence. He hadn't asked about my meeting with Marilee, but then again, there was a lot on his mind. But part of me felt that if I was so important to him, that I should be on his mind, too. It was all one big chaotic jumble, so I finally pushed my thoughts aside and watched the water as we crossed the bridge. The whitecaps were churning on one side, as they always did, while the other side seemed still as glass. As rain broke and pounded down the windshield, I leaned my head back against the seat and closed my eyes, lost in my thoughts.

Chapter 9

GINTY WAS A dwarf who owned a Waystation bar and grill on the Eastside. It was right off Paradise Lake Road, near Bear Creek. Rustic on the outside, it looked to be single story, until you went inside. Built from brown lumber, with bronze trim everywhere, it was a popular go-to joint with the SubCult. As we entered the massive parking lot, the place appeared to be jumping. The lot could hold at least forty cars, and it was over half-full.

As Herne and I unbuckled our seat belts, I pulled out my dagger to peace bind it. We wouldn't be allowed in the door with open weaponry, but peace binding was allowed. I had been here once before, and though I thoroughly liked both the bar and the owner, it was too far out of the way to put on my go-to list.

A very large bouncer stood at the door, watching us as we approached. After inspecting our weapons to make certain they were peace-bound, he cleared his throat.

"You are now entering Ginty's, a Waystation bar and grill. One show of magic or drawing a weapon will get you booted and banned. Do you agree to abide by the Rules of Parley, by blood and bone?" He was massive. His muscles had muscles, and he was staring down on us as though we were ants. I wagered he was part giant, or perhaps full ogre. He had a knobby face, with a forehead that seemed too large for his skull, and his squinty gaze seemed to dart around toward every sound.

"We do, by blood and bone," Herne said, giving the standard return. It basically meant we were putting our lives on the line if we broke our word.

The bouncer stepped back, ushering us in.

The bar was busy, with most of the booths filled. There was a bustle in the air that spoke to autumn and seeking warm shelter and bright hearth fires after a cold day's travel. As if reading my thoughts, a huge rush of wind rattled the windows from the parking lot as the rain turned into a deluge. I shivered, staring at the sky out of the massive bay window. The clouds were dark and heavy, and didn't seem in any hurry to go anywhere.

Herne led me over to the bar. Ginty was on the step-rail behind the counter, which raised him up to see his customers with a clear line of sight. He was polishing the beer taps, and when he saw us, his face lit up.

"Ah, Herne and Ember. I wondered when you would be dragging your asses in here." He rolled his eyes toward the ceiling. "They're already here."

The bar was single story outside, but once you entered the Waystation it was obvious that it extended well into other realms. A staircase led into another dimension, which offered private chambers for those coming to parley. It also, I had found out, held protected rooms for those seeking sanctuary until they could either escape or be fairly tried.

"Already? They're early." Herne glanced at the clock on the wall. We still had ten minutes until we were supposed to show up.

"Well, you know the way they are. But yeah, do you want to go right up?"

Herne snorted. "I don't want to go up at all, but my mother insisted. Ember, do you want a beer to take with you?"

I shook my head. "I'd rather be alert and sober when we talk to them. I can get drunk later." I leaned against the bar. "Hey, Ginty. I appreciate you remembering my name, by the way."

Ginty laughed. The dwarf was handsome, with mid-back flowing blond hair. He was well-proportioned, muscled to perfection, and as married as they come. His wife was named Ireland, and from what Talia told me, she kept a tight rein on her husband and he had no problem accepting it.

"Not hard to remember the name of someone with your reputation." He paused, turning as a buzzer sounded. He glanced at a tablet that was hooked up to the counter. "They're waiting. You two better get a move on before they decide to come down here and drag you up there by the scruffs of your necks."

He called out for Wendy, his second in command. She was six-two, built like a brick house, and had apparently opted for a Mohawk, because her head had been shaved on the sides, and a row of platinum spikes glimmered against her earthen-brown scalp.

"I have parley to deal with. Watch the bar."

She nodded. "Sure, boss. Mind if I toss out the rotter over at table three? He's grabbed Teresa by her ass three times."

Ginty scowled. "Spank him, toss him out, and he doesn't come back. Make sure Jona knows he's been banned."

Wendy swung around the counter, a feral smile on her face, and she stomped over to one of the corner tables. A man was sitting there. He looked like a shifter to me. He was drunk off his ass, and when Wendy said something to him, he gave her the finger. She had him up, his arm wrapped around his back, faster than we could blink. He yelped but she hauled his ass to the door where the bouncer opened it with a laugh.

"Come on, they'll take care of him," Ginty said, leading us behind the bar over to the staircase. The stairs were roped off, but he waved his hand and it opened on its own, closing behind us. I wasn't sure if it was a tech system, or magical, but whatever it was, it worked.

We took the steps to the landing before they turned to the left. The passage was, like last time, misty and filled with fog. The stairs kept ascending, seeming to go on for some time before they opened in a long hallway. Ginty led us to the first

door on the right—a different door than last time—
and opened it, allowing us to enter first.

Saílle and Névé were there, all right.

Saílle, Queen of Dark Fae, was dressed in a
gown of ice blue, beaded and shimmering. Her
hair flowed like a river of black lava, and she wore
a crown of diamonds and sapphires. Névé was her
opposite, with hair the color of spun platinum, and
she was dressed in green, and dripping with em-
eralds. The pair were brilliantly beautiful to look
at, and as deadly as they were mesmerizing. They
had brought their guards, of course, but there was
someone else there, someone I recognized.

Callan. The statue who had taken form.

I uttered a curse under my breath. How much
better could this meeting get? I glanced at Herne.
He was pissed. Even though he tried not to show
it, it read in his eyes and stance.

Herne cleared his throat, giving a polite nod to
the women. Technically, he outranked them, but
there was a delicate balance that we had to maintain in dealing with the grande dames of Fae, and
if we screwed this up, Herne's father would probably whip the lot of us.

"Your Majesties, thank you for meeting with
me."

Oh yeah, his words were polite but his tone was
as frosty as a winter morning.

Saílle allowed herself a bemused smile. "Welcome, son of Cernunnos. Lord Herne, I see you
brought your...associate."

I knew exactly what she intended with her re-
mark—both courts wished I didn't exist and I was

a blight on their egos. I gave them a grumpy nod, deciding that I'd forgo playing *who's the biggest bitch* with the cornerstones of Fae society.

Herne stared at Callan. "I see you've saved us some trouble."

"Hold on," Ginty said, standing and holding up his wand. It was gold with a dark crystal attached to the end—smoky quartz. "I need to establish the rules and hear your oaths. So shut up, all of you."

Saílle and Névé gave him dirty looks but quieted down. Herne snorted, but he, too, gave the dwarf a gracious nod.

Ginty cleared his throat. "I hereby declare the Mabon Parley, Part 1 of the Courts of Light and Darkness, in the year 10,258 CFE, open."

"Why 'part one'?" Saílle interrupted.

"I have a sneaking suspicion you may be requiring more than one this season." Ginty gave her a smoldering look that would have withered any normal person. Saílle just flashed him a toothy smile. "May I continue?"

"Please do, Master McClintlock," she said.

"Under this mantle, all members are bound to forswear bearing arms against any other member of this parley until the meeting is officially closed and all members are safely home..." He paused, then said, "I hate all this shit."

"Then why go through it?" Névé asked, examining her nails with a bored look.

He shook his head. "Because you are who you are."

"Then carry on and get it over with." She didn't even glance at him.

Ginty gave her a nasty look, but continued.

"I also remind the Courts of Light and Darkness that they are forsworn by the Covenant of the Wild Hunt from inflicting injury on any and all members of the Wild Hunt team, under the sigil of Cernunnos, Lord of the Forest, and Morgana, Goddess of the Sea and the Fae. Let no one break honor, let discussions progress civilly, and remember that I—Ginty McClintlock, of the McClintlock Clan of the Cascade Dwarves—am your moderator and mediator, and my rule as such supersedes all other authority while we are in this Waystation."

He held up the scroll I remembered from last time. "If you stay, you agree to the rules. If you disagree, leave now, or you *will* be bound to the parley. I have spoken, and so it is done." He let out a long breath. "Okay, it's settled. Herne, you have the floor."

Herne stood, nodding to Ginty. "Thank you, Master McClintlock. Queen Saílle, Queen Névé, I am here to take Callan into custody and return him to the past, where he belongs. If you hand him over now, we'll call it good."

Saílle and Névé gave each other a long look, then Saílle dropped her head back, laughing.

"What's so funny?" Herne asked.

"You think that's why we're here today? To hand over Callan to you?"

Looking confused, he nodded. "Of course. You knew we were looking for him. You know Cernunnos and Morgana feel he'll upset the balance and cause repercussions in the human world. Why else would we be here?"

Saílle motioned for Névé to take the floor. Herne sat down when Ginty motioned to him.

Névé stood so gracefully that it looked like she floated up from the chair. "The Court of Light wishes to announce that it has come to a truce with the Court of Darkness, enacted as of the beginning of the Harvest Moon, in the year 10,258 CFE, to last until both parties feel the desire to dissolve it. We jointly sponsor the warrior Callan to lead our defense against Elatha, the Fomorian King, and any and all of his armies. We have requested sanctuary from this Waystation for Callan. We do not recognize the power of the Wild Hunt to extradite him. Any attempts to remove him from our custody will result in breaking the Covenant of the Wild Hunt."

And with that, both the Queen of Light and the Queen of Darkness gave Herne and me smugly satisfied looks.

NEEDLESS TO SAY, things went downhill from there. Herne bolted to his feet, but Ginty jumped up on his footstool and held up the golden wand.

"I remind you all we are under the rules of parley. Watch your tongues lest I be forced to censure you." He gave Herne a long look. "This means you, Herne."

Herne sputtered. "But I have a direct order from both Cernunnos and Morgana to apprehend Callan if he shows his face and I call *this*, showing his face."

Ginty squinted at him. "I remind you, this is a *Waystation* that offers Sanctuary. Callan is staying here," he said, looking like he'd rather not admit to that. "As long as he sleeps under this roof and has asked for Sanctuary, I have no choice but to offer it to him and do everything in my power to protect him."

Saílle laughed again, which wasn't the wisest move in my opinion.

"What do you find so funny?" Herne turned on her, furious.

"You see, Herne, we thought ahead about this. We need Callan, now that Elatha is forcing his way into the United Coalition. He has already effected one attack on the Fae race, and still your precious Morgana and Cernunnos allow him free rein. So we have no choice but to protect ourselves."

I said nothing, watching the interplay with growing apprehension. If we walked out of here with Callan in tow, irreparable damage would be done. And leaving him here also insured the same.

Ginty pointed to their chairs. "Both of you, sit down. Everybody sit down."

Herne reluctantly returned to his seat. Saílle gracefully sank into hers, and Névé joined her. The two queens gave each other crocodile smiles. I wondered just how long their little peace treaty would last, considering they hated each other's guts.

"So, where do we go from here?" Ginty asked. "Herne, you cannot walk out of here with Callan. Even with direct orders from the Lord of the Forest and the Lady of the Sea, I cannot break tradition and violate Sanctuary. This Waystation is sacred. The only way I can hand over Callan is for a Triamvinate to be called, and that can only happen with official petitions and within the prescribed perimeters."

I gulped back a gasp. A Triamvinate was a major undertaking and the results were final. Even I knew that.

"That's going to require time to set up," Herne said. "You know that Cernunnos and Morgana will manage it, so why you bother, I have no idea. The Dagda, Danu, and Eriu must stand in attendance as the judges and you *know* they'll side with my mother and father."

"But," Saílle said, "as you said, that will take time. Meanwhile, we have Callan to lead us to safety. As long as he walks with Ginty's sigil on his back, he's forsworn for you to touch." She leaned back, looking satisfied. "Are you willing to break the Covenant, son of the land?"

Herne's eyes flashed dangerously. "*I* do not break oaths, unlike some people. We will be back, with the date for the Triamvinate, and you will see just how far you get with this scheme. You know how this will play out. Yet you are willing to put the human population at risk."

"It's a risk I'm willing to take, when *my* people are on the chopping block," Saílle said, once again shooting to her feet.

Névé joined her. "We're done. We've indicated our line. It's in your court, Herne." And with that, the pair of them turned and swept out of the room, followed by Callan and their guards.

I glanced at Herne. "We can't stop him?"

He shook his head. "Not unless we want a war with the Fae on our hands. Cernunnos is going to be pissed."

Ginty worried his lip. "You aren't going to start something, are you? No raiding my Waystation to drag Callan away in handcuffs?"

Herne let out a mirthless laugh, his gaze still on the door. "No, Ginty. I won't do that. I'm not authorized to start a war and that's what it would do." He motioned to me. "Come on. Can you drive? I need to put in a call to my father and mother."

Wordlessly, I took his keys and we bid Ginty farewell and headed to the car. There was no sign of either Fae Queen. For that, I was grateful. Herne might promise not to cause trouble, but it was difficult for me to believe that he would let it go if they were outside, waiting to taunt us.

BY THE TIME we got back to the office, Morgana had called telling us to "do nothing" about the incident, and that she would arrive at the Wild Hunt in the morning to discuss the matter. Meanwhile, it was going on five. As I took off my jacket, I realized that it was as cold inside as it was out and then I noticed that Angel had her coat on, and as Talia trundled into the waiting room from her office, she had her jacket and gloves on.

"What's going on?" Herne asked.

"The building's furnace went belly-up and the owner won't be able to get to it till the weekend. So dress warm or you're going to turn into a Popsicle." Angel shivered. "If anybody has any space heaters at home, bring them in tomorrow because we're going to need them."

Herne grimaced. "Well, hell. Okay, space heaters it is. By the way, we need to be here by seven-thirty. My mother's coming to discuss this fucking mess with Callan."

Yutani was sitting on the sofa, staring at his tablet. He jerked his head up. "What happened?"

Herne shook his head, rubbing his hands together. "We're going home early. Time enough tomorrow to tell you, except that Saílle and Névé have just earned themselves a special spot in hell in my heart." He turned to me. "Love, I'm sorry, I promised to spend tonight with Danielle. I'm taking her around town to show her the sights."

I shrugged. "I expected you'd be busy, anyway." That came out more abrupt than I wanted, so I quickly tried to smooth it over. "Besides, Angel and I can use a girls' night in. And I haven't been to the gym in a week—way too long."

The elevator doors opened and Celia stepped out. "Am I early?" she asked.

Yutani gave her a bright smile—I'd never seen him smile that warmly for anybody—and shook his head. "Nope. I'm ready to go. We're closing shop early. Come on, I made reservations at Oui on the Pier for dinner."

"Fancy," Talia said, teasing him. "Oui on the Pier is pretty pricey and do you even *own* a suit jacket?

They have a dress code, you know."

Yutani stuck his tongue out at her. "Someday we'll go out on the town and I'll show you just how well I clean up." With that, he escorted his aunt into the elevator again and Talia dashed in behind them, waving at us. As the car doors closed, I turned back to Angel.

"That gives me an idea."

"Oh no, I do not feel like dressing up and crashing their party." She gave me a look that told me just how much she had appreciated sitting in the cold all afternoon.

"Neither do I, but since we're both free, why don't we go to a movie? We haven't done that in ages." We usually streamed them at home, but I felt like doing something different.

She shrugged. "What's playing?"

"I think the new Ghost Rigger movie is out." Ghost Rigger was a movie franchise that we both loved. They were cheesy, with outlandish dialogue and ridiculous plots, but something about them never failed to make us laugh.

"I'm on it. Stop by Burger-Burger for dinner?"

"I'll buy." I waved at Viktor, who had just emerged from the back. Herne gave me an expectant look, and even though I wasn't feeling all that charitable, I moved to his side and gave him a kiss good-bye.

"Say, you're sure you're not mad?" he whispered.

"Everything just feels topsy-turvy, and I've never liked that feeling," I whispered back.

"Love you." He pressed his forehead against mine, staring into my eyes.

I relented then, and let out a long sigh. "I love you, too. I'll see you tomorrow morning. Have fun tonight, okay?"

"You and Angel, too," he said, then slowly let me go after another kiss.

As Angel and I headed out, I couldn't help but wonder how much longer things would be in the muddle they'd gotten themselves into.

THE MOVIE WAS a blast, and Angel and I arrived home in much better moods than we had left work in. We had the remains of a pizza—which we had opted for in place of burgers—with us, and she placed the last four slices on a plate and stuck them in the microwave so we could snack on them.

I picked up Mr. Rumblebutt and gave him a squeeze, kissing his nose, as Angel set out his dinner. Then, as he squirmed his way out of my arms in order to go eat, I dropped into one of the kitchen chairs.

"So, what do you think Morgana will have to say tomorrow? You really think we have to let them protect Callan?" Angel handed me a couple napkins, and then carried our plates over.

I held up a slice of pizza, taking a big bite of it and immediately regretting it as I burned my tongue. "Damn it. Thermodynamics of pizza strikes again." Wincing, I got myself a glass of ice water. "That's better, though I think I raised a blister."

"You never could wait till it cooled off," she said with a laugh.

"Yeah, I know." I wiped my lips and sat down, blowing on the rest of it to cool it. "Honestly, I don't know. I thought Herne was going to blow his stack today. Ginty did, too. I have no clue if they've ever pulled this sort of thing before, but it seems to me that it was as close as they've come to an outright declaration of independence from the Covenant. I don't know what will happen if they continue to refuse the extradition order. Seriously, they're both a piece of work."

Angel answered more slowly. "But Ember, can you blame them? They see Callan as a chance to save their way of life. And frankly, with Elatha and his kind gaining access to the United Coalition, you know he'll do what he can to undermine your people." She held up her hand. "Don't even start. Like it or not, you're Fae and you have to accept it."

I nodded. I had been thinking a lot about that very subject lately. For so long, I had hated my lineage. My grandparents had killed my parents. Neither side—Light or Dark—wanted to claim me. I was considered *tralaeth*—a mongrel combination of both. But the truth was, I was Fae and, as Angel said, like it or not, I had to accept it. I was just beginning to think I might be able to create something new...forge a new path for those like me.

"I know. And I see what you're saying. Elatha is an inherent danger to both sides of my people, and I can't believe the UC is accepting him into their ranks, given what happened." I paused. "I don't think they can help it, though. They would be slapped with discrimination suits so fast and furious. Until now, the ogres and giants haven't thought to voice resistance, but Elatha can unite them. From what legend reads, he's terribly persuasive. An orator supreme."

"Yes, well, we've seen in the past what that can do." Angel shuddered. "Remember Hitler? He was supposed to be charismatic, too."

"I know." Finally, I shook my head. "All right. We have a long day tomorrow and we need to go in early. I suggest we get some sleep." As we gathered our plates and carried them over to the sink, I asked, "Did you hear from DJ today?"

A smile blossomed across Angel's face. "Yeah, I did. He won first prize in a science contest." She sighed. "I wish I could be there to watch all these milestones, but he seems happy with Cooper and his family. I suppose I should just be grateful."

I wrapped an arm around her shoulder and gave her a squeeze. "He won't forget you. You're his sister and he loves you. Come on, now. Let's get to bed."

As she turned off into her room, I hoped for her sake that I was right.

Chapter 10

I DRESSED WITH extra care the next morning, given Morgana was supposed to show up in the office. Since I was bound to her, I didn't want her to see me looking sloppy or acting petulant. I wore dark jeans, as usual, but slipped into a shimmery silver corset-top, fastened a black belt around my waist, and then added a black denim overshirt, leaving it open. Ankle boots finished the outfit. I brushed my hair back into a ponytail, slid silver hoops into my ears, and did my makeup.

"You look sharp," Angel said. "But don't forget the power's out so take an extra warm jacket."

"Thanks, I almost forgot. Morgana's going to be there. I'd *better* look sharp." I accepted the breakfast sandwich she handed me, and the travel mug filled with steaming latte. "I hope the building superintendant can get to the furnace earlier than he said he could."

"Take a jacket you can move in. I have a feeling you'll be out on the prowl today. Just a hunch... plus yesterday I heard Herne mention to Viktor that you guys were going to go body-hunting." She grabbed her purse. "Let's take both cars, just in case."

"I'd better bring a different top then, so that I don't rip this one up if we have to wade through a tangle." I darted up the stairs to my room and grabbed a long-sleeved microsuede tunic that never caught on brambles or briars. Stuffing it in my backpack, I returned to the foyer where Angel was waiting. She had found a couple spare space heaters to take into the office.

Patting the charm on the wall by the door—it had become a ritual of mine every day when I left to press my hand against the good luck talisman I had made for our home—I followed Angel out the front door. Waving to her, I climbed in my car and pulled out behind her, as we headed toward work.

BY THE TIME we got to the office, everybody else was there and it was still freezing. We had encountered an accident that led to a detour, which led to being fifteen minutes late. But luckily, Morgana wasn't there yet. Herne hustled everybody into the break room except Angel, who would wait for Morgana and escort her in. He set up one of the space heaters we had brought. Angel put the other one by her desk.

"While we're waiting, let's hand out assignments. Ember? I want you and Viktor out hunting through UnderLake Park today. Talia and Yutani are researching the other missing Fae to see if they can pinpoint any connections between Ulstair and them—any correlations at all. I'm not sure why the cops aren't on this, but maybe it has to do with Saílle's court. If you have any connections in the Court of Darkness, see if they can find out any dirt on the missing men." Herne paused as Angel tapped on the door.

She peeked into the room. "Lady Morgana is here."

"Show her in, and bring your notes. Lock the elevator for now."

Angel led Morgana into the room. The goddess was looking lovely. Dressed in a long gown of periwinkle layers, each filmy and as sheer as silk, she glided into the room. A black cloak hung around her shoulders, trailing the ground, and her hair was caught back in an intricate knotwork of braids, held by a silver clasp. She filled the room with her power, and I could hear the call of the ocean, the roar of the waves as they crashed against the shore as she passed by me to stand by Herne.

"Well met, my son." She turned to the rest of us, nodding. Her gaze fell on me and she smiled. "Ember, child. How are you faring? Marilee tells me that you are coming along nicely in your preparations for the Cruharach."

I nodded. "I've met both sides of my heritage, so I guess she's right, milady."

"I will talk to Cernunnos and we will arrange the

final rituals for you." She paused, then motioned for Herne to sit down. As he pulled out a chair for her, then sat down, she took her seat. "Have you told your crew what happened yesterday?"

"Not in so many words," Herne said. "To recap in case anybody didn't hear yesterday. Saílle and Névé have decided to unite under a truce. They're protecting Callan and giving him lead over their combined military forces in case Elatha makes any more threatening moves their way. They refuse to hand him over, he's claimed Sanctuary and is staying at Ginty's Waystation. While we could stake out the Waystation to try to catch him when he steps off the property, both Courts have indicated they will consider such an act a breach of the Covenant with Morgana and Cernunnos. I wasn't sure what else to do." He turned to Morgana. "So, what have you and Cernunnos decided?"

She twisted her lip, her eyes flashing. "While I understand their fears, I'm not at all happy with their choice. They *could* have petitioned us about it. But such is not the nature of the Fae Queens, and this I also realize. Cernunnos asked me to approach them last night. He thought they would listen to me more than to him. Unfortunately, neither side will listen to reason. So, while we work on setting up a Triamvinate, we must either allow them to shelter Callan, or break the Covenant, and centuries of work will be undone. Obviously, we're leaving this alone until we can petition for a Triamvinate."

I raised my hand.

She pointed to me. "Yes, Ember?"

"They may claim to be under a truce now, but you know how much the Light and the Dark hate each other. How long do you think this truce will last? When it breaks, Callan will be yanked in both directions. Don't you think we can just wait for them to be their own undoing, so to speak?" It made sense to me. I doubted they could go a week before starting to squabble again.

Morgana laughed. "Yes, I *do* think that's what will happen. We walk softly for now, and leave them alone. But that said, I'm worried they're going to go a step further and plot revenge against Elatha, which will—of course—spill out into the human community." She leaned back. "I don't appreciate having to cave in to them—it vexes me. But Cernunnos and I agree that we're doing the only thing we can at this time. Meanwhile, I'm consulting my father to see if he can be of any assistance. He's in Spain right now, hanging out with Rasputin."

I blinked. "*Rasputin*?"

"Yes, another member of the Force Majeure."

"I thought Rasputin was killed," Talia said.

"No, that was a great coverup. He's alive and well and still stirring up trouble. If I can pry my father away from the chess tournament they're playing in, I'll ask his help."

I gulped. Morgana's father was *the* Merlin, who belonged to the Force Majeure—a secret society of mages, witches, sorcerers, and enchantresses. There were only twenty-one of them at any given time in the world, and they were hand picked for entry into the society. The only way out was death.

Elatha—the Fomorian King—had a mistress who belonged to them. Ranna had been the one to create the iron plague that had threatened the Fae a couple of months back.

"Meeting Merlin would be like meeting a rock star. A very scary rock star." I stared at the table, both hoping and dreading it would come to that.

"Yes, well, my father's a blustery sort, that's for sure." Morgana rose.

"Is that all, Mother?" Herne stood along with her.

"For now, yes. Walk with caution and do nothing regarding Callan until we give you the word." With that, she swept toward the door, stopping to pat me lightly on the shoulder before she vanished into the waiting area.

Angel dashed after her, but returned, blinking. "She's gone, but the elevator's still locked."

"She's a goddess. What do you expect?" Talia said with a cackle.

"So, I guess we have our marching orders," Herne said. "All right then. We focus on Raven's case. Ember, you and Viktor head out to the park now. Grab your lunch while you're out. I want you to scour the park. See if there's anything we missed, or the cops missed. We know they didn't look very hard. Talia and Yutani, go ahead and get to work on your research. Angel, come into my office with the ledger for last month. We need to go over the accounting and make certain everything's square and set."

Given our tasks, we broke the meeting and got started for the day.

VIKTOR AND I stared at the vast expanse of foliage around us. Luckily, all the men had went missing in one area, which gave us a place to start, but searching for clues that the cops might have overlooked or evidence that might have been buried was a far cry from easy.

"Where do we start?" I asked, staring around me. The air was saturated with moisture and it was due to rain again. I shivered, even though I had on a warm jacket and my microsuede shirt.

"I'm not certain. Are there any bodies of water close enough for you to contact an elemental and maybe get some information?"

I frowned. "Well, there's the beach, but since Ulstair went missing about a quarter mile from there on the Beach Trail, that's too far. We *might* gain some help from an Elemental, but I doubt it." Truth was, I didn't even know if there were any elementals around the area.

We began the hunt from the spot where we had found Ulstair's phone. The cops hadn't been out here in a while. Viktor had found out that there hadn't been any real investigation into *any* of the missing men, which meant the park hadn't been searched thoroughly. On the down side, that meant there was close to two hundred acres of land to search through.

"Where do you want to start?"

I was about to say "Pick a place" when a tingle at

the back of my neck stopped me. I closed my eyes, holding up my hand. As I slowly turned, reaching out to search the currents of air, something whispered to head north—directly off trail from where we had found the phone, into a deeply wooded part of the park.

"That way," I said, pointing.

Viktor was staring at me. "You look different."

"I feel different," I said softly. The voice that had told me which way we should look was strong and firm and decisive. I picked up my walking stick—this time I had remembered to bring one—and headed up the sloping side of the ravine into the dense undergrowth. The trees grew thick here, their trunks within touching distance, and the ferns were knee-high. Brambles wove through the area, their thorns wickedly sharp. I tried to avoid them, stepping around patches, but still, they caught at our clothing as we made our way around them.

Viktor let out a soft curse and I turned. He held up his hand. He was bleeding. "Didn't see a bramble cane and it got me."

"Do you need to go back?"

He shook his head, pulling out a handkerchief. "I'll wrap it up and it will be fine till we're done. Just hurts like hell."

As we set off again with me in the lead, I began to fall into the energy of the forest. It was seductive, dark and dangerous with shadows lurking everywhere, and eyes peeking out from the depths of the gloom. There were creatures here, watching us, and they snuck along beside us as we passed by them. Creatures from *my* realm—from the Fae realm—that bore no semblance of humanity. They were sub-Fae, the beings who lived between the world of the forest devas and the world of the Fae. Back in Annwn, they lived in the realm of Elphame—ruled by Nicnevan, one of the numerous queens of the realm.

Here, they lived in the woodlands and the wilds, and they kept no connection with the Dark or the Light Fae, being thoroughly untamed. They were younger than the Ante-Fae, but older than the Light and the Dark, and the more the world crowded in, the more they fled back to Annwn to avoid the infiltration of their territory. They were hunters and tricksters, predators and jokesters, ruled by chaos.

I seldom had business with them, for they didn't care much for their Light and Dark cousins. In fact, I seldom noticed them when I passed through the woodlands. But now I felt them all around us, running loose in UnderLake Park. They watched as we passed by, and I lightly reached out with my thoughts, trying to touch them like I did the water elementals, but all I encountered was a flurry of energy, a wild dance of color and sound and dangerous laughter.

I withdrew my thoughts, shielding myself, wondering if I could feel them more than I had before because I had met and accepted my Dark Fae blood. Surely, the Autumn Stalkers would know the sub-Fae of the forest? If so, perhaps I was able to sense their presence now.

I said nothing to Viktor, not wanting to worry

him. I wasn't sure if he could sense their presence, and it occurred to me that out here in the tangle of wild brambles wasn't the best place to broach the question. Instead, I focused my attention on the whispering voice that urged me on, tapping me on the shoulder like a ghost.

After about fifteen minutes, I paused, halfway up a ravine, and looked back at Viktor. "I still get the sense to go on."

"Then we might as well, because otherwise I have no clue exactly what Herne expects us to do. You want to keep leading? I'm fine with it, unless you need a break."

"Let me. I feel like I'm on the verge of remembering something. It's like a memory that I can't quite grasp, but I know it's there and if I just pay attention long enough, it will come into clear focus."

I knelt, placing my hands against the soil. There were no water elementals within close proximity, but after a few minutes, I was sinking deeper into trance, and the smell of the soil, the tang of the earth, was feeding my senses. I opened my eyes, scouting along the ground, cautiously brushing back the brambles and ferns. A few minutes later, I found what I had been searching for.

"Here. See the ground here? Someone's been dragged through here, though the plants rebounded afterward. But...I know it. See this? There's a depression along the detritus, about the width of a body. I think that somebody was dragged up this slope."

Viktor stared at me for a moment, then nodded

for me to move on ahead.

As we continued, with me stopping every few minutes to kneel and keep my focus on whatever signs I could see, it occurred to me that a month ago, I wouldn't have been able to do this sort of reconnaissance work.

Another fifty feet and I stopped. We had been hunting through the ravine for about half an hour and I wasn't sure how far off the trail we had gone. I was about to shift direction when something caught my nose—a faint scent.

"Do you smell something?"

Viktor shook his head, frowning. "No, what does it smell like?"

"Sweet, cloying like old perfume." I glanced around. Out of the corner of my eye, I caught sight of what appeared to be the mouth of a cave or very large hole, jutting deep into the side of the ravine. "There."

The last ten yards to reach the hole were steep, and I pressed closer to the side of the slope, almost clawing my way up. I could see the drag marks clearly now that showed something heavy had slid through the area.

"Those?" Viktor pointed them out.

"Yes," I said. "The smell is getting stronger."

Viktor took another sniff and his eyes lit up. "I can smell it too, now."

We reached the hole and Viktor pulled out a flashlight. While I waited, he flashed it inside to make certain there wasn't a coyote or other critter holing up in there.

"Uh oh," he said.

I glanced over his shoulder.

Inside, were several prone figures, and the cloying scent of decay was thick around them. One was still recognizable as the corpse of a man. He was bloated, covered with flies and his skin was turning a mottled green. The other three were in worse stages of decomposition, their skeletons covered with tattered bits of remains.

I turned away, my stomach churning, and pressed my knuckles to my lips.

Viktor pulled the light away. "I'll call Erica at the station. We can't chance messing up a crime scene, and it has to be that. I doubt they all crawled in there and died together." He wasn't being flippant. He placed a hand on my shoulder. "You okay?"

I stared at the forest around us.

Was I okay? Death wasn't foreign to me, and I had caused the death of a number of creatures—most of them trying to kill me. But it never got easier. From the time I had discovered my parents on the floor of our home to now, staring at yet more dead bodies—it was all a reminder of how frail life could be. Even when your life spanned a thousand years or more, all it took was one misplaced step, one blow to the head or heart, to cut that short.

I dropped back on my ass, leaning back against the sloping ground.

"Am I okay? I don't know how to answer that. I'm better off than those poor souls, whoever they were." I paused, then added, "Do you think we've found Ulstair? Do you think that's him? He's only been missing a week or so."

"I think the freshest one could be him, but it's

hard to tell with a flashlight and with…" Viktor shone his light in the hole again, then turned back to me with a grim look. "I think we can assume it is. He has long red hair and I caught a glimpse of a gold tooth. I'll call the cops now. Erica has me on the Where's My Friend app. She'll be able to track us to where we are. We'll have to wait for her."

I nodded. "Do you think she'll be able to come? Won't the cops in this jurisdiction get pissed if another precinct sends in people?"

"She can call them and figure something out. Either way, we have to wait to talk to them." He scooted closer to me as I rolled up to a sitting position and wrapped my arms around my knees. "Hell of a job, isn't it?"

"Oh, yeah. But then again, my life before I came to work for you guys wasn't all that glam. I killed my share of goblins and other creepers. I was out in the field every week, chasing down sub-Fae, mostly. But until I came to work for the Wild Hunt, I really didn't have to deal with more…*humanish* deaths. Goblins and some of the other sub-Fae liquefy after death. At least over here, they do. It's easier to kill your opponent when there isn't much of a reminder left behind."

A thought occurred to me and I eased my dagger out of the sheath. "How do we know whoever killed them isn't still around?"

Tensing, I glanced around, an edge of fear creeping in around the edges. Then, what I can only describe as a feeling of confidence washed through me, and I took a deep breath, letting it out slowly. Viktor and I could take on most opponents, and the half-ogre was mega-strong. If someone showed up with a gun, we'd figure out a way to deal with it.

Viktor scouted around the area. "I'm not see-ing anybody, but there's a good-sized huckleberry bush over there. Why don't we hide behind it until the cops get here?"

Grateful for the cover, I followed him over to hunker down. As we squatted behind the brush, the rain began to pound down and I pressed fur-ther beneath the boughs of the huckleberry bush. Viktor reached in his pocket and pulled out two squares of folded plastic. He handed one to me and I shook it out into a very thin, lightweight, plastic rain poncho. Grateful, I slid it over my head and pulled the hood up. The ponchos weren't warm, but they forced the rain to roll off, and kept us dry.

I closed my eyes again, trying to reach out to the forest Fae around me. The creatures of Elphame's realm were watching us closely. I opened up more, trying to break down some of my barriers and walls.

"Do you know what happened? Do you know who the dead men are?" I whispered, forcing the question into a whisper on the wind.

There was a scurry to the left, and then another to the right. Someone had heard me. I waited to see if they would answer.

Follow us...

The thought entered my mind and there was a part of me that was uncertain whether I had imag-ined it or not. But I turned back to Viktor. "They want me to follow. Stay here."

"No, you shouldn't go alone—" Viktor started to

say, then he stopped and nodded. "Do what you need to, but call me if you need help. The cops won't be here for at least another forty minutes, given they'll have to trek through the woods."

Half-wishing he would have tried to persuade me to stay more, I skulked away from the cave in the direction the urging had come from. They were all around me now, the woodland sprites. I wasn't sure what they were or what to call them, but that would work for now.

As I focused on the ground, I realized that I could see them. They were everywhere, in the shape of leaves and creatures wearing mushrooms on their heads, riding on the backs of dragonflies that darted through the woods, still alive even in the chill weather. They were rising up off the ground, looking like curling autumn leaves, which were actually massive sails attached to their backs. The world shifted and writhed with their movement.

I blinked, afraid to take a step. But the words *Follow us* echoed in my head again, and I began to wade through the undergrowth, trying to avoid thinking about how many of the tiny sub-Faefolk I was stepping on. I felt like a giant, a behemoth monster striding out of the water and onto a city.

The snaps and chattering sounds around me magnified till my head was awash in a whir of white noise. I crept along, balancing myself on the slope with my walking stick, trying to keep my balance. And then, as quickly as it had overwhelmed me, the noise faded and I was once again standing alone in the forest, all signs of the sub-Fae gone.

I could still feel them around, but they had faded back into whatever in-between realm they lived in.

I sucked in a deep breath and let it out slowly as my gaze came to rest on a crow that was perched on a low limb in a cedar tree. It stared at me, then let out one long, low caw, and dropped something from its beak. As it flew away, I approached the cedar. There, on the ground, was a ring of silver. I picked it up. Pulling out my flashlight, I glanced at it more carefully. The ring was engraved.

Ulstair—All My Love—Raven

I stared at the ring, then clenched my fist around it. Ulstair was dead and one of those bodies back at the cave was his. I bit my lip, thinking that at least I had something tangible to give to Raven.

Returning to where Viktor waited, I showed him the ring.

"Should I give it to the cops? A crow had it in its mouth, so it could have come from anywhere." I didn't want to hand it over. I wanted to give it to Raven because I had the feeling she'd never see it again if we gave it to the police.

Viktor must have sensed what I was thinking because after a moment, he shook his head. "No, not right now. We'll ask Herne when we get back to the office." His phone jangled and he answered. "Erica and her partner are almost here. The medical examiner isn't far behind."

I pocketed the ring, and we stood back as the cops began to appear from down below. I stared at the hole, not wanting to think about the bodies inside. It seemed such a cold way to spend eternity—hidden out of sight. How many more bodies were out in the woods, stuffed into caves and holes and buried in shallow graves? Wondering just who—or what—we were dealing with, I turned as the cops appeared and went into full steam.

Chapter 11

WE HEADED BACK to the office well before the coroner was done examining the scene and the bodies. Before we left, Erica pulled us aside and told us—unofficially—that Ulstair was one of the victims as far as they could tell. With the gold tooth and the red hair, identification was fairly certain.

Though Erica was Fae, she didn't give me any side-eye, which surprised me. In fact, she seemed pleasant enough and, with a glance over her shoulder to make sure no one else was listening, she motioned for us to follow her over to one of the fir trees.

"Listen up," she said in a low voice. "If these are the men who were missing, and I think they probably are, there's a reason why their disappearances went uninvestigated. Look into their connections with Saílle's court. Look for what caste they belong in. You'll understand why we couldn't follow up on the cases. We've got standing orders that any-body falling into this particular caste is a *no-show*. Meaning we don't show up for their calls for help, if we know who they are, and we don't follow up on any trouble they have. I know it sucks, but I don't make the rules. I try to do what I can on the side, but—"

"Erica, get your ass over here. We need your help!" one of the cops by the dump site shouted, sounding grumpy.

"I've got to go. I'll tell them I interviewed you and that I got all the info I could—that you were just out here scouting around for Raven."

"True enough," Viktor said.

"Yeah, but it will keep them from calling you down to the station." She slipped her notebook back in her pocket and gave us the go-ahead to leave.

I jerked my head down the slope. "We'd better take her advice. I don't think they're happy about this and I don't want to be around a bunch of un-happy police."

We began to make our way through the under-growth, leaving the cops to finish sorting through whatever they found in the hole. I hoped that Erica would come through with information on anything else they managed to find.

When we reached the car and were safely inside, I turned to Viktor, who had opted to drive back to Seattle.

"How did you two meet? You and Erica?"

"At a bar. She was working on a case that Herne

had taken on, and it involved the Light Fae. Erica's Dark, by the way, but she's not tied to Saílle's apron strings. She's one of the few who seems to feel it would be better if the two sides worked together. She's all right."

He eased out of UnderLake Park. I realized we were near Raven's house. "Should we stop and tell her about Ulstair?"

"Better ask Herne first." Viktor shrugged. "You still have the ring?"

I nodded, fishing it out of my pocket. It was pretty—either silver or platinum, I wasn't sure which. I sighed, realizing that the tenth anniversary of the engraved date was coming up shortly. "She bought this for him almost ten years ago." I paused, thinking about relationships. "So, how's Sheila doing? It was nice to finally meet her at your Labor Day picnic."

"She's fine. She was happy to meet you, too." Viktor laughed, signaling before pulling over into the middle lane. "She's a ripsnorter, I'll tell you that."

I smiled, grateful for the chance to laugh. "She seems it. That woman has no problem with speaking her mind."

Sheila was forty-three years old, and she was a kitchen witch, one of the magic-born though not connected to the Force Majeure. She taught geology at a local community college and, according to Viktor—and borne out by the basket she had brought to the picnic—she grew the best tomatoes in town.

"She's started volunteering at the Chapel Hill

Homeless Shelter in the U-District every other weekend. She's one of the cooks there, for the soup kitchen." A light danced in his eyes that told me Viktor was in love with Sheila, whether he knew it or not.

"I'd like to see her again," I said. "Angel and I will throw a party soon. Let me know what weekend is good for her."

I was suddenly hungry to know my coworkers better. We had become friends, but there was so much to each person's life that just six months was an impossible amount of time to get to fully know somebody. I wasn't sure what was behind my desire to deepen our friendships, but whatever it was, I didn't want to deny it.

As we headed back to the office, Viktor began to open up a little more, and I pushed the thoughts of the dead out of my mind for at least a little while.

BY THE TIME we got back to the office, Erica had called Viktor to tell him they had proof that Ulstair was the freshest victim out of the four. The other three would take longer to identify, but they found evidence on the body to prove it was Ulstair. The cops asked us to inform Saílle's court and Ulstair's family.

"I wonder why they won't do it themselves," Angel said, scowling.

"I know why." Yutani pushed a button on his laptop. "I just sent you all the info I found. Looks like our missing Fae boys are all on the outs with Saílle. Two of them were found cavorting with Light Fae women, and while the relationships were nipped in the bud, they were added to her persona non grata list, so to speak. The third was caught pilfering from the royal coffers and was punished by being exiled. So when they went missing, since the three were on the bad-boys list, the cops were instructed to back off the investigations."

"What about Ulstair? Was he on the list, too?" If he had been, then we had an answer as to why some cases never got picked up by the cops.

"Yeah, he is, because of his mother. His mother is dying. Earlier, she had the audacity to refuse a position as one of Saílle's ladies-in-waiting. Apparently, she wanted to stay home and raise her children. That put Ulstair's entire family on Saílle's shit list."

The more I learned about Saílle, the more I didn't like the bitch.

"Lovely. All right, then. We have a connection between all four of the victims. They were all on the outs from the Dark Fae Court. Could their murders be retribution? Is someone targeting those on Saílle's list?"

"I doubt it," Herne said. "If the murders were officially sanctioned, the bodies would just vanish when the offense was made. The Fae Queens don't tend to waste time."

"I have another thought," Angel said. "What if the killer is targeting them *precisely* because he knows the cops won't look into it and neither will the Dark Fae?"

"True that," Yutani said. "But I think we're overlooking the fact that the four men looked a lot like each other. Serial killers follow patterns. All of the men had red hair, or close to it. They all had slender, strong bodies. And their bone structure in their face? Close. They aren't exactly carbon copies, but there's a pattern there."

"Or, the choice to abduct them could come from a combination of things." Herne stared at the pictures on his tablet, shaking his head. "Who knows why people do the things they do? We can reasonably assume that the police won't actually investigate the murders. Viktor, care to ask your friend Erica for whatever info she can spare? We were hired to investigate this case. I suppose, technically, we've finished our work with it, given we've found Ulstair. Or rather, his remains. But I don't feel right just dropping it, especially since the cops aren't going to do anything."

"I feel the same way," I said. "I like Raven, and I don't want to just walk away after we tell her that Ulstair was murdered. It doesn't seem right."

Herne nodded. "*Right*. It isn't the right thing to do. We'll stay on the case, and see what we can find. While I don't want to step on the toes of the cops, if they aren't going to bother, then we are going to do what we can. Yutani and Talia, interview whomever you can find who was close to the other three men. Ask them about their habits. What were their names, by the way?" He glanced on the document that Yutani had sent us.

"Trey, Wirral, and the thief was named Rand." Angel ticked off the names as I jotted them down on a notepad.

"Very well, look into their backgrounds. Find out everything you can. We know they all seemed to use the same trail in UnderLake Park, but why? Were there other runners as well? What kind of schedule did they keep? Were they out there randomly, or did they go to the park on specific days of the week?"

"They all seem to have the same physique so it's quite possible they all jogged that trail," Viktor said.

"I'd like to tell Raven the news," I said.

It wasn't that I really *wanted* to be there—that sort of news was never easy to deliver. But I liked Raven and it might help to hear it from someone she was comfortable with.

"I'd like to go, too," Angel said. "I liked Raven, too. I've never been engaged, but I know what it feels like to find out someone you love has been killed. When the cops told me about Mama J., I was alone. I called Ember right afterward, but it's really hard to handle when you first hear the news and there's nobody else there."

"Unfortunately, I found my parents after they were murdered, but Angel's right. And the fact that her fiancé was murdered is going to make it worse. I'm not saying that one death is better than another, but hearing that somebody killed the person you love? Well, it doesn't get much harder than that." I glanced at the clock. It was going on six o'clock already. "I suppose we should go over there now."

Herne nodded. "Ember, you and Angel and I will

talk to her. Then I think we're going to take the weekend off. We'll pick the case up on Monday. Before we finish, speaking of Monday, can you all stay late? Charlie will be coming in that evening and I'd like everybody to be here to welcome him."

"Not a problem," Yutani said, closing his laptop and gathering up his gear. "By then my aunt will be gone. But, if you're in the mood, she asked if we could have a barbecue with everybody. She'd like to say hi to you a bit more." He rolled his eyes. "I don't need to tell you that I'm going to have to ask for some help, given I don't have an outdoor space right now."

Yutani lived on a three-acre parcel of land, in a mobile home. But the county had recently slapped him with several fines for not being up to code on a number of his jury-rigged systems, so he was renting an apartment while having a house built. Luckily, he had saved enough money over the years to actually create something pretty spectacular. When I had asked him why he hadn't hired contractors earlier, he just shrugged and said that it had seemed like way too much trouble.

Herne cleared his throat. "I'd invite you over to my place, but I don't know if Danielle is ready to meet everybody."

"Okay, we get the message." I glanced at Angel and she returned my grin. "We can have the barbecue at our place. We have plenty of space, although we don't have a good grill. You'll have to bring that equipment yourself."

Herne laughed. "I can bring the grill. Yutani, you bring the meat. Say six o'clock?"

"Why not make it four-thirty?" I asked. "It gets dark early and that way we can be inside tucked away with our hamburgers and corn on the cob before it gets too dark."

After we agreed to meet at four-thirty at our house, Angel and I waved the others out. Herne hung back, waiting with us. Angel called Raven to make sure she was home and told her we were coming over. When everybody was gone, we gathered our things.

"I suppose we better get this over with." Herne looked like he wanted to do anything but that.

"Well, let's get a move on." I slipped into my jacket, having changed back into my silver top. The other one was covered with gunk from the woods, and I didn't want Raven to see it. "Make sure all the space heaters are turned off so that we don't start a fire in here."

Angel made one more round, making sure all of the space heaters were unplugged, and then we headed down the elevator after locking our floor. Herne held my hand as the car descended, and I gave him a long look, missing him dreadfully. I wanted to go home with him, to make love to him, to stretch out in bed and snuggle. But that wasn't possible. Reluctantly, I let go of his fingers as we stepped out of the elevator.

Angel headed toward the door but Herne reached out, grabbing my hand again. He pulled me to him and gave me a long kiss, wrapping his arms around me.

"I want more than anything to take you home with me." He stared into my eyes, his gaze piercing my heart. "But with Danielle there, I just..." His expression said everything there was to say. He was torn, wanting to do the right thing for his daughter and wanting to do the right thing for me.

"I'll make it easy for you," I said. "I'll see you tomorrow for brunch. We'll find some time this weekend. Maybe we can sneak away while Yutani is grilling the hamburgers. I love you, Herne. I'm not happy about all this, I'll be honest. But I love you, and I'll make this as easy as I can."

He kissed me again and then, with Angel calling us from the front door, we headed out into the night, off to Raven's.

RAJ WAS WAITING out front when we got there. Herne was in the front and Raj's leathery shoulders stiffened the moment he saw us. He hunkered down, his eyes glowing. Herne stopped, holding out his hand, but I stepped around him. When Raj saw me, the gargoyle straightened up, padding over to me with a happy look on his face. He held up his paw, or hand—I wasn't sure what a gargoyle's front appendages were called—waiting for me to shake it. I knelt, a smile forming on my lips. I had never had much to do with gargoyles, but if Raj was typical of them, then I was glad we had met.

"How are you doing, Raj?" I reached out to hesitantly stroke his ears. He let out a satisfied moan, ducking his head and blinking at me.

"I've never seen a wingless gargoyle before," Herne said.

"I wasn't sure if they had wings or not. I didn't think to ask last time I was here." I motioned for Angel to join me and Raj gave her a suspicious look, but at my coaxing, he let her stroke his head.

"His skin feels like hardened leather," Angel said. "I thought he'd be smooth, but it's bumpy."

At that moment, the door opened and Raven came out. She smiled when she saw Angel stroking Raj's head.

"Welcome to my home," she said, but behind her smile, I could see the worry. She knelt beside Raj. "Angel and Herne are friends, just like Ember. They're okay, Raj. You understand?"

Raj let out a grunt, and nodded. Then he turned, padding back into the shadows, where he settled down beside what looked like a very large food dish. Raven stood and led us into the house.

"Please, take a seat. Would you like a drink? I have some wine, if you like. I also have sparkling water."

Herne shook his head. "Perhaps in a little while, thank you." He paused, glancing at me, but before I could say anything, Raven interrupted.

"It's about Ulstair, isn't it? Did you find him? Is he alive?" By the quiver in her voice, I had the feeling she knew he wasn't.

"We found him, yes. Viktor and I also found the three others who were missing." I wasn't sure how to tell her—or how much to tell her.

Raven stared at her hands, sitting still on the sofa. Her back was straight, so straight she looked like a statue. Her hands were on her knees, clutching at the velvet of her skirt. She sat frozen, barely breathing.

"He's dead, isn't he?"

I remembered that moment. That single moment when you *know* something is coming, and you know it's going to be bad, but it hasn't quite hit you yet. It's that moment when you prayed for something to interrupt, to turn the clock back ten minutes, or make time stop altogether, or for someone to wake you out of a nightmare. I had felt it when I found my parents' bodies. I felt it when I saw the back door was open and pushed it wide just enough to see the trail of blood. I had stood there, staring at the drops on the floor, wanting to step back outside, to return to five minutes before, when everything was normal.

I let her breathe another moment. I let her freeze time for just a little longer. Then I reached out and put my hand on top of hers.

"Yes, he's dead. Viktor and I found his body."

She clutched my fingers. Angel sat on the other side, putting her arms around Raven's shoulders. We sat there for a moment, the three of us, in silence as the tears slowly began to trail down Raven's face. I glanced up to find Herne watching the three of us, a sadness in his eyes that I seldom saw from him. It occurred to me that in his world, death of a loved one didn't happen very often. The gods were essentially immortal, removed from loss. And yet, were they? Gods *could* die, although it was rare. And when they formed attachments with mortals, surely then, death touched them.

After a moment, Raven shuddered. "I knew he was dead. I knew it in my heart, but I didn't want to believe it. How did he die?"

"We're not sure," I said. "The police took away the bodies."

"Where did you find him?"

I hesitated, not wanting her to traipse out into the woods in hopes of speaking with his spirit. But then, I decided that she wouldn't be able to find the place if I spoke in generalities.

"We found him in UnderLake Park, well back in the woods. He was in a hole that had been dug into the side of the ravine. There were three other bodies with him."

She squeezed my hand even tighter, then taking a deep breath, she let it out slowly and let go of our hands. Angel and I sat back a little ways, giving her space. After a few minutes she looked up, reaching up to dry her eyes. I poked through my purse and came up with some tissues, handing them to her.

"So," she said, her voice shaky. "What happens next? Do you think the police are going to investigate?"

Herne cleared his throat. "Unfortunately, I don't think so. Did you know that Ulstair was on Saílle's shit list, so to speak?"

Raven blinked, then gave a half shrug. "I had the feeling that something was wrong between him and the Court. He never mentioned it, though, and every time I approached the subject, he dodged my questions. I just assumed it was a touchy area and let it go. It didn't seem to matter, given I'm Ante-Fae. I have no real ties to either court."

"Apparently his family ticked off Saílle at some point, and she put the entire line on her list," Herne said. "The other missing Fae were also on her list, and the police were given explicit instructions to ignore any calls concerning them. Since the Dark and the Light Fae both own a good share of the cops, for lack of a better word, any calls about people on their pariah lists are pretty much ignored. Which leads me to believe that these deaths will be swept under the rug."

Raven's eyes flashed, and for the first time, anger replaced the sorrow. The look on her face was terrifying and I shrank back as she straightened her shoulders and pressed her hands against the seat cushion.

"Oh, how lovely they are. This doesn't surprise me. Petty warring bitches." Her nostrils flared. "Would you continue to look into his death? I want to know who killed him. I want revenge. The Dark Fae can suck balls for all I care. If they won't find his killer, then I will."

Herne simply nodded. "We'll do everything we can. I'm so sorry we didn't have better news."

"It's not your fault. But I want to know who did this. They will learn what it is to fear the Ante-Fae."

As Herne stood, Raven cringed. I knew what she was thinking.

"Raven, would you like Angel and me to stay for a while? Herne has to get home, but we can stay and keep you company for a while."

As quickly as the rage had crossed her face, it fled, and she gave me a grateful look. "Thank you.

I'd like that. I'd like both of you to stay."

I walked Herne to the door while Angel stayed behind.

"Are you sure it's a good idea? She is Ante-Fae, and they're highly unpredictable," Herne said in a low voice.

I glanced over my shoulder, then back at him. "I know what it's like when someone you love dies. I know what it's like to feel alone. Angel and I like Raven, and I don't think she'll do anything to us. Trust me, my gut tells me that she needs us right now."

"All right, but call me if you need me. Otherwise, I'll see you tomorrow morning around eleven?"

I nodded. "Love you. I'll see you tomorrow."

Herne gave me a soft kiss, then headed out to his car. Raj watched him leave, growling softly, but keeping his place in the undergrowth. As I shut the door against the night, I wondered if we would be able to find out who killed Ulstair and the other men. Who was out there, hunting the Dark Fae. And why?

Chapter 12

BY THE TIME Angel and I were ready to go, we had met Raven's ferrets. Templeton was black and he was hot to trot and quite a handful. Elise was a beautiful sable brown, and she was quite amenable to being petted. Gordon was white, and he seemed to be the broody one of the bunch.

"Where did you get Raj? I thought all gargoyles had wings," Angel said as she snuggled Elise and then handed her back to Raven.

Raven smiled for the first time that night. "I won him in a poker game with a demon. Poor Raj had been tortured. The demon had cut off his wings when he was a baby, a little like docking a Doberman's ears, only worse. Most gargoyles have flight as an innate power, but they are taught when they're babies. I don't know where the demon found Raj, but he hadn't learned to fly by the time that freakshow got hold of him. He didn't want Raj running away, so he cut off his wings."

That made me sick to my stomach. I bit my lip. While gargoyles weren't animals, the thought of some sadist docking Raj's wings so he wouldn't run away made me spitting mad.

"What did you do?"

"The stupid demon got drunk during the game and I decided to get even. I'm a *really good* poker player, and I had two friends with me who were more than willing to help. We fleeced that demon till he was broke. He was drunk enough to demand a chance to get his money back, I offered double or nothing. If he lost, he'd give me Raj. If he won, I'd give him double his money. We made certain he lost." She laughed, her eyes darkening.

"So he gave you Raj?"

"Yeah. I brought Raj home and he's been with me ever since. I called in some favors and they healed his scars so you can't really see where his wings were. I also asked another friend to mind-wipe his memory. Raj has no memory of the time he spent before he came to me, or of the pain he endured. The only thing he knows is that he's always been with me, and that's all he'll ever know."

It was my turn to catch my breath. "That's quite a story. Where did you run into the demon? I'd like to steer clear of there. I thought it was bad enough dealing with goblins and other creatures from the sub-Fae."

Angel tapped me on the shoulder. "Don't forget, you've dealt with demons before. Wasn't Kuveo a demon?"

"Sort of. And then, of course..." I stopped, sud-

denly realizing it might not be wise to talk about
the King of Thorns to another one of the Ante-Fae.
I had no clue whether she had heard about Blackthorn and his son, but now was not the time.

Raven appeared not to notice the interplay
between Angel and me. She seemed lost in her
thoughts. "Where did I run into the demon? It was
in a charnel house." She pressed her hand against
her lips then, and gave a little cry. "Ulstair's really
dead, isn't he?"

I nodded, not knowing what to do. But Angel moved in, holding her arms open and Raven
leaned against her shoulder, weeping. We stayed
for another half hour, until Raven fell asleep on
the sofa. Angel found a throw and spread it over
her, and we headed out, locking the door behind
us. Raj watched us go, giving a little grunt as we
passed. I knelt to look at him.

"Your mama needs you. Watch over her. You're
one lucky gargoyle, you know that?"

He grunted again, and I had the feeling he
understood what I said. I wasn't sure just how
intelligent gargoyles were, but Raj seemed to have
a semblance of understanding. I patted his head,
scratching his ears before Angel and I headed back
to our cars.

As we stood there, on the side of the street, I
realized I didn't feel like going home just yet.

"I really need a drink. Do you want to go to
Medinos?" We had found a bar a couple months
before, thanks to Talia. A great number of the Sub-
Cult gathered there, and it was usually jumping.
It also happened to be the perfect place to grab a

drink, sit in the corner, and just relax.

"I'll meet you there," Angel said. "I don't want to go home yet, either."

As we headed out, over to West Seattle, I thought again about Raven. I hadn't warmed up to somebody that fast in a long time. I had a feeling Angel and I had just made a friend for the long haul.

MEDINOS WASN'T EXACTLY packed, but there were enough people there to bring the noise level up to a moderate drone. I glanced around, looking for anybody that we might know. In particular, I was looking for Talia, but she didn't seem to be there. However, just as I was about to head up to the bar, Angel tapped me on the shoulder. She pointed to one of the booths, and I glanced over at the man who was sitting there. He gave us a little wave and motioned for us to join him.

It was Kipa.

I glanced at Angel again, grimacing. Leaning in so she could hear me, I said, "Are you sure?"

Kipa was essentially Herne's cousin. Which wouldn't be a problem except that Herne and Kipa weren't exactly friends. At one point in the past, Herne had discovered Kipa in a compromising position with his girlfriend and that had put an end to any friendly family banter. Kipa was just as gorgeous as Herne, with golden skin and eyes as dark as the dregs of the coffee cup. He was tall and striking, with long rich brown hair and a full beard and mustache. Kipa believed in piercings—his ears were a trail of aquamarine studs, his lower lip sported two silver hoops and a dolphin bite piercing. And he loved women.

But Kipa had spotted us. It would be rude to ignore him.

"It will be fine," Angel said. "Herne knows that you love him and that his cousin isn't going to get anywhere with you. And Kipa seems to understand that you're hands off."

I let her lead me over to the booth, and as we sat down the waitress swung by.

"May I take your order?" she said, her eyes firmly glued on Kipa's face. He just grinned at her and leaned back as Angel and I ordered.

"I'll have a goblin blaster," I said, deciding that I needed at least one stiff drink.

Angel blinked. "That's pretty strong, even for you."

"I know," I said, "but I need it right now."

Angel glanced up at the woman and said, "I'll take a beer. Microbrew if you have it. I like dark ale."

The waitress meandered off, glancing over her shoulder at Kipa once again.

"She sure fancies you," Angel said grinning.

Kipa shrugged. "Fancy is as fancy does. A lot of women give me those looks but I don't go home with them." He gave Angel a long look. "Not that I wouldn't fancy a little fun with a beautiful and intelligent woman. It's been a while since I've played in the dating scene."

Angel snorted. "I rather doubt that, but you do a good job of laying on the charm." She laughed, leaning back against the seat. "We had a hard day."

I let out a sigh, my thoughts returning to Raven. "Hard day doesn't begin to encompass it."

Kipa's easy smile vanished, and he leaned forward. "What happened?" he asked, a serious note filtering into his voice.

I shrugged. "We had to tell someone that her fiancé was murdered. And unfortunately, Viktor and I were the ones who found the bodies. Her fiancé, and three other Dark Fae men who looked like him, were killed. We don't know why, or who did it."

Kipa ducked his head, staring at the table. "It's never easy. I'm sorry. This woman whose fiancé was murdered, is she a friend of yours?"

"Somewhat," I said. "A new friend, I guess you could say. A client. Angel and I like her a lot. She's one of the Ante-Fae, but she's nice, and it really sucks to have to tell somebody that the person they love is dead and gone."

Kipa stared at us, then pushed the basket of potato chips our way. "Here. You need food. You need junk food," he added. He motioned for the waitress and she returned with our drinks, sliding the bubbling green cocktail in front of me.

Goblin blasters were a mixture of three types of rum, pineapple juice, a burnt sugar caramel syrup, and lime. It wouldn't have been so potent if one of the rums hadn't been Dahayshun rum, a liqueur made by the Dark Fae that could knock you off your ass with one shot.

I took a sip and felt a shudder run through me. Dahayshun rum was expensive and rare and the archenemy of sobriety.

Kipa looked up at the waitress. "Three pieces of cheesecake, another basket of potato chips, a plate of nachos fully loaded, and some chicken wings, please. A double portion appetizer of the wings, if you would. Moderately spicy." He glanced at us. "That work for you girls?"

I groaned, but nodded. Angel broke into a wide smile.

"That sounds wonderful," she said, taking a long pull on her beer. "Bring me another beer as well."

I decided I might as will make a night of it. "I'll take another goblin blaster."

"Oh girl, you're asking for trouble." Kipa laughed again, and he pointed to my drink. "I seriously hope that you have another way home besides driving."

Angel spoke up. "I'll limit myself to two beers. I never drink more than that anyway, or at least not usually. In a couple hours I'll be able to drive without a problem."

Halfway through the wings, I ordered my third goblin blaster. I was feeling no pain by then. The room seemed a lot brighter, and Kipa seemed a whole lot cuter, and the music made me want to dance. I glanced at the dance floor where a few couples were getting their groove on.

"Kipa, dance with me." I motioned for Angel to get out of the booth so I could slide out.

"Are you sure—" Angel started to say but I waved away her protests. I wanted to dance, and since Herne wasn't there, Kipa would do.

Kipa gave me a speculative look, then glanced at Angel. "You think I should?"

Angel cleared her throat. "I don't think a dance will hurt, but you'd better leave it at that. Herne wouldn't hesitate to beat you to a pulp if your hands wander."

"Quit talking about me like I'm not here," I said. "I want to dance."

The room was spinning as Kipa took my hand and led me onto the dance floor. The music was techno-dance, but as I tried to match my movements to the rhythm, I almost tipped over. Maybe the goblin blasters were stronger than I thought they were.

Kipa pulled me toward him, putting his arm around my waist, and we danced slow and easy. He smelled wild, a little like Herne but more feral. There was a musky scent to him that wasn't unpleasant. He smelled like wet cedar on a cold day, and the mist rising in the forest at night. Kipa was Lord of the Wolves, and right now I could almost hear them howling around him. Chilled, and a little turned on, I nestled into his arms and leaned my head against his chest. As the song ended though, he gently pushed me away and led me back to the booth. Angel scooted over so I could slide in on the end.

"I want another drink," I said, stumbling over the words.

"You don't *need* another drink," Angel said.

"What's going on, Ember? I've never seen you like this." Kipa glanced over at Angel, and I saw him question her with his eyes.

"It's been a sucky week, and I hated having to tell Raven that Ulstair was dead. She was so in love with him. And tomorrow I've got to meet my boyfriend's daughter and I don't know how to act. I can't believe Herne's got a daughter." I suddenly burst into tears, and my nose began to run. Angel handed me a napkin.

"Oh, ho! So that's what's going on. Herne's past has come back to haunt him." Kipa arched his eyebrows as he leaned back, popping another potato chip into his mouth. "Everybody makes mistakes, Ember. Even Herne."

"What if she doesn't like me? What if she doesn't want him to see me anymore?"

Oh gods, I was sounding like a needy, clingy girlfriend. I rolled my eyes, staring at the ceiling. My stomach lurched around as I ate the last bite of my cheesecake. Grimacing, I pressed my hand to my stomach, hoping that everything would stay down.

"Trust me," Kipa said. "Herne has it bad for you. If Cernunnos himself told him to break up with you, he wouldn't do it. He's not going to throw you over just because of a daughter whom he knew nothing about. Who knows, maybe she'll love you? Maybe you two will become best friends."

"I've already got a best friend and she's sitting right here." I turned to Angel. "I would *never* throw you over for Herne's daughter. You know that, right?"

Angel shook her head, laughing. "Girlfriend, it's time to get you home and into bed. You are not driving."

"I can drive her back. How are you doing?"

Angel pointed to the empty bottles. "It's been two hours since I drank those and I'm quite sober. I ate enough to cushion the alcohol. If you can drive her car, let's pour her into it and get her back home. If she throws up, it's going to be in her own vehicle, not mine."

The conversation was becoming a blur, and I wasn't sure exactly what they were talking about. The next thing I knew they had me up and heading toward the door. My stomach swayed dangerously, but I managed to keep everything down.

When we reach the parking lot, Angel and Kipa got me strapped into the passenger seat of my car. Angel found my keys and handed them to Kipa and then headed for her own car. Kipa waited until she was safely inside and had started the ignition, then he started up my car. I didn't protest—even in my drunken stupor I knew I was far too drunk to drive. I leaned back against the headrest on the seat, closing my eyes.

"Ember, I want to ask you something." Kipa took the turns nice and easy as we followed Angel back to our place.

"What?" I tried to focus on his voice.

"Are you and Herne happy? Or rather, are you happy with Herne?"

I let out a loud belch, wincing as the taste of the goblin blasters hit my throat again. Everything might be blurry, but I had no doubt about how to answer his question.

"I love Herne. I'm scared of being in a relationship with him, because hey, he's a god. But I love him."

"That's all I wanted to know," Kipa said, easing the car off the road, parking behind Angel.

I almost made it to the front door before I threw up. Luckily, I managed to avoid splattering either one of them with the remains of my goblin blaster orgy. Kipa picked me up in his arms and carried me in, and Angel directed him up the stairs. He set me down on my bed, turning me over to Angel at that point.

"Take care of her. Call me if you need me. Here's my cell number." He jotted down something on a piece of paper and handed it to her. "Do you need help getting her cleaned up and into bed?"

I could barely hear Angel's reply, and the next thing I knew someone was washing my face and stripping me out of my clothes. I didn't know who it was, but as my head hit the pillow, I saw Mr. Rumblebutt laying beside me. I wrapped my arm around him, and groaning softly, passed out for the night.

"EMBER, TIME TO wake up." Angel was shaking my shoulder.

I didn't want to open my eyes. I felt like crap and I could tell it was going to be a rough morning. I tried to wave her off, but then she opened the curtains, letting the light splash into the room. While it was overcast, the brightness of morning still hit me right between the eyes. I groaned, trying to roll over and pull the covers over my head.

"No," I moaned. "Me no get up."

"Sorry. You have to take a shower because you've got to be over at Herne's in ninety minutes and you reek of rum. Come on, upsy-daisy." She yanked my covers off of me, and I began to shiver in the chill morning air.

"You're enjoying this far too much," I managed to say as I rolled to a sitting position. My head was throbbing, and I felt like something had crawled into my stomach and died. "What the hell did I do last night?" Everything was a little fuzzy, although I seemed to remember dancing with Kipa.

"You drank three goblin blasters. Or maybe four. I'm not sure. Remember? We went to Medinos?"

It was starting to come back. The bar. Dancing with Kipa. Eating way too much junk food and drinking way too much booze. I groaned again, and glanced at the other side of my bed.

"Please tell me that I didn't do something that I'm going to regret."

Angel snorted. "Kipa was more of a gentleman than you were. You were flirting pretty bad, but you didn't cross any lines you shouldn't. And he was very careful to maintain boundaries. You should thank him because knowing Kipa, it was probably pretty hard."

My mind still in the gutter, I laughed. "I bet it was."

"*Shower. Now.* Then I'm making you breakfast."

My stomach revolted at the thought of food. "I'm not hungry."

"You need to eat something to calm your stomach before you go over there for brunch."

"Can't I just call and plead sick?" But, at the look on her face, I knew Angel wasn't going to let me out of this. "Oh, all right. I'm up. Lead me to the shower."

As I stumbled toward the bathroom, Angel began stripping my bed. I glanced back at her.

"What are you doing?"

"You didn't throw up in bed, but I'll tell you this, your sheets smell like old booze and stinky armpits. Go take your shower."

"Have I ever told you how much I love having you as a roommate?" I said, darting into my bathroom as she threw a pillow at me.

I stripped off my nightshirt, turning on the water so it was comfortably warm. Grateful for the shower seat, I sat down and lathered up a body sponge with vanilla scented shower gel as the water poured down on me. I angled the shower head directly toward me, cautiously sitting back down. I was still woozy, and didn't want to risk slipping. But the water hit me full force, and I was able to scrub all of the funk away while sitting there, trying to remember everything that I had said and done.

I seldom drank that much. In fact, Angel and I had been on several benders over the years, but they weren't frequent and they usually entailed some breakup or personal disappointment.

By the time I was finished washing my hair, I had to admit that my frustration over Herne and the situation with his daughter had finally come to a head. Though it was better that the emotions had surfaced while I was with friends, and not with Herne and Danielle.

I combed out my wet hair, and sat down at the bathroom vanity to dry it. I took extra pains with my makeup, partially because I was still shaky, and partially because I wanted to look as good as I could. As I stared at myself in the mirror, drawing on my eyeliner, I heaved a sigh and stopped, facing myself square on.

"You're an insecure mess right now. No matter what Kipa or Angel say, the fact is Danielle is Herne's daughter. And children usually come first."

By the time I finished putting on my makeup and drying my hair, Angel had stripped my bed, changed the sheets, and made it up nice and tidy again. I owed her one. If she had not been there, Kipa might not have been such a gentleman. He wasn't a bad person, but he was carefree and footloose, unless he wanted to impress somebody. And while Angel refused to date him, he seemed to still want her respect.

After carefully choosing my underwear and bra, I slipped into a pair of jeans that rode low on my hips, lacing a black leather belt through the loops. Next came a corset top that zipped up the front. I zipped up a pair of the new ankle boots I had bought. They had three-inch stilettos and were studded with hardware and a silver chain that looped around the ankle. I even took the time to polish the crow necklace that Morgana had given me before fastening it back on my neck. After adding silver earrings and a silver bracelet, I swept my hair back into a high ponytail and headed down-stairs.

The kitchen smelled wonderful. I wasn't sure exactly what Angel was making, but for the first time since I'd opened my eyes my stomach gave a little rumble and I realized that I actually was hungry.

"Whatever that is, it smells wonderful," I said, entering the kitchen. Angel pointed over toward the table. There, at my usual place, was a large coffee cup next to a plate with a waffle and bacon on it.

"The carbs of the waffle will help soothe your stomach, and the bacon will give you some energy. I figured you'd only need one, given you'll be eating again in an hour." She joined me, carrying her own plate and a cup of tea.

"Was I really that terrible last night?" I gave her a repentant look.

"Well, you weren't at your best. You were down-right funny at times. But sweetie, I gotta tell you this. You really shouldn't go out partying with Kipa. At least not while you're upset at Herne. That's not the best way to handle this situation."

"I know," I said, diving into my food.

Chapter 13

I STOOD, MY hand poised over the doorbell, as I ran over what I planned to say. I had been standing there five minutes when the door opened abruptly in my face and Herne leaned against the door frame, a grin on his lips.

"So, were you planning on ringing the bell? Or are you just going stand outside my door all day?" His smile was easy, and he sounded happy to see me.

"Can I let you know about it when I've thought it through?" I pushed past him into the house, wanting to stop and give him a long kiss, but not sure about the protocol in front of his daughter. But he caught me by the wrist, pulling me back and wrapping his arms around me.

I slid into his kiss, letting out a gentle sigh as he embraced me. I had missed this so much, even though it had only been a few days it felt like it'd been forever since we'd had time to ourselves.

"I've missed this," Herne said, reading my thoughts. "We'll get through this, I promise." He touched his forehead to mine, and then pulled back as a woman entered the room.

While I knew that his daughter was older than I was, technically, the fact that she was young in terms of the gods had made me expect a child. But the woman standing in front of me was no little girl. At least not in body. She was lovely, statuesque with broad shoulders and long golden hair bound back in a braid. She was wearing a pair of white jeans and a pale blue tank top. While she looked to be in her twenties, I began to wonder about Herne describing her as a teenager. Could he have read things wrong? But when she opened her mouth, I realized he was spot on.

"Is this her?" Danielle stared at me, her eyes flashing. "Are you my dad's girlfriend?"

Oh yes, no doubt at all that she wasn't thrilled to meet me. And it wasn't just icy politeness. She sounded like a petulant teenager.

"Ember, I want you to meet my daughter Danielle. Danielle, this is my girlfriend Ember. *Be polite.*" The last was stated with a warning note.

Danielle let out a loud sigh, then shrugged. "Whatever. I'm going to go watch Supetube again." She turned and flounced off.

The confusion must have shown on my face because Herne let out a short laugh.

"Don't mind her. I told you she's pretty much the proverbial teenager, even though she doesn't look it. She may look grown up, but I guarantee you, that's one moody kid."

As the prospect of spending an hour eating brunch with Danielle stretched out in front of me, I wanted to turn around and walk out the door. All thoughts of getting along with Danielle had fled. In that one brief moment, I had seen exactly what she thought of me, and it wasn't pretty.

"Are you sure you want me here? She doesn't seem happy to meet me. In fact, I'd say she's downright hostile."

"I know, I know. But please stay? You can leave in an hour if you want, I promise. I just think that if she spends enough time with you, she'll come to love you just as much as I do."

I wasn't banking on it, but I didn't tell Herne that. Instead, I followed him into the dining room where the table was set for brunch. The sideboard held all sorts of dishes.

"Did you do all this yourself?" I asked, crossing over to look at the spread. There were muffins and waffles and stacks of pancakes, hard-boiled eggs and sliced ham and bacon, fruits and jams, and various breakfast rolls and croissants spread out along the walnut surface.

"Are you kidding? I can cook but I'm not *that* interested in cooking. No, I had this catered."

Thank gods that Angel had made me eat something because my stomach had finally calmed down. I settled in at the table next to Herne, and he called to Danielle.

"Brunch is ready, get your butt to the table!"

I blinked. "That's not the most congenial invitation."

"I have already discovered that just asking elicits no response." Herne rolled his eyes.

Danielle reluctantly entered the room, dragging her feet. "Do I have to eat with you guys?"

Herne gave her a long look. "Yes. Ember's important to me and I want you to get along. Or at least, I want you to give it a try."

Danielle rolled her eyes, but shrugged and flounced over to the table. It was still hard for me to make the mental jump between her looks and her actions, but it was getting easier. Herne had been right. She was a petulant child, and I wondered just how long this adolescence would go on.

I added ham and bacon to my plate, and a croissant, and some grapes and strawberries. Then, pouring a glass of orange juice, I headed over to the table and sat on the opposite side of Danielle. Herne joined us, sitting at the head of the table. His plate was piled high with pancakes and eggs and bacon, and he turned to Danielle.

"Get yourself some breakfast." He held her gaze. "Please."

"All right. Don't have a stroke." She sighed, dragging herself to her feet. "I'm not that hungry." But once she was at the sideboard, she didn't spare any space on her plate. She returned, sitting closer to Herne so that she was kitty corner to me.

I broke open my croissant, spreading butter and jam on it. As I bit into it, she gave me another look, again rolling her eyes and shaking her head. I swallowed the bread, then dabbed my lips with my napkin.

"Is there a problem?" I asked. I would try to

be nice, but I wasn't going to allow myself to be walked over, especially by a whiny brat. It didn't matter whether she was the daughter of a god or an Amazon or the kid down the street.

Herne glanced at her. "Answer her."

Danielle gave him a glowering look. "You told me to be polite to her. If I answer her, I'd be breaking my promise."

So we were playing the passive-aggressive game, were we? I decided to quit mincing words. I set down my fork, propped my elbows on the table, and leaned my chin on my hands, staring directly at her.

"Danielle, You don't know me. You don't want to talk to me. Fine. But the fact is that I'm your father's girlfriend, and we have been together for over six months. *I don't care* if you like me, or what you think about me. That means squat to me if you're going to be a snot about it. I would *like* to become friends, but I'm not going to play all nice-nice while you treat me like shit. *However*...for the sake of your father, how about you and I both show some civility to each other?" I wasn't feeling particularly diplomatic today, and at this point I didn't really care what the girl thought about me.

She blinked, the sneer sliding off her face. "What makes you think you can talk to me that way?"

"If you act like a snot-nosed brat, I'm going to treat you like one regardless of who your parents are. Now, let's change the subject and make brunch as pleasant as we can."

I glanced at Herne, surprised by the laughter behind his veiled eyes.

"I agree with Ember," he said. "Brunch is a civil event, or it's supposed to be. Let's relax, enjoy the food, and be polite." He turned to stare at Danielle. "*No matter what you're feeling.*"

She seemed to be gauging her chances. Then, with a shrug, she said, "Whatever," and dug into her food, ignoring the both of us.

Herne's phone rang at that moment, and he stepped away from the table to answer it. I finished my croissant when Danielle wiped her mouth on her napkin.

"My father says that you're part Dark Fae, part Light Fae. I didn't think the two courts could inter-breed." It wasn't so much a statement as a question.

I shrugged, wiping my own mouth. "Both sides would prefer that people believe that, but the truth is, Light or Dark, we're all the same race. The Fae can interbreed with each other, with humans, and with some other members of the SubCult. Saílle and Névé just don't like that fact, and they do their best to cover it up. Neither court recognizes me as legitimate."

The surly look began to slide off her face. "How did your parents meet?"

"To be honest I'm not quite sure. My mother promised to tell me when I was older, but they were murdered when I was fifteen, before she had the chance. So I never found out." I held Danielle's gaze, still hoping that we could establish some sort of common ground.

She recoiled, wincing. "They were *murdered*? You were only fifteen? That was probably tough," she said, a slight hesitation in her voice.

"Oh, it gets better than that," I said. I seemed to be getting through to her by being blunt, so decided to go for it. "My grandparents on both sides ordered my parents' assassinations. I found them when I came home from school, on the floor, stabbed so many times that they had bled completely out."

Danielle let out a little bleat. She glanced at me again, her cheeks flushing, then she stared down at her plate, toying with her food. I felt like this was a good time to change the subject.

"So, are you having fun getting to know your father?"

Again, she gave a little shrug, but this time she didn't seem so snarly. "It's okay. It's not quite what I thought it would be." She looked me in the eye. "I didn't even know who my father was until last month."

"Your mother never told you that Herne was your father until now?" I knew the answer to that one, but I had the feeling that Myrna might be using Danielle as a pawn.

Danielle shook her head. "No. In fact, for years she told me she didn't know who my father was. Then all of a sudden she changed her tune and start talking about how she'd found him, and that I really should meet him. I guess I'm glad to know, and at least he's not some pervert or war god. But we got along just fine without him. In fact, everything was just great until she met Thantos. Then everything fell apart."

Hmm, what was Myra looking to get out of this?

If she had never felt the need to look up Herne
before, what had caused the change?

"Who's Thantos? Obviously her boyfriend but..."

Danielle shrugged again. "He's one of Zeus's
sons. I don't know who his mother was, some
woman I guess. Thantos is a demigod, like Herne.
But then he got all pervy, and he came onto me.
My mother caught him trying to feel me up, and
they got in a huge argument. He said some really
nasty things and stomped out. I guess she blames
me. I don't know why, because I can't stand the
thought of him touching me. He's gross." She
paused, suddenly looking up as though she hadn't
realized she had been talking out loud.

"So that's when she contacted Herne to see if he
would take you?"

Ten to one Myrna was trying to get Thantos
back, now that her daughter was out of the way.
It surprised me that any Amazon would knuckle
under to a man like that. If Danielle had been *my*
daughter, Thantos would have been nursing a broken pecker.

"You think she's trying to get rid of me, too,
don't you?" Danielle's eyes crinkled, and I could
see the wounded child beneath the exterior. She
might look like an adult, but we were truly dealing
with a young woman.

I paused, trying to frame my answer so it
wouldn't reflect too badly on her mother.

"I think your mother might be a little mixed up
right now. Maybe she needs some time to think."
Part of me wanted to pay a visit to Myrna and set
her straight, but that would be a huge mistake. But

I couldn't just let this go.

"Mixed up is right." Danielle shook her head. "I wouldn't have let him touch me," she said, a pleading note in her voice. I wondered just how much her mother had believed her. "No matter what my mother thinks. I haven't told her this yet, but I like girls." She said it almost shyly.

I smiled, then, nodded. "Also, you told him *no* and he didn't listen. What he did was wrong, Danielle. You weren't to blame. And because he's an adult, it means he's totally at fault." I stopped as Herne returned to the table.

He glanced at Danielle, and then at me, his brow crinkling. "So you two haven't been beating each other up, I hope?"

Danielle shrugged, but this time she smiled a little. "No."

I finished my bacon. "Who was that on the phone?"

Herne's eyes flashed as he stared at me. "Kipa. Ember, can I talk to you in private?"

Oh crap, I thought. Kipa had ratted me out. I said nothing, but stood and followed Herne into his study.

HERNE SHUT THE door behind him as I crossed to the window, leaning against the sill. He sat on the corner of his desk, staring at me with his arms folded across his chest.

"So, you were partying with Kipa last night, were

you?"

I kept my eyes on the birdfeeder out back. It was blustery outside, pouring rain and the wind was rising. The trees surrounding Herne's rental were swaying and I could feel the storm growing. Unfortunately, I had the feeling that I was in for quite a storm of my own.

"Angel and I went to Medinos. Kipa happened to be there, and we had a few drinks with him. Why do you ask?"

"Kipa told me you got shit-faced drunk. He said he helped take you home and pour you into bed. Now, normally I wouldn't think to ask this but given it was *Kipa*, and given you're my *girlfriend*, I feel it necessary to ask if he poured you into bed alone?"

Swinging around, I pointed my finger at him. "You listen to me. *I'm not Nya.* You know I love you, and I've told you that I have no interest in bedding Kipa. I'm insulted you feel you have to ask that."

Herne couldn't look straight at me, but his voice was gruff as he said, "Kipa said you danced together."

"Yes, we danced. I like to dance and you weren't there. I'd dance with Angel if she wanted me to, or Viktor, or Talia, or Ginty. Dancing isn't fucking. Not that I feel I owe you an explanation, but here it is, all laid out. Yes, I flirted a little with Kipa—all in fun. He was the perfect gentleman. He kept his hands to himself. I was drunk off my ass and feeling horrible over breaking the news about Ulstair to Raven. *You* weren't there. But Angel and

Kipa were. If you don't believe me that nothing happened, ask her. Except she'll bust your ass for suspecting me."

Herne's eyes flashed, but then he began to deflate. "Kipa told me nothing happened. But he wanted me to know just in case anybody saw you two and decided to spread rumors. Were you at least going to tell me?"

I still didn't like his accusatory tone, but I knew how badly Kipa had hurt him before.

"Yes, I was. But not in front of your daughter. We haven't had any time alone since I got here until now. What *more* do you want to know? Do you want to know what song we danced to? Because I can't remember. I do remember how crummy I felt. First, finding those bodies, then telling Raven, and let's not forget finding out my boyfriend has a daughter. Apparently, I broke down in front of Kipa and Angel last night and ugly cried. So, yes. I got drunk. I got shit-faced drunk. I danced with Kipa. I drank three goblin blasters... Maybe four."

Herne coughed. "You drank *three* goblin blasters? No wonder you were three sheets in the wind."

I let out a long sigh. "Herne, I'm terrified you're going to drop me because of Danielle. And there's absolutely nothing I can say because... *Family*. Your family comes first, and she's your blood. We're not married. We're not engaged. You owe your daughter...well...I don't know what, but *she needs you*. After talking to her in there while you were on the phone, I see that. So if I'm coming between you two, I know the score. And I'm angry at *myself* because I feel so insecure."

He held out his hands. I stared at them, wanting to take them, but I couldn't. Not just yet.

"Ember, there's room in my life for you and for Danielle. Even if she doesn't like you, we'll find a way."

I dropped to the sofa. "Look, I have to say something. Yeah, we've said *I love you* but until now, I didn't realize just how truly in love with you I am. And that scares me because it makes me vulnerable. I've been alone most of my life, except for Angel. I don't like needing other people. It's scary, being invested in somebody else's life, when they might just toss me aside. I've always had to rely on myself. And lately I've come to rely on you. And that scares me too."

Herne sat beside me, pulling me into his arms. He lifted my chin and pressed his lips against mine. His strength flowed through me as the kiss swept me up, back into his world. He lingered, and the longer he kissed me the more I realized that I had truly lost my heart to him. After a while, he let me go.

"I will *always* tell you where we stand. I won't lie to you. I give you my word, as the son of Cernunnos. I give you my word on my mother's magic. If something *does* happen, I'll tell you. I'm not sure how all this will play out, but Ember, you have the key to my heart. And I promise you that I won't let *anybody* tear us apart."

I leaned back against the window, relieved and yet still afraid. Being vulnerable meant being open to pain. But I trusted Herne and decided to release the worry that had crept into my heart. Herne had given me his promise on all that was sacred to him, and that was all I could ask.

After a moment, I nodded. "All right."

"So what did you and Danielle talk about while I was gone?"

I licked my lips, not wanting to break her confidence but feeling that Herne should know about Thantos.

"Actually, it was okay. But, Herne, I think I know why Myrna contacted you. And your daughter needs reassurance right now." It might not be my place to tell Herne what Danielle had told me, but he was her father and I felt he should know. If Danielle went back to Myrna's while Thantos was there, she'd be in danger. And there was no way I could let that happen.

"What do you mean?" Herne asked.

I motioned for him to sit down. "You have to promise me that you won't tell her I told you. I don't want her to think that I'm carrying tales, but this is important."

He nodded. "I promise."

I told him what Danielle had said. "Thantos obviously doesn't care about her age."

Herne's expression darkened. "I can see I need to have to have a talk with Myrna. I'll keep you out of this, but there's no way I'm letting my daughter go back to her mother if that pervert is around. Unfortunately, this is a big problem in the realm of the gods."

At that moment my phone rang, and I glanced at it. It was Raven. "I need to take this," I said. "I'll meet you back at the table."

Herne nodded, heading out the door as I answered the phone.

"Ember, I wanted to ask if you and Angel would come over this afternoon? I'm holding a ceremony to mark Ulstair's passing, and really, we didn't have many friends in common. Very few of my kind understand my desire to be with someone who isn't Ante-Fae. And he didn't have a lot of connections from the Dark Court. He had a few work friends, but they wouldn't understand this kind of ceremony. So I thought..."

"I'll be there. What time?" I understood her feelings of isolation.

"Three-thirty? Will that work?" There was a frailty in her voice that touched my heart.

"That's fine. Have you called Angel yet?"

"I did. She said she could come. I really appreciate this. I just can't face this alone and I didn't know who else to call."

Reassuring her I would be there, I hung up and returned to the table. Herne and Danielle and I finished our brunch on relatively good terms, and I made my good-byes.

As I drove home to change clothes and pick some flowers to take to Raven's, I thought over everything that I had learned about Danielle. She really wasn't that bad, once I understood where she was coming from. And if Herne had to have a child, at least she wasn't a toddler. On the other hand, I wanted to bitch slap Myrna. Any woman who blamed her daughter for a grown man coming onto her had a few screws loose.

All the way home, I thought about Danielle, and how she had suddenly become a part of my life. It wasn't something I had planned on, but as long as Herne and I were together, she would be a factor in our relationship.

Chapter 14

"**WHAT** SHOULD I wear?" Angel said. "I've never gone to something like this before."

"Yes, you have. Remember, I held a small cord-cutting ceremony for my parents. You were the only one there." I was sitting on Angel's bed as she foraged through her closet. "I suggest wearing a dress in either purple, red, or black. Long and floaty would probably be the most appropriate."

Angel sorted through her clothes, sliding the hangers one by one across the pole until she stopped, removing a dress from the closet. She held it up for me to see. "How about this? Do you think this will work?"

The dress was beautiful, a long gauze dress in a coral color. It had smocking on the back, and embroidery on the front, looking Bohemian. Yet it wasn't flirty enough to be inappropriate.

"That's gorgeous, and it will be perfect. Pair it

with a black shawl."

"What are you wearing?" Angel asked.

"A purple skirt, and a black corset top. The skirt has a cropped jacket that goes with it. I'll go get dressed now. We should take some flowers, and maybe a bottle of wine."

I pushed myself off her bed, feeling exhausted. The combination of my drunken debauchery and the emotions of the morning had left me tired and spent. I told Angel about what had happened.

"I'm glad at least you and Danielle came to some sort of peace."

"Yeah, but it wasn't easy."

Angel shimmied out of her jeans, and pulled off her top. I stared at her stomach, thinking you could grate cheese on her abs. My own stomach muscles were just as defined, but they were covered with a nice layer of padding. I was muscled and fit, but I had curves, where Angel was tall and willowy.

"Me too, and I hope it lasts." I headed toward the door. "I'm going to go change. Can you make me some coffee?"

"Roger that. I could go for a cup of tea, myself."

After we changed clothes, we decided to save time and stop at the nearest Starbucks drive-through. There was a flower vendor on the corner, and while I ordered my coffee and Angel's tea, she ran over to pick up a bouquet of rust-colored mums. We made another quick stop at The Grape Vine to pick up a bottle of their best merlot, and then headed over to Raven's.

"You don't think she's going to try to summon

up Ulstair's ghost, do you?"

Given Raven was a bone witch, I was hesitant to say no, but logic won out.

"I sincerely doubt it. I can't vouch for the Ante-Fae because you never know with them, but if she has any sense at all, she won't attempt it. The only way I can see her doing so is in order to find out more about his murder, and right now, since we're on the case, I doubt if she'll try." I paused. "You know, she truly loved him."

"You sound surprised."

"Raven's made me rethink my assumptions about the Ante-Fae. I guess I can't base my opinions on Blackthorn and his son. Stereotyping is pretty stupid, when you get down to it. Everyone is different, and that means it's always a crapshoot when you're dealing with someone new."

Angel nodded. We had spent a lot of hours over the years discussing discrimination and stereotypes, since both of us had been on the receiving end of hard-nosed bigotry. We passed the rest of the drive in silence as dusk began to creep up on the city. Even in September, dusk was coming earlier. It wouldn't be long before it would be dark in the mornings when we got up for work.

We parked in Raven's driveway, next to her car. As usual, Raj was peeking out from his nook off the sidewalk. When he saw me, he came loping out. I patted his head, greeting him. He allowed Angel to pet him too, and as we were cooing to him, Raven opened the door.

"I thought I heard you out here," she said, motioning us in. "Come on, Raj. It's chilly out tonight, so come inside."

"Does he usually stay outdoors?" Angel darted out of the way as Raj went bounding past, his tongue hanging out. He looked so delighted that Angel and I couldn't help but laugh.

"He prefers it, usually. But it's chilly tonight, and I'd like him present for the ceremony. He adored Ulstair, and I don't think he quite understands where he went. I tried to explain it to him, but gargoyles have a different sense of the passage of time, and of loss. While they grow to full size quickly, like the Fae and the Ante-Fae, their aging process slows down so drastically that it almost seems to stop. As time goes on, and eons pass, some gargoyles become almost immobile. A number of the statues on the cathedrals are actually alive, but caught in stasis. They watch and listen, and sometimes when they're summoned, they wake up."

"I don't know much about gargoyles," Angel said. "My experience with the SubCult has been fairly limited. Except for Ember, of course, and my brother."

"You have a brother?" Raven asked.

I glanced at Angel, starting to shake my head. We tried to keep any talk of DJ off limits to outsiders. There were certain people who would find him a handy tool to use as leverage if they ever wanted to get one up on Angel or the Wild Hunt.

But Angel gave me a long look and then shrugged. "It's all right. She's safe. I *know*, and you know enough to trust me."

Raven gave Angel a curious look.

"I'm an empath," Angel said. "I'm extremely good at reading people, whether they be Crypto or not." She paused, then continued. "I have a little brother who is half wolf shifter. He no longer lives with me, for his own safety. And for his own growth."

If Raven had any thoughts on the subject, she kept them to herself. Instead, she led us into the living room. She had pushed back the furniture and set up a circle of white roses on the floor that almost filled the room. In the center of the circle sat a skull—which looked to be humanoid of some sort, with a candle attached to the top of it. The skull rested on a tray, in a bed of sand, surrounded by crystals. The tray was on a low table, along with the wicked-looking dagger, two taper candles—one black, one white—and a silver chalice filled with wine. A picture of Ulstair was propped up along the side of the table, its frame black and covered with silver runes.

"We have to wait for Ulstair's brother. Most of his family doesn't care for me, but his brother—Rafé—and I get along well. Rafé is the black sheep of the family. They considered Ulstair eccentric, but Rafé is almost an outcast."

"Herne notified Saílle about Ulstair's death. I assume they told his family?" Angel said.

Raven shook her head. "No, they wouldn't, given the circumstances. I told Rafé and he broke it to them."

The doorbell rang, and she moved to answer it. Raj danced up to me, his butt wiggling. I stared at the gargoyle, shaking my head, wanting to laugh but feeling like it might be out of place in such a somber moment.

He truly didn't seem to remember his earlier life, that much was apparent.

"You're a happy gargoyle, aren't you?" I knelt down to pat his back as he leaned against me. He was so heavy that I almost tipped over.

Angel laughed as I fumbled for balance.

At that moment Raven entered the room with a tall, lithe man behind her. He looked a lot like Ulstair, with pale skin and red hair, and a brief thought ran through my head that we should warn him to be careful, given the resemblance and the fact that there were three other dead men who had looked a lot like Ulstair.

"Rafé, I'd like you to meet Ember and Angel. They work for the Wild Hunt Agency." Raven swung around the circle and took a seat on the sofa that had been pushed to the side.

Rafé gave us both a deep bow. "I'm pleased to meet you, ladies." His voice was smooth, like velvet, and I wondered if he sang.

I held out my hand and he clasped it firmly. "I'm Ember Kearney."

He shook my hand, and then gently let it go. If he thought anything about the fact that I was a tralaeth, he was gracious enough to say nothing.

"And I'm Angel Jackson." Angel held out her hand.

As Rafé took it, I saw little spark of light. Angel inhaled sharply, and he held her hand longer than he had held mine as they stared at each other.

"And you are an incredibly beautiful woman,"

Rafé said, then suddenly blushed. "I'm sorry if that was an appropriate but…"

"No," Angel said. "Thank you, I appreciate the compliment." She still hadn't let go of his hand and, as if she suddenly realized it, she stepped back, releasing him. Angel seemed so flustered that I stepped in to cover up her embarrassment.

I motioned to Raven. "Where do you want us? And where can we put these mums? We also brought a bottle of wine."

"Why don't you take them in the kitchen? I'll come with you so I can find a vase for the flowers. They're perfect for the ceremony tonight and I thank you for bringing them."

And just like that, Raven hustled me into the kitchen, leaving Angel and Rafé to talk.

"Angel's human, you know," I said, glancing back toward the living room.

Raven found a vase and ran water into it.

"Here's a pair of scissors to trim the stems. And yes, I know, but Rafe's a good-hearted man. He loved his brother very much. Rafé and I got along from the very start, and he's never made one untoward movement toward me. He doesn't share a lot of the Dark Court's views toward humans or anybody else that they might see as a misfit."

She gave me a long look, telling me everything I needed to know. I peeked back at Angel and Rafé, who were already into deep discussion.

"They seem to be hitting it off."

"Angel's a good-enough empath that she'll be able to tell he's on the up and up. He won't be able to slide anything past her. And my guess is that he wouldn't even try."

Raven opened the wine as I cut the stems of the mums down to fit the vase. She pulled a silver tray out of a cupboard, directing me to retrieve four goblets from a built-in. We carried the flowers and wine back into the living room, and Rafé quickly took the tray from me, setting it on a side table. Raven lowered the lights so they were dim in the background.

"Well, I guess we're ready. As you know, I'm a bone witch and I work with the dead. But I don't want you to worry that I'm trying to summon Ulstair's spirit tonight. There's a part of me that wants to, I'll admit that. I'd like to ask him who killed him, to find out so I could have my vengeance. But I'll let the Wild Hunt try to figure it out first. Tonight is simply about saying good-bye to someone I love, with friends here to support me."

Raven stepped into the circle, motioning for us to join her. Raj settled down under the table, while Raven asked me to sit on her left side, Angel in front of her on the other side of the makeshift altar, and Rafé to her right. We sat on the floor.

Raven reached for my hand. I reached for Angel's, and Angel reached for Rafé. He completed the circle by taking Raven's other hand.

I call upon the spirits of the dead to hear me.
I call upon my ancestors to guide me.
I call upon the gates of the Veil to open.
I call upon the magic of the forgotten to fill my heart.
I call upon the dust of the grave and the bones

of the dead to attend me.

All that was, all that has passed, all that lies in the shadows, hear me.

I am Raven, the Daughter of Bones, a Daughter of the Grave.

Let the mysteries reveal themselves to me.

Let the Haunts remember my name.

Let Arawn, Lord of the Dead, clear my vision.

A mist began to rise around the edges of the Circle, not crossing the ring of roses, but so thick we could barely see anything else. There were figures in the mist, faces and bodies so veiled I could barely make them out, but they were there nonetheless. Angel caught her breath, but said nothing and continued to hold tight to my hand. I looked at Raven. Her eyes were glowing, alight with dancing flames. The energy running through her fingers snapped and crackled against mine, and the power that was pouring from her was palpable.

"We have come here to bid farewell to Ulstair. My love was lost too soon, stolen from me, stolen from his brother Rafé. We come to mourn his death, we come to say good-bye, we come to bid his spirit an easy transition. We come to promise justice, however long it may take. We come to cut the cords that bind his mortal presence to this world so that his immortal spirit flies free. We set his spirit free to sail back across the great Sea, to the world of his ancestors."

She turned to Rafé and nodded. We were still holding hands, and she showed no sign that we should let go.

Rafé cleared his throat. "Ulstair, my brother, I miss you so much. Our family fell apart, but you and I had a strong bond. You will *always* be in my heart, and I will tell the stories of you to the next generations. Once my brother, always my brother. One day, we will meet again across the great Sea. I give you my oath that I will watch over your beloved. I promise on all that is sacred that I will be Raven BoneTalker's brother, here for her however she needs me and whenever she needs me. Farewell, until my own path fades and I join you."

By now, tears were running down my face, but I wasn't alone. Angel was crying, and Raven, and Rafé as well. Raven looked at me.

"I know you didn't know Ulstair, but do you have any words you wish to say?"

I cleared my throat. "I hope, that in finding your mortal body, I helped to set you free. I promise to do everything in my power to find your murderer. I pledge myself as a friend to Raven. Rest easy across the Great Sea, Ulstair."

Angel spoke next. "May you rest with the peace of the valiant in your heart, and the knowledge that we will do what we can to help Raven. I too pledge my friendship to her. And to her brother, Rafé." The last, she said quickly, almost as though the words spilled out unbidden.

Rafé gave her a quick look, and smiled at her softly. "I thank you for that, Angel Jackson."

No one else had anything to say, and so Raven spoke last.

"Ulstair, you will always rest in my heart. I will miss you forever, and yet I must let you journey into my past, to remain a memory." She was sobbing now, so hard the words were like barbed darts. "We have made our good-byes. We have sent our best wishes and our love across the great Sea with Ulstair. May the guardians watch over you. May the gods lead you on your path. May the bountiful waters of the great sea carry you home swiftly and safely. *Ashamane*."

"*Ashamane*," I murmured, along with Rafé.

As we softly repeated the *Turneth*—the Dark Faespeak—expression bidding a respectful farewell—a sudden gust of wind rushed through the room, blowing out the candle, and Raven let go of our hands.

"He's gone," she said. "I felt him journey through the veil."

Rafé nodded. "Thank you for doing this. Our mother's too sick to do anything for his memory, and I'm afraid the rest of my family is so messed up that they don't care anymore." He stared down at his hands. "I miss my brother."

"I know," Raven said, brushing a strand of loose hair back away from his face. "He loved you, Rafé. He always told me, if anything goes wrong, go to Rafé and he'll help."

"He was right." Rafé let out a sigh, then stood. "I brought some pastries. They're in the kitchen. Why don't I get them?"

"I'll help," Angel said, jumping up to join him.

While they were in the kitchen, I helped Raven clear away the altar. We spent the next hour just hanging out. Angel and Rafé chatted. I played with Raj and helped Raven feed the ferrets. Finally,

Angel and I made our farewells and headed to our car.

As we buckled our seat belts, I glanced at her. "So, did you get his number?"

"You did not just ask me that." She glared at me, but as I kept my eyes trained on her face, she blushed and broke into a wide smile. "Yeah, I got his number. And he's calling me tonight to set up a date. Anything else you want to know?"

"No. I'm just glad that you actually took him up on it. You guys had a spark. I could tell."

"Well, just because we sparked doesn't mean there's anything there. I'm not getting my hopes up, or at least not more than I think I can handle."

As we pulled out of Raven's driveway and head-ed down the street, I felt a gloom from the shad-ows. We were close to UnderLake Park, and part of me wanted to drive through it, just to see if I could feel whether Ulstair's killer was there. But that would be stupid, especially just coming from his farewell ceremony.

As we drove across the 520 floating bridge, Angel and I kept our chatter deliberately light, and all the way home, we didn't mention the ceremony again.

I SUDDENLY GROANED as we neared our house. "Marilee—I've got a session with her to-night and I forgot. I'm late." I had gotten so wrapped up in Raven's ritual that I had forgotten I was supposed to be at Marilee's a half hour earlier. I pulled into my parking space, grabbed at my phone and called her.

"Let me guess, you're late." She didn't sound enthusiastic.

"I'm sorry. I totally forgot. We went to a farewell ritual for our friend whose boyfriend was murdered and time just got away from me. I can come over but I'm not prepared."

"No, we'll skip it tonight. Wednesday was important, but tonight we were just going to do some follow-up. But try to be here next Wednesday, or at least call me if you can't make it."

"Damn," I said, hanging up. "I hate disappointing people and I don't like breaking my word."

"Everything will be fine. Come on, we have to get ready for the barbecue tomorrow. We need to make sure that we've got enough paper plates and supplies."

"Right. I almost forgot." I paused as I unlocked the door. "Do you think we should ask Raven and Rafé?"

"I was thinking about it, but I doubt if either one of them would feel up to it. But I'd like to throw a party soon, and we could invite both of them then." Angel hung up her jacket in the hall closet, and I followed suit.

We spent the rest of the evening watching movies while Angel texted her brother DJ. We were both tired, and by the time we turned in it was barely ten PM. I was grateful that sleep came easy, without dreams, and I slept like the dead until morning light.

YUTANI ARRIVED EARLY, along with his aunt. They carried in a big bag filled with hamburger, hotdogs, and salmon. Celia bustled around the kitchen, insisting on helping Angel. They made the salad and shucked the corn while Yutani began preparing the marinade for the salmon.

Viktor and Sheila arrived, and we left Sheila to help in the kitchen as Viktor and I headed out to the patio to clear a place for the grill. Ten minutes later, Herne arrived, and he and Viktor wrestled the massive grill out of the back of the truck and over onto the patio. I looked around, but Danielle was nowhere in sight.

"Where's your daughter?"

"She decided to stay home," he said, giving me a look that told me there was more to that story.

"I know things have been rough lately, and I haven't been as much help as I could be. I'm sorry." I wasn't sure why I felt the need to apologize, but it seemed to be the thing to do.

"This isn't anything you need to apologize for." He paused, then said, "I had a long, straightforward talk with Myrna, and I made it clear that things aren't working out. The simple truth is that Danielle doesn't really like me that much. I'm her father, and at first I thought she wanted to get to know me, but we don't get along much."

"It takes time, you know."

"Yes, and we'll work on it, but I realize that right

now, I'm just a place for Myrna to store her daughter so she can carry on with that pervert. I warned her that if she lets Thantos back into her house, I'll report her to Artemis. And trust me, the Amazons *won't* take kindly to knowing that one of their own not only chose a man over her daughter, but actually chose a man who put her daughter in danger. Myrna was pissed, but she had no choice but to agree. It occurred to me that Danielle might want to spend some time with the Amazons. She's of an age where she can train with them and I think it might do her some good."

"That sounds almost like sending her to military school." I shuddered, not wanting to think about the kind of discipline they probably meted out.

"Not at all. They'll treat her well, and she'll be away from her mother. And let's face it, I'm not the best at parenting, even though I'm trying. She's too close to adulthood to want to listen to a man she never knew was her father."

I nodded. That made sense. Danielle had a lot of resentment built up, beyond the legitimate anger at her mother.

"I talked to her and she's actually excited about the idea. But I told her that if she ever gets into trouble, she can come to me. Well, as long as she didn't cause it deliberately." He gave me a bittersweet smile. "Cernunnos and Morgana aren't terribly thrilled about all this—and they're pissed at Myrna too—but they will keep tabs on Danielle. She's their grandchild. But when I told them about Thantos, they agreed that this might be the best choice all the way around."

I tried not to show him how relieved I was. At that moment, Celia joined us on the patio, bringing out a tray of hamburger patties.

"Celia, it's so good to see you again," Herne said, taking the meat. He paused, then asked, "So, have you heard anything from Coyote lately?"

Celia shook her head. "He's been making himself scarce in my life, but I wouldn't be surprised to see him show up again soon."

I had turned away to layer charcoal briquettes in the grill, so I could only hear the conversation over my shoulder.

"Do you think Yutani will ever figure it out?" Herne asked. "There have been several incidents lately that make me think it would be a good thing if he knew."

Celia sighed. "I keep hoping that the Great Coyote will tell him, but I'm beginning to think you're right. I'm beginning to think that someday, we're going to have to tell Yutani that Coyote is his father."

There was a sudden silence, then the sound of metal hitting the concrete. The hairs on the back of my neck stood up. I turned as Celia gasped.

Yutani was standing there, a platter of salmon on the patio in front of him. He was staring at Celia and Herne, a wild-eyed look on his face, his mouth agape.

"Oh my gods, I didn't know you were there," Celia said.

"What did you say?" He stared at her, his eyes blazing. "Coyote is my *father*?"

Herne and Celia glanced at one another, and

Celia moved a step closer to Herne.

"I didn't want you to find out this way," Celia said. "I thought you were still in the house."

"Obviously," Yutani said. He crossed his arms, staring her down. "Tell me again, do you mean what you say? Are you seriously telling me that the Great Coyote not only dogs my heels but that he's my blood?"

Celia paused, paling. She glanced at Herne, who put his hand on her shoulder to steady her. Finally, she whispered, "I'm afraid it's true. Coyote is your father."

Yutani stared at her for another moment, then he turned on his heel and ran toward the house. Before we could stop him, he slammed through the door. I raced toward the side of the yard just in time to see him hop in his car and screech away from the curb. As he roared off down the street, I turned back to see Celia crying. Herne wrapped his arm around her.

So much for the barbecue, I thought, as I headed inside to tell the others what had happened.

Chapter 15

THE REST OF the evening was a spectacular bust. Viktor and Sheila ended up driving Celia back to Yutani's place. By the time they got there, there was still no sign of Yutani, but he had left a note telling Celia to go home, that he needed some time to himself.

Herne was pissed at him, I could tell that much, but he said nothing. Talia went over to Yutani's, helped Celia pack, and then drove her to a hotel near the airport. Celia decided to leave on the next flight home, but begged us to talk to Yutani for her.

Angel and I froze the meat, cleaned up the patio, and ended up eating hot dogs for dinner with Herne until he went home an hour later.

The next morning, we drove in to work together, not feeling very cheery. The past week had been one intense clusterfuck. The only bright spot was meeting Raven, and the fact that Rafé had called

Angel as promised, and the pair arranged to go out to dinner.

We arrived at work at the same time as Herne. He was looking all sorts of grumpy.

"I still haven't heard from Yutani. Damned jackass, running out on his aunt like that." Herne unlocked our stop on the elevator and we entered the office.

We immediately noticed that the superintendent had fixed the furnace, so Angel gathered up the space heaters and put them in the storage room for the next time the furnace failed.

"Meeting as soon as Victor and Talia get here. Ember, find out if there are any messages from Yutani." Herne turned to Angel. "Can you make a pot of strong coffee? And if we don't have any pastries, order some in." With that, he shut his office door behind him.

I knew he was out of sorts over Yutani's behavior, but I had to admit, if I had been Yutani, I would have been pissed, too.

While Angel headed into the break room to take care of the coffee, I sat down at her desk and checked the messages. There were a few from clients and one from Raven, but none from Yutani. While I was sitting there, I decided to give him a call. He didn't answer, so I texted him.

YOU NEED TO GET YOUR ASS BACK HERE. HERNE IS PISSED OUT OF HIS MIND. I KNOW WHAT YOU FOUND OUT WAS A SHOCK, BUT THIS IS NOT THE BEST WAY TO DEAL WITH IT.

I didn't expect an answer but a few seconds later, Yutani surprised me.

EMBER, I DON'T EXPECT YOU TO UNDERSTAND. BUT YOU NEED TO KEEP YOUR NOSE OUT OF THIS.

TOO LATE. I'M ALREADY NOSE DEEP IN IT. I'M SERIOUS. IF YOU COME BACK AND TALK, WE CAN FIGURE THIS OUT.

HERNE KNEW, DIDN'T HE? AND SO DID YOU, RIGHT?

I hesitated before answering. Finally, I texted back.

HERNE SUSPECTED AS MUCH. I'M NOT SURE IF HE ACTU- ALLY KNEW, OR IF YOUR AUNT TOLD HIM. HE DIDN'T TELL ME THAT, BUT YES —HE TOLD ME THAT HE BELIEVES THAT YOU ARE COYOTE'S SON. I BELIEVE HE FELT IT WASN'T HIS PLACE TO TELL YOU.

YET HE FELT PERFECTLY FINE TELLING YOU. AND IF HE TOLD YOU, HE PROBABLY TOLD THE OTHERS. YOU SEE, THAT'S WHAT I CAN'T QUITE FORGIVE HIM FOR.

I let out a sigh, and then tried one more time.

THEN COME BACK AND TELL HIM THAT. YOU NEED TO TELL HIM WHAT YOU'RE FEELING. OTHERWISE THIS WILL CAUSE A PERMANENT RIFT BETWEEN THE TWO OF YOU AND I DO NOT BELIEVE THIS IS UNFIXABLE. YUTANI, YOU'RE SMART ENOUGH TO KNOW ALL THIS. WHAT'S THE REAL REASON YOU RAN OFF?

I waited for a moment, thinking that he wasn't going to answer. But as I stood up to give Angel back her seat, one last text came in.

WHAT IF I AM COYOTE'S SON? WHAT THEN? TELL HERNE I'LL BE BACK BY TOMORROW.

Angel glanced at me. "Yutani?"

I nodded. "He's pissed at Herne, but I think more than that, he's terrified this is real. I wonder if Danielle went through that when Myrna told her that Herne was her father? I suppose finding out that one of your parents is a god can be terrifying. Finding out that you're a godling must be even more so." I glanced over my shoulder at Herne's closed door. "He's not in a good mood today, so watch your step around him. There's a message from Raven, and a couple others from potential clients. I'm going to head in the break room, so when —" I stopped as the elevator opened and Viktor and Talia entered the room. "Herne wants us all in the break room as soon as you guys get settled in. I wouldn't take too long, because he's not happy today."

Viktor nodded. "Good, because I've got news. I got a phone call from Erica this morning. There's been another abduction attempt. This time, the man escaped."

WE WERE GATHERED around the break table,

with Angel's super strong coffee and two boxes of designer doughnuts. Looking at the doughnuts made me think of Ray, and part of me wanted to find out how he was. Part of me was afraid that he might find out that I had checked. I decided after the meeting to put in a quick phone call to the hospital, and ask them not to tell him.

Herne scanned the table, frowning. "Obviously, we're down a man—"

"I talked with Yutani. He'll be back tomorrow morning." I glanced across the table at Herne. I had no desire to tell him how pissed off Yutani was, and decided to let them sort it out.

"He all right?" Herne asked.

"I guess so. As okay as you can get when you've just found out your father's a god." The words spilled out of my mouth before I realized what I had said. Herne stared at me, an incredulous look on his face. I realized that my words had hit too close to home.

"You know that wasn't meant personally. But face it, Yutani has just had a big shock. He wasn't sure how to take it and I think he's terrified."

Talia let out a cackle. "You *know* she's right. The poor kid is probably petrified. And ten to one, he's embarrassed that he's the last one to know."

I gave her a quick nod. "Right on both scores. He only texted me a few times but I could tell that he's feeling pretty crummy right now."

Herne set down his tablet, pushing it back from him. "Neither Celia nor I realized he was there. We were stupid, yes, but we didn't mean any harm, and I hope you can believe that. Is he really that pissed at me?"

I shrugged. "As far as I can tell, yes. But I con-vinced him to come back and talk to you instead of just running off. So I suggest you go easy on him. Anyway, he said he'll be back tomorrow morning."

Herne held my gaze for a moment, a faint grin on his face. "The day *you* are playing diplomat is the day that I know I went too far. All right, I'll play nice and apologize. I really didn't want him to find out like that. I'm worried about his aunt as well. Celia was truly between a rock and a hard place on this one. Maybe I can help patch things up between them. All right, onto business. Viktor, you have news?"

Viktor nodded. "As I said, Erica just called me before I came in. There's been another attack. This time, the man got away. Erica interviewed him. While she can't tell me what he said, she did give me his name and suggested we pay him a visit. Apparently, he fits the victim profile. She also confirmed, unofficially, that the department isn't investigating the deaths in any way that matters. Saílle told them that the Dark Court would take care of it. Which we know is bogus. They have no intention of doing anything. So I suggest we ques-tion him."

Talia held up her phone. "Text me his number and I'll set something up."

"Excuse me," a voice echoed from the door. "May I join your meeting?" Before we could turn, Morgana walked up to the table and sat down, reaching for one of the doughnuts.

"Mother! What are you doing here?" Herne

looked as startled as the rest of us.

Morgana laughed. "Can't I visit my son and his girlfriend when I want to? Actually, I have some information about the Triamvinate."

As I stared at her, I realized what struck me as strange. Morgana was wearing a pale blue pants suit—high-waisted trousers over a cream-colored shirt, and a matching jacket. Her flowing hair had been pulled up into a high chignon, and she was carrying a Louis Vuitton handbag. Her dress seemed so at odds with what she normally wore that I had to blink twice in order to take it in.

"Are you going shopping?" I asked, suddenly realizing the words had actually left my mouth and not just stayed inside might brain. I blushed, sinking down in my seat.

But Morgana just laughed. "Actually, I have a luncheon to attend. I'm meeting with several of my high priestesses at the Space Needle. This attire is a better fit than my regular gowns."

I nodded, zipping my lips shut.

"You look lovely," Viktor said. "If I may be so bold as to say so."

"And I thank you, Master Viktor." Morgana gave him a gracious nod.

Herne looked a little nonplussed. "What about the Triamvinate? Are they going to grant it?"

"Well, here's the rub." Morgana's expression darkened. "Apparently, since the United Coalition has seen fit to allow Elatha and his minions into the fold, Danu is convinced that the Fae *do* need to defend themselves against him and she has convinced the Dagda and Eriu to go along with her."

"So they're not going to convene a Triamvinate?" I asked.

She shook her head. "Since Danu is the mother of the Tuatha de Danann, I can't go up against her on this. Neither can Cernunnos. We're at a standstill. Unless we can convince some of the other gods that this is necessary, the three of them overrule us all. This means trouble for humans and Fae alike. Saílle and Névé have no idea exactly what they are getting themselves into with this."

"What do you mean?" Talia asked.

"Callan was more than just an extraordinary warrior. He was a beast, vicious and cruel to his own men. He sacrificed hundreds of lives in pursuit of his obsession, which was to drive the Fomorians back. I truly fear this decision, but there's nothing I can do about it. When I tried to argue, the Dagda questioned as to whether the Wild Hunt is necessary at all at this point. Cernunnos and I believe that if we push this matter, they might dissolve the agency. Cernunnos is livid—not at you or me—but he's truly unhappy with the Triad."

"Triad?" Viktor asked.

"The Dagda, Danu, and Eriu. They have the final say over matters amongst the Celtic gods. Although at times Arawn insists on being included." Morgana looked pissed as hell. I had thought that Herne looked angry when he was out of sorts, but seeing her smoldering expression made me grateful that I'd never gotten on her bad side.

"Well...this isn't good." Talia poured herself another cup of coffee and held up the pot. "Would you like some?"

Morgana nodded. "Half a cup, please. I have to leave soon."

"Then what do we do?" Herne asked. "Callan is untouchable and you know the moment Elatha finds out he's back among the living, there's going to be hell to pay."

"That's an understatement. Elatha *never* forgets an enemy. And he already hates the Fae. When he finds out that Névé and Saílle have summoned Callan's spirit back among the living, I fear open warfare. The only thing I can advise is that you keep your eyes open. Be alert. Look for any signs that the Fomorians and the Fae are going up against each other."

While Morgana took a bite of her doughnut and sipped the coffee that Talia gave her, the rest of us fell into a melancholy silence. We all knew that the Fae had no self-control when it came to spilling their troubles into the human community. And Elatha wouldn't be any better. He might be sneakier, but that just made things worse.

"What are you working on now?" Morgana asked.

Herne motioned to me, and I told her about Raven, and Ulstair.

"There's also something I wanted to ask you about, but it's more of a personal matter. I'm seeing crows and ravens in visions, and they're showing up a lot in my life. In fact, one of them brought me Ulstair's ring." I brought out the ring. I had totally forgotten to show it to Herne.

"I wonder... Hand me that."

Morgana held out her hand and I dropped the

YASMINE GALENORN

ring into her palm. She closed her eyes, shuddered, and shoved it back across the table.

"There was a lot of love invested in that ring. I think you're right about Raven. I encourage you to keep up your friendship with her. It can't hurt to have one of the Ante-Fae in your corner. But there's more."

"What?"

She licked her lips. "The ring is invested with a great deal of pain, the type that comes from torture. I believe Ulstair was wearing it during the moments he was murdered. Whoever killed him is seething with envy and hatred. And, I might add, psychosis of the worst kind. You must locate the murderer and eliminate him. There's no coming back from the shadows in which he's steeped himself."

I picked up the ring, grateful that I hadn't given it to Angel. Her psychometry was too good, and the last thing I wanted to do was inflict that kind of pain on her.

"Do you know anymore?" Herne asked.

Morgana shook her head. "No. But I know the gods are involved in this somehow, though not encouraging or inflicting the murders. Anyway, I have to get on for my luncheon."

As she gathered up her things, she turned to me. "I'll summon you soon. I've talked to Marilee and Cernunnos, and we're preparing for the final ritual to take you through the Cruharach. I'll be in touch through Aoife." And with that, she vanished through the door.

TALIA GOT HOLD of Hassa, the man who had almost been abducted, and arranged for Herne and me to visit him at two PM. Meanwhile, we discussed how to approach the mess with Callan, the Fomorians, and the Fae.

"So, we aren't allowed to interfere with Callan. Does this mean we're no longer allowed to stop any dangers that threaten to trickle through the human community?" Viktor asked.

Herne shrugged. "I don't know. And I don't think my mother knows either or she would have said something. We're going to have to talk with her and Cernunnos to get this straightened out. If we go against the Dagda and Danu, even accidentally, we might as well pack up and move to the ends of the earth."

"That bad, huh?" Angel asked.

"Oh, they may *seem* congenial on the outside, but there's a reason they lead the pantheon. And Eriu is the very spirit of Ireland. She's...well...like the Gaia of the island. The Fae, at least the Tuatha de Danann, are part of her very makeup. Until we know more, just keep your eyes open and report anything you see. And somebody make certain Charlie knows about this. He's enthusiastic, and I don't want him making any wrong moves. Also, remember, we're throwing him a party to make him feel included. So don't put anything on your calendars."

I rolled my eyes. "I'll cancel our date," I said,

with a laugh.

We spent the next few hours tidying up loose ends on some of the cases we'd recently closed. There was a never-ending amount of paperwork that came with the job, and I never seemed to finish my reports on time.

Herne tapped on my office door at one. "Let's go. Hassa lives on the Eastside, in Woodinville close to TirNaNog."

I slipped on my leather jacket, grabbed my purse, and followed him out. I realized I had forgotten lunch, I had gotten so immersed in dealing with the paperwork.

"Can we stop for a burger on the way? I forgot to eat, and the doughnuts I ate this morning during the meeting aren't going to hold me. I could also use more caffeine."

Herne snorted. "You can *always* use caffeine, woman. I swear, the next time you get cut during a fight I want to collect some of that blood and test it. My guess is that it's pure coffee. Hurry up. We don't have much time, so we'll stop at Starbucks and you can grab a sandwich and coffee at the same time."

As we headed toward the freeway, my coffee and sandwich in hand, I glanced at him. "So, Danielle's really going to the island of the Amazons?"

He nodded, looking serious. "She's excited. She loves the idea of learning her people's ways. Since her mother has no objection, I'll send her off this weekend. It's really better this way." He sounded like he was trying to convince himself more than me. "Danielle's not going to learn a whole lot from me. This way, she'll have education, physical training, whatever she wants. She did ask to come back and spend spring break with me." He glanced at me. "Do you think I'm a horrible father?"

I shook my head. "No, I don't. You're putting her needs first. She needs more than just a place to stay. That's all she had with her mother, and that's what she has with you. This will give her a purpose in life. Funny thing is, now that she's going, I think I'm sorry. I know we didn't hit it off but I think after a while we could have become friends. At least now that I know her background."

"It's been an eye-opening experience." Herne paused again. "I just want to say how much I appreciate the fact that you stuck by me during this period. Reilly would have been out the door at the first breath of trouble. None of the women that I knew would have even tried to understand. Thank you, for not giving me an ultimatum."

I took a bite of my sandwich and swallowed, chasing it down with a slug of coffee. "What kind of person would I be if I had done that?" I decided to change the subject, because really, there wasn't much more to say. "You promise to take it easy on Yutani when he comes back?"

Herne nodded. "I gave you my word, and I'll keep it."

As he shifted gears, merging into the left lane and speeding up as we headed out on the 520 bridge, I glanced out the window.

The rain was heavy and cold—that bone-chilling cold that only drenching rain can bring. The skies were overcast and it was forecast to rain through the night and the next few days. I leaned my head back against the seat, my thoughts drifting. So much had happened in the past couple weeks that it felt like life had become a whirlwind, a vortex sweeping up everybody in its path, including me.

I was approaching the Cruharach, and while I was still nervous, I wasn't as afraid as I had been. I was feeling stronger as both my mother's and father's sides had risen in me. As my father's blood rose, my mother's had ebbed some, but they were both still there and they seemed to have made peace. Morgana and Marilee had reassured me that the transformation would just make me a stronger version of me, and I hoped they were right.

"What are you thinking of?" Herne asked after a few minutes.

"This, that, a little bit of everything. I was thinking about Yutani and Raven. And the Cruharach. It seems like during September the world picks up pace. Even before I came to the Wild Hunt, it felt like that. Autumn seems to bring a renaissance, a renewal of sorts. My energy always has risen during the autumn months and now I know why—it's because of my father's blood. I'm attuned to the season."

"That you are," Herne said. "So, changing the subject...I know you love me. But if you had it to do again, would you still get involved with me? Given everything that's happened?"

I laughed. "You have to ask? Herne, you're one of the best things that's ever happened to me. Granted, you're also a pain in the ass, but sometimes you can't have one without the other. Which reminds me, I need to call the hospital and ask them about Ray. I don't want him knowing I called, but I need to know if he came through surgery, for my own peace of mind."

Herne said nothing as I pulled out my phone and gave the hospital a call. I got hold of one of the nurses who had been looking after him, and asked her how he was doing.

"Mr. Fontaine came through his surgery without incident. But he's going to be in the hospital for at least another month. There were extensive internal injuries. Are you sure I can't tell him you called? He's been asking every day."

"No, please don't. Did you take me off of his chart as his next of kin?"

She checked. "I see the request but it doesn't appear that your name has been removed. I can take care of that if you like." She sounded unsure, as though she was trying to give me a second chance to think it over again.

"Please, remove it. I'm not his next of kin. We aren't related and I'm not his girlfriend." I thanked her, and hung up.

"What are you going to do about him? If you won't let me take a baseball bat to him, then you have to do something." Herne didn't sound pleased.

"Marilee is working on a spell to counter his obsession with me. That should take care of any remaining problems."

Herne turned onto a back road, and before long we pulled into the driveway of a small house in

Woodinville. He cut the ignition, and unfastened his seat belt.

"We're here. Let's go talk to Hassa."

As we headed toward the house, I hoped that Hassa could provide us with something that would lead us to the murderer.

Chapter 16

THE FIRST THING I thought when Hassa opened the door was that he could have been Ulstair's twin. He was tall, with red hair and a runner's body. He glanced at me, frowning for a moment, but said nothing as he let us in.

His house was small but tidy, with everything in its place with neat precision. Even the magazines on the coffee table were stacked with the edges matching. He motioned for us to take a seat on the sofa.

"If you'll excuse me, I was making tea. Would you care to join me?" His voice was higher than I would expect, but even timbered.

"Yes, please," Herne said, and I indicated the same with a nod.

Hassa vanished through the archway and we heard the clinking of china. I glanced around the room. It was small, but the built-ins made it easier to store all of his books. Other than the archway leading into the kitchen, there were two doors. From the size of the house, I assumed they led to a bedroom and bath. Hassa returned, carrying a tray with a teapot, three china cups and saucers, a sugar dish and creamer, and a plate of what looked like whole-grain cookies.

"I wasn't sure if you took lemon, but I'm out, so I apologize if you do." He seemed like a serious young man, but given the fact that he'd almost been abducted, I wasn't surprised. An attempted kidnapping had a way of sobering the mood.

"Did the police tell you that we would be investigating?"

He nodded. "Officer Erica said you would probably be by. She said you are investigating a case where several men have been abducted?"

Herne nodded. "Yes. Actually, several men had been murdered after they were abducted, so consider yourself fortunate. It's important that we gather as much information as we can."

"Why didn't the cops talk to me more then?"

"The men who were murdered are on Saílle's... list, if you get my meaning."

I was glad Herne answered, because I wasn't sure how to be diplomatic about it. But Hassa seemed to understand.

"I hear you loud and clear. So while the cops took my complaint seriously, they aren't working the other aspects of this case given the nature of the victims?" He rolled his eyes. "I'm not going to comment on that, given you never know who's listening, but I'm glad somebody's on the case."

"Why don't we get down to facts? You were running in UnderLake Park, correct?"

Hassa nodded. "Yes, I was headed down the Beach Trail when I tripped over a wire. I didn't see it, obviously. The moment I fell, a figure rushed out of the bushes. It was a man, and he seemed pretty strong, but he wasn't as quick as I am. He tried to attack me with a stun gun, but I managed to roll out of the way. I scrambled up, and he tried again. I don't think he expected that I was carrying pepper spray, but I always do because I've been attacked by stray dogs on occasion. I keep it clipped to my belt when I run. I sprayed him in the eyes. He screamed, and I managed to dodge around him and get away. He tried to come after me, but that pepper spray is *really* concentrated. I managed to get back to my car and drive off."

Herne and I glanced at each other. Hassa had saved his life thanks to his foresight.

"Be grateful you had that spray," Herne said. "Can you tell us anything about your attacker? Anything at all that you noticed about him. You said he was big and burly. Can you estimate how tall he was? How much he weighed?"

Hassa took a sip of his tea.

"I got a good look at him, actually. He was about five-ten, and I'd say he weighed around 175 pounds. He had a lot of muscle—I could tell by the way he moved. I can also tell you that he's Dark Fae. He had some strange tattoo work on his face, and from what I could tell, also his hands."

"This is very helpful. Do you by chance remember what the tattoos were of?" I asked.

He nodded. "Not the ones on his hands, but he had a crow tattooed on his right temple, curving around his eyebrow, and he had some strange markings on the left side. I remember thinking they looked like a series of triangles. His hair was light brown, down to the nape of his neck. He was wearing a black sweatshirt and a pair of torn jeans. I saw the tattoos on his knuckles when he tried to stun me, but I can't tell you what they were." He paused, then added, "Oh, the tattoo of the crow was black, and the arrow-like tattoos were red. The tattoos on his knuckles were black and red."

Herne paled. I could have sworn a light went off in his head. He leaned forward.

"You said a series of red arrows? Or red triangles? And that the man had a crow tattooed around his temple?"

"It could have been a raven. It's hard to tell."

Herne sat back, and I glanced at him. He closed his eyes, shaking his head.

"You recognize something?" I asked.

He nodded. "We'll talk about it later." He glanced at the man. "Is there anything else you can tell us? You said he used a tripwire to catch you?"

Hassa nodded. "Is that important?"

"It could be. Tell me, do you go running on that trail on a regular basis? Would someone recognize you if they watched the trail every morning?"

"Actually, yes. I go running there four times a week. I always run on the same days because it correlates with my work schedule. You mean that he's been watching me?" Hassa blanched. "Should I worry that he's going to come to my house to finish the job?"

Herne chewed on his lip for a moment. "I'd like to say no, since all the abductions happened in Un-derLake Park, but I'd be careful for a while. Vary your routine. Try not to go out alone, and don't go running for a while. Lock your doors and windows. I really doubt that he'll come after you. That's not his MO. But for the sake of caution, take some extra care." He glanced around the room. "Do you live here alone?"

Hassa nodded. "Yes, just me."

"You might go to one of the local magic shops and ask for a protection spell. As I said, it isn't this man's MO to hunt his victims outside of the park as far as we know. But we aren't dealing with someone who's sane. His pattern could change at any time. Chances are he has no clue what your name is or where you live, but err on the side of caution."

"Can you tell me why I was targeted? Is it per-sonal?" Hassa paused, then added, "It couldn't be, could it? Not if he confines his hunting to the park."

"No, it's not personal. You fit the physical type that he's looking for. We're not sure why he's targeting men who look like you, but you've given us a lot to go on. The fact that you remember what his tattoos look like helps a great deal. Is there anything else? Any nuance that you noticed? Every single thing you can tell us will help us find him faster. Did he say anything? Even under his breath?"

Hassa took a moment to think. Then, he

straightened. "There was one thing. He said something when he jumped out at me. I thought it was garbled, but maybe it was a name. He yelled out 'garrison.' That's all I can remember him saying. He cursed when I got away and when I sprayed him with the pepper spray he yelled, but it was more grunts and swearwords. That's everything."

I thought of a question. "Can you tell us where the tripwire was? You said it was on the Beach Trail, but do you remember the spot?"

Hassa nodded. "Yes, actually. It was by the side of a ravine that slopes up. I know that sounds vague, but it looked like there had been activity there recently. A lot of the undergrowth had been brushed aside, and looked like it had been bent and folded." He then went on to describe what sounded a lot like the place to me where we had gone off the path to find the bodies.

Herne and I thanked him for his time, and Herne gave him his card.

"If you think of anything else, or if you need to call on us for any reason, here's my number. My forwarding number is on there as well. As I said, I don't think you'll have any more trouble from him again as long as you stay away from the park. We'll let you will know when we find him. Hopefully, we *will* find him." And with that, we headed out.

Once we were in the car, I turned to Herne. "All right, what is it? You recognized something when he was talking about the tattoos. What is it?"

"We have a serious problem on our hands, Ember. When we get back to the office, I'll drop you off and then I've got to go see my father. I'll give you a rundown that you can tell the others. There's not much more we can do today, but tomorrow I want you to be prepared to go meet one of the gods." He began to fill me in, and my heart sank.

HERNE DROPPED ME off, and immediately headed out again. I hustled myself into the elevator, and the minute the doors opened into the waiting room, I motioned to Angel.

"Into the break room. I'm going to grab Talia and Viktor."

Angel blinked, but jumped up. I headed back to Talia's office, poking my head through the door. Viktor was there, and they were going over something that she was showing him on the computer screen.

"Break room, now." As I poured myself some coffee, Angel and the others trickled in. I motioned for them to sit down. Carrying my coffee to the table, I settled in.

"Herne will be back in a while. For one thing, we have to prepare for Charlie's party. But we found out something important from Hassa. This could be the break we need in the case."

"That would be helpful, given we have nothing else to go on." Talia shook her head. "I still can't believe the cops. Four dead men, and they aren't doing anything. But then again, the powers behind the local police aren't always out for justice."

"True that," I said. "All right, here's the thing.

Hassa remembered what the man looked like. According to Herne, his would-be abductor has the markings of a priest of the Morrígan." I told them everything Hassa had said, adding, "Herne recognized the description of the tattoos right away. He dropped me off, and he's on his way to talk to Cernunnos. He wants to set up an appointment with the Morrígan tomorrow. She'll know all of her priests. We also know that the man is Dark Fae, so it shouldn't be too difficult to pinpoint suspects."

"Crap. *The Morrígan*? A priest of the Morrígan is going to be one hell of an opponent. I wonder if she knows about this? The Morrígan doesn't require sacrifices. Not in that sense." Viktor scratched his chin. "Did Herne say anything else?"

"Yeah, he said to get things ready for Charlie's party. Which means basically somebody has to go to the store and bring back a bunch of goodies." I glanced at the clock. It was going on four-thirty. Charlie would be arriving in about three hours. "Viktor, run out and pick up a bunch of snacks, please. Don't forget bottled blood. Talia, if you could dig up some information on the Morrígan, and on her priests? And Angel, is there anything else we need to deal with?"

"I've got three messages from potential clients. I'm wondering when I should schedule them for meetings with Herne. Two of them seemed fairly simple and straightforward, but one might be somewhat convoluted."

"Why don't you schedule them to come in on Thursday and Friday? That will give us a couple days to deal with this matter, and Herne can reschedule if need be."

She nodded. "Sounds good."

And with that, we headed back to our respective desks. Viktor signed out money from petty cash, and took off for the store. While Talia was researching the priests of the Morrígan and Angel returned calls, I sat at my desk, putting more paperwork to bed.

BY THE TIME Herne returned, Viktor was back. He had picked up a fruit tray, a vegetable tray, a cheesecake, some chips and dip, some premade sandwiches, and a six-pack of bottled blood. Angel helped him set up in the break room, while Talia and I followed Herne back into his office.

"The Morrígan will meet with us tomorrow, Ember, you'll go with me. It's vital that you be on your best behavior," he said, looking straight at me. "The Morrígan doesn't mess around, and she doesn't have the best sense of humor. Get it?"

"Got it," I said, suppressing a smile. I knew when to mind my manners, but sometimes people had to remind me. "Is she coming here?"

"No, but neither are we going into Annwn. She'll meet us at my place." He paused, glancing at Talia. "Did you find out anything about the priests of the Morrígan?"

She nodded. "They have a code of honor they're supposed to live by. They're an intense group and they deal, of course, with death. But they don't mete it out. As you know, crows are scavengers. Morrígan picks up the dead from the battlefield and carries them off. So she's not the one who hands it out, and her priests aren't required to make sacrifices or anything of that sort. If it *is* a priest of the Morrígan committing these murders, then he's really fucking up."

"That jibes with everything I know about her," Herne said. "All right, we'll table this until tomorrow. Charlie should be here soon. Make him feel as comfortable as you can. Most of what I have him doing is some of the backup paperwork. This should lighten the load on everybody. In fact, when he's here, we'll discuss what you should fax over to him. We do *not* send the actual files off site, though. There's a lot of data entry he can do, as well. Okay, why don't we get back to work?"

Talia and I headed back to our offices, but Angel stopped me on the way.

"I just got a call from Rafé. He asked me out tomorrow night. We're going to dinner and a movie." She tried to make it sound casual but excitement danced in her eyes.

"You really like him, don't you?" I smiled, grateful for a bright spot in an otherwise gloomy day.

Angel gave me a little shrug. "Well, yeah. There was just something that seemed to click between us. I've never dated one of the Fae before. I've actually never dated anybody who wasn't *human* before. Is there anything that I should know about? Any customs that I make sure I don't break?"

I sat on the edge of her desk, thinking. "I'm not exactly the best source of information for this, but... The Fae are sexual. Make it clear up front that you might want to wait before you sleep with him, if you do. Sleeping together isn't a big deal in TirNaNog and Navane, so he may come on to you pretty quickly. Don't take it as an insult, but be clear about your boundaries. If he's a good guy, he'll respect them, regardless of his race."

WHEN CHARLIE ARRIVED, I almost didn't recognize him. He had been the roommate of one of our suspects on an earlier case. He was definitely a vamp, though he didn't fit the stereotype.

Charlie looked like a surfer dude, or even a computer geek. He was gangly, tall, and thin, and had hair that brushed the top of his shoulders. But he had definitely spruced up since we last met. The polo shirt and jeans were gone, and in their place, he was wearing a pair of cargo pants, and a V-neck blue sweater. The lens-less glasses were also gone. For a while after he had been turned, Charlie had continued to wear his glasses, sans lenses, almost like a shield against the world. All in all, he was a pleasant fellow. He had been a math major until he had been turned by a rogue vampire. He hadn't collected enough money to be independently wealthy yet, and so he had welcomed the job with Wild Hunt.

Viktor shook his hand and clapped him on the back. He had become friends with Charlie first, before Herne hired him on.

"Where's Yutani?" Charlie asked, glancing around.

"Long story. He'll be back tomorrow. How's it going?"

I wasn't terribly comfortable around vampires, but Charlie made it easy. He only drank bottled blood, was squeamish about attacking anyone, and refused the bloodwhores who offered their services.

"Okay, I guess. My parents still refuse to talk to me. I have to give up the hope that they'll ever accept me back into the family." He looked dejected. Charlie had been disowned by his family once he was turned, and it weighed heavy on his heart.

"You know, we're a family here," Talia said, patting his hand.

He stared at her fingers on his, and then shot her a pale smile. "I appreciate that. And I appreciate you throwing this get-together for me. I don't get out much. Truth is, I find it hard to make friends in the vampire community. Maybe I just haven't met the right people yet."

"Did you get the night job that you were going for?" Viktor asked.

Charlie had been itching to land a job on the side with the Vampire National Bank. He had hoped to work his way up in the vampire community that way.

He shook his head. "No. Unfortunately, given my sire was a rogue who's now dust, and I have no one to vouch for me, they said I need to find a sponsor before they'll even consider taking me on. Which means I need to make friends in the community. I've joined a couple of clubs, but developing relationships takes time and I don't want to jump into anything that I might regret later. I have to accept what I am, but I want to accept it on my terms."

We filled him in on Raven's case, and spent the next couple hours eating and chatting. Finally, Angel and I said our good nights, and headed home. It'd been a long day, and I was looking forward to going to bed.

I WAS STANDING on the field, under the moon. As I looked up at the sky, the stars wheeled overhead in a panoramic expanse, dancing to the music of the universe. I held my arms out to the side, breathing deeply. The air was chill, and I could smell winter around the corner. There was something on the wind, coming my way...*transformation.*

As I stood there, two figures approached me, one from either side. I held out my hands, beckoning to them. I knew who they were—these ghostly figures clouded in mist. They were both whispering to me, trying to convince me that I needed them.

And I knew I did need them. I needed them as much as I needed the blood in my veins, as much as I needed the breath in my lungs.

They approached me, neither one taking on full form. Yet, I knew exactly who they were. Both were blood of my blood, flesh of my flesh. On one side, the Leannan Sidhe whirled in a dance, sinuous and seductive. And on the other side, the Huntress prowled through the treetops, crouching, watching for her prey. Both Leannan Sidhe and Autumn Stalker tried to seduce me to their side. But I couldn't choose—I *would not* choose.

I raised my arms overhead, a flurry of energy surrounding me as a pale mist rose from my body. I opened my mouth to let out a long echoing cry. It was a call to action, a call to arms.

"You will coexist," I said, my voice reverberating through the night. "You will *both* coexist because *I exist.*"

The figures stopped, still enveloped in the fog that embraced the autumn night. They waited, hesitating, and I could sense they were almost ready to come to me, almost ready to balance within me. But it wasn't time yet. There were still rituals to be done before they could merge.

Part of me wanted to urge them on now, to finish this and see it done. But a voice inside insisted that I wait. That I not force the matter.

All things in their own time.

And so I dropped my hands, and the figures halted, still out of reach but *oh, so close*. I turned and walked away, knowing that I would return to this spot. Knowing that it was only a matter of time before I finally felt whole and complete.

Chapter 17

I WOKE UP feeling somewhat disoriented, then remembered my dream from the night before. Obviously, the Cruharach was coming closer, and my subconscious was trying to get ready for it. But the dream had given me a valuable warning. It wasn't yet time, and I shouldn't force the issue.

While Angel made breakfast, I took a walk out back, into the gardens. As I sat on the bench, the mist rolled around me. I could see my breath in front of my face, and even under my warm jacket, I shivered. It had rained during the night, and the sky was still overcast and dark. The dampness chilled to the bone in a way that dry, cold weather couldn't match.

The mist rolled over the ground, as fog lurked in the trees. It felt like I was breathing in vapor, and I stuck my hands in my pockets. But it felt good to be outside, though the calling of the crows unsettled me.

I turned around, staring at the house. Ever since Kipa had cleansed it for us, the ghosts seemed to have vanished. They had moved on, and now it seemed warm and inviting even though it had been a murder house. The light inside beckoned, and with a glance over my shoulder at the raw earth of the garden, I stood and hustled back inside. As I took off my coat and hung it near the door, Angel called to me from the kitchen.

"Breakfast!"

I headed toward the kitchen, Mr. Rumblebutt running up to join me. He wove in and around my legs, almost tripping me up until I leaned down and scooped him into my arms, snuggling my face into his long fur.

"Are you hungry, you little twerp?" I asked.

He answered with another purr, and what sounded almost like a burp. I put him down next to his food dish, and as Angel plated our breakfasts, I filled Mr. Rumblebutt's food dish. I made sure he had clean water, and then followed Angel to the table, helping her carry the food.

"How do you think it's gonna work out between Yutani and Herne?" she asked as we settled in at the table.

I loved the kitchen. The dining space was large enough to hold a large table and a wide bay window overlooked the front yard.

"I don't know, to tell you the truth. Yutani was really pissed. But I know he values his friendship with Herne, and he was freaked out. There will probably be a rocky time ahead, but I think they can get through it. I hope they can." I scooped a forkful of eggs, closing my eyes as the robust flavor hit my tongue.

"So you get to meet the Morrígan today? I don't envy you." Angel shook her head. "If anybody had told me six months ago that we would be hanging out with the gods and investigating murder cases, I would have laughed them out of the room. So much as happened since then. Oh," she added. "I got a text from DJ today. He wants to know if he can spend Thanksgiving with us. Or if I can go down to spend Thanksgiving with him and his new family. Quite frankly, while I'd love to have him here, I think maybe I should go down to Cooper's. It would help DJ to adapt by spending Thanksgiving with his foster family. But I wanted to ask what you thought first, given we always spend T-Day together."

The thought of spending Thanksgiving without Angel made me sad, but she was right. He'd do best to have both his sister and his foster family around him on the holiday.

"Why don't you go down there? I can host Thanksgiving here for the others in the agency, if they don't have anywhere to go."

"Are you sure you don't mind?"

"Of course not. You need to be with DJ, and I agree that it's best if he's with his new family. Why don't you text him back right now and tell him you'll be there? Maybe he can come up here for the winter solstice."

With a smile on her lips, she pulled out her phone and texted her brother.

WE DROVE INTO work separately, given we had no idea how the day was going to play out. By the time we arrived, Yutani was with Herne in Herne's office, talking things over.

"I wouldn't interrupt them," Talia said. "Yutani's in a dark mood, and so is Herne."

I was about to head back to my office when the pair appeared. They both looked resigned, but neither looked angry. Yutani glanced over at us.

"I'm sorry I ran off like that. I realize that it wasn't the best way to handle things. Herne and I've talked things over. I was just so surprised and shocked, especially that I was the last one to know. To be honest, I suspected for some time that this might be the case. But I had no clue of what to do about it, or whether to even follow up on my suspicions. I still have no clue what to do. The next time Coyote talks to me, I suppose I'm going to have to ask. Anyway, I'm going to call my aunt and apologize and ask her to come back up when she's able."

He was wearing his usual somber expression, but his words sounded genuine, and I suddenly felt sorry for him. Herne had always known he was a god. He was brought up to be one. But Yutani was the son of a god and the son of a shifter, and he was totally unprepared for what had happened.

Talia clapped him on the back. "You'll find your way. Coyote should have talked to you years ago. And for what it's worth, we didn't know for sure.

We only suspected, just like you."

"I suppose we had better get to work," Herne said. "While we were talking, I filled Yutani in on what we've discovered so far. Ember, we need to leave to meet the Morrígan in about an hour. As I said, she'll be coming to my house. I want to get there before she does, because I don't want Danielle to be alone when she arrives. Trust me, the Morrígan is frightening enough for an adult. Hell, she even frightens the other gods."

I had dressed carefully, in a pair of black jeans, with an embroidered indigo tank top and a black jean jacket. I was wearing a silver belt, and my necklace marking me as Morgana's. I brushed my hair into a tidy ponytail, and made sure my make-up was spot on.

"Do I look okay to meet her? Should I wear a dress or something?" I was never sure how to appear in front of the gods. They all had such varying personalities and formalities.

Herne gave me the once-over. "You look wonderful." He held out his arms and as I slipped into his embrace, he gave me a quick but firm kiss. "Nervous?"

"Shouldn't I be?" I glanced up at him.

"Honestly? Yes. Don't joke around, be respectful and polite, and don't interrupt her when she's speaking." He glanced around the office. Everybody had moved off to their desks. His arm still around my shoulders, he walked me back into his office and closed the door behind us. Once we were alone, he pulled me in for a longer kiss, trailing his lips up the side of my neck. I let out a soft moan, wanting to do more than just kiss.

"It's been too long," I whispered.

"Soon," he said. "I promise you. And I want you too. More than you know."

I broke away from his embrace and dropped into the chair next to his desk.

"How did it go with Yutani? You guys okay again?"

He shrugged. "I apologized. He apologized. We did our best to talk things over and I think things will be fine. It's just going to be a little uncomfortable for a while. But it's not like we haven't gone through arguments before. At some point, though, he's going to have to confront Coyote. This isn't something that he can let sit, not now that he knows about it." He glanced at the clock. "We should get going. I really meant it when I said I don't want Danielle to be alone when the Morrígan arrives."

As we headed out, my nerves went into overdrive. I didn't know much about the Morrígan, but what I did know was enough to terrify me. I only hoped that she wouldn't live up to her hype.

DANIELLE SEEMED HAPPIER to see me then she had before. She took my coat, hanging it on the coat rack. "Did my father tell you? I get to go live with the Amazons! I'm going to train with them and learn to use a sword and martial arts." She seemed truly excited, and her eyes sparkled with the fire I hadn't seen there before.

"I heard, yes. And I'm excited for you. You seem really happy."

She danced around, and even though she looked like a grown woman, I could see the gleeful child inside. "I've always wanted to go to the island of the Amazons. My mother would never let me. I don't know how my father got her to agree, but however he did, I'm grateful. I leave on Sunday." She hesitated, then added," I'm sorry that I acted so snotty last time. I've just been..." She seemed to run out of words, and blushing, she stared at the floor.

"Don't worry about it. You've had a lot of up-heaval lately, so it's not surprising you've been out of sorts. I'm just glad that you're finally getting to do something that will make you happy."

"Danielle?" Herne said, joining us. "I want you to go to your room and stay there. Trust me, you do not want to meet the Morrígan. At least not yet." His tone left no room for argument, and she mumbled her good-bye, and dashed off her room.

"Boy, when you go authoritarian, you go author-itarian."

"You'll understand why in a few minutes. Would you like a drink?" He moved toward the bar. "Oth-er than caffeine, that is?"

I shook my head. "As I told you the other day, I don't drink much alcohol, and after the other night, I'm not all that keen on it. Apparently, I pay for my indulgences." The doorbell rang, startling me. I gave Herne an inquisitive look. "She uses the doorbell?"

"Not all of the gods are bereft of manners, love."
He went to answer it.

When he returned he was followed by a woman
who stood at least six-five. Dressed in black leather, she was wearing a black pea coat over a pair of
black leather pants. Her hair was flame red, cop-
pery as the autumn leaves, and she had caught it in
a high, tight braid. Her face was angular, her dark
eyes flashing as she set her gaze on me. The energy
around her was so fierce that it almost knocked me
over. I took a step back, bumping into the coffee
table. I was grateful that I hadn't fallen over it.

"Ember, allow me to present the Morrígan. Morrígan, this is my consort and coworker, Ember Kearney." Herne swung around to stand beside me.
Just having him next to me made me feel better.

The Morrígan stared at me for a moment, then a
feral smile swept across her face.

"Well met, Ember." She held out her hand and
Herne poked me in the side.

Hesitating, I accepted her clasp. Her skin was
surprisingly warm, but the energy racing through
her fingers almost launched me backward. I *really*
didn't want to find out what it would be like to be
on the receiving end if she was deliberately directing her power.

"Well met," I managed to squeak out. I wasn't
sure what else to say so I decided to keep my
mouth shut.

"Won't you have a seat," Herne said, sweeping
his arm toward the sofa.

Without a word, the Morrígan crossed over and
sat down. She sprawled against the back of the

sofa, stretching her legs out. Her boots were plat-form, studded with wicked spikes, and they looked like they could stomp a person to mush.

Once again I shivered, wondering how the gods managed to live within their own skins.

"So, Cernunnos told me this is urgent? I don't have much time to spare, so get down to business." She pointed to the chairs opposite the sofa.

Herne and I quickly took our seats.

"Actually yes it's an emergency. We need to know where to find one of your priests." Herne explained what had happened, and the Morrígan listened attentively. "So, we're wondering if you can tell us who this priest might be? We need to stop him, providing, of course these mur—*deaths* aren't being carried out under your directive."

I bristled, but tried to keep my reaction to my-self. Whether a god had ordered the murders to be carried out or they were the actions of a psycho-path didn't seem to matter. And it wouldn't make any difference to the victims, either.

The Morrígan cleared her throat. "First, any priest of mine who committed such an act would be disowned. As you should know, I do not require living sacrifices. My job is to cleanse the battlefield. The only souls we take are those who are ready to transition. However, I think I know of whom you are speaking."

I caught my breath, hoping she'd have a name for us.

"About six months ago, I expelled a member of my priesthood. His name is Lucius, and he's Dark Fae. He had been convicted of attacking several members of TirNaNog. Before they could punish him—they consulted me before meting out a sentence, and I agreed that they could impose whatever they wished—he vanished. He managed to escape his captors, and vanished into the city. A little over two months ago, he came to me, pleading for sanctuary. I expelled him from the ranks, and replaced him with another priest, named Garrison. Unfortunately, Lucius tried to attack Garrison. Again, he got away before I could punish him."

"Garrison—that's the name Hassa mentioned hearing his attacker say."

"I'm not surprised. Lucius was devoted to being my priest, even though he grew addled." She leaned forward, pointing to the pictures of the murdered men that Herne had laid out. "They all have the same build and look as Garrison. If he's murdering lookalikes, then he's totally off his rocker. I believe your murderer is Lucius. He also fits the description given by your witness. He's tall and burly, although not overtly tall. He bears my symbols on his face and his hands."

"Is there anything else we should know about him?" Herne asked. "What kind of magic can he use?"

"Actually, he doesn't have much magic of his own. Some very basic spells but nothing that can do much. But he does have a way with crows and ravens, and I know he collected them as pets. If he's siccing them against his victims, that would anger me greatly, given crows are my chosen creatures. But he's intelligent, and crafty. If he truly has devolved to the point of murdering substitutes, consider him a deadly enemy. I keep track of where my priests live, and I can give you the last address I had for him. I hadn't bothered going after him, thinking the attack on Garrison was a final exit, if you will. I'll text it to you when I get back to my palace." She looked so grave that I almost wanted to comfort her.

"I'm sorry we had to bother you with this," Herne said. "But we have to put a stop to him, and the local authorities are doing nothing, given the men murdered were all on the outs with Saílle. But then again, most of the Fae who aren't on the outs with the queens live within TirNaNog and Navane."

"Honestly, sometimes I like to strip the entire Fae race of their powers." She glanced at me, adding, "No offense intended, Ember, but your people make it hard to empathize with them. The fact that they are encouraging the authorities to look the other way turns my stomach."

"It turns mine too," I said. "I may be Fae, but they don't accept me as one of their own."

She nodded. "Understood. I'll be going now, but I'll text you as soon as I have that address. Oh, and when you catch him, if you catch him *alive*, turn him over to me and I'll take care of punishment." Her eyes grew dark, and the tone of her voice told me that Lucius had better pray he didn't come out of this alive. I shuddered as she stood and, without another word, vanished from Herne's house.

WE WERE ON the way back to the office when the Morrígan's text came through. Herne asked me to check his phone when the notification sounded, and sure enough, it was from her. It still boggled my mind that the gods used cell phones, but it made sense to keep track of technology in a world in which you were worshipped. Which brought to mind another thought.

"Are the gods worshipped on other worlds?" I frowned. "You guys don't necessarily live in this particular physical realm. Take Annwn, for example. Can you reach it from other worlds?"

Herne glanced at me, a faint smile on his face. "Yes, you can. You can reach most of the realms through the astral plane. So it stands to reason that if someone on another planet is able to dimension-shift, they could find Annwn. Or Valhalla, or a number of other realms."

"You didn't quite answer my first question." I wasn't sure whether to repeat it. I wasn't entirely sure how to process the answer if it was yes.

"Why don't we save that discussion for another time," Herne said. "So, was that the Morrígan who texted?"

I noticed how quickly he dodged the issue, but decided not to push it. For one thing, it wasn't important right now. For another, one thing I knew about the gods: if they didn't want to answer something, they wouldn't, regardless of how hard you pushed.

"Yes, it was. Lucius's address is located in—wait for it—the UnderLake District. No surprise there."

I paused, then asked, "So, head there next?"

"No. We go back to the office now that we have his name and address. I'll have Yutani and Talia look him up first, and probably send Viktor out to check out the house from the exterior. Lucius is crafty and dangerous, and the fact that he's a psycho just makes it worse. I want to know what we're getting into before we rush in."

When we arrived back to the office, we filled them in on what it happened. Herne assigned Viktor to take off and see if he could pick up on Lucius's trail, cautioning him to stay out of sight. Yutani and Talia went to work on researching his background.

Herne turned to me. "Why don't you and Angel leave early? You guys have been pulling a lot of hours. Since I'm tied up with Danielle until Sunday, that gives you a little breathing space." He paused, gently placing his hands on my shoulders. "I want to spend the evenings this week with her. This may be the last time I see of her for a while."

I nodded. "Understandable. Tell her I said hello."

Angel and I headed for home after tidying up our offices. As Angel sat on my bed while I hung up some clothes I had washed the night before, she tried to figure out what she was going to wear for her date with Rafé.

"He said we're going out to dinner. I can't decide between jeans and a nice top, or a dress. He said it's casual, so I don't want to overdo it. But I don't want to look like a slob, either."

I laughed. "Let me tell you something, woman.

You never look like a slob. *I* look like a slob sometimes, but I have never once seen you appear anything but neat and tidy. Why don't you wear that sparkly gold top over a pair of white jeans? You'd look striking."

I followed her into her room, where she tried on the outfit in question. Against her ebony skin, it looked absolutely stunning. She threaded a black belt through the jeans, and it set off both the gold lamé of her tank top and the crisp white of the denim.

"You're right. This is perfect. It will work on the dance floor as well as in a restaurant. I'll pair it with a pair of black ankle boots." As she sat on her bed to pull on the boots, I sorted through her handbags and pulled out a white hobo bag. It was blinged out with plenty of gold hardware, and would look good with the outfit.

"There you go. Take this. What are you going to wear for a jacket?"

She frowned, then shrugged. "Maybe my short brown trench? If so, I'll change my belt to a brown one."

I concurred, and in another five minutes, she was ready to go. She had pulled her hair back into a chignon and added thin gold hoop earrings and a crystal necklace for finishing touches. As she fastened the necklace around her neck, the doorbell rang.

"I'll get it. That should be Rafé." I dashed down the stairs, dodging Mr. Rumblebutt who was splayed out at the bottom. Sure enough, it was Rafé.

"Come on in. Why don't you wait in the living room? Angel will be down in a moment." I paused, then turned back to him. "Listen, dude. Angel's probably going to kill me for this, but I don't care. She's my best friend. She and I have history."

"Okay. What is it?"

"Just this. If you hurt her, I hope you can run fast and far. Get it?"

Instead of acting insulted, Rafé smiled. "Loud and clear. I promise, even if for some reason it doesn't work out, I'm on my best behavior. But I like Angel, and I want her to enjoy herself tonight." He paused, then added, "I know that this may be a touchy subject, but don't think that I looked down on you because of your parentage. Because I don't."

I held his gaze for a moment, but saw nothing but sincerity in his eyes. I nodded, then turned as Angel joined us.

"I'm ready," she said. She glanced at Rafé, then at me. "Ember, did you give him the warning?"

I laughed, shrugging. "I'm sure I don't know what you mean. I'm just doing what you and I have done for each other for years."

"I'm sure." She snorted. "Come on Rafé, let's head out."

Laughing, he joined her, and they both waved as they left.

I shut the door, silently wishing them a wonderful evening. Angel deserved find someone worthy of her, and I hope to hell Rafé meant what he said. Turning back to Mr. Rumblebutt, who was staring up at me with a look that said "dinner time," I scooped him up in my arms.

"Are you hungry? Come on, babe, I'll get you some food."

I carried him in the kitchen, nuzzling him as I went. Once there, I put him on the counter as I pulled out a can of cat food. I set the dish down and refilled his water fountain, thinking that it was almost time to clean it. Then I decided to take the easy way out for dinner and phoned to order a pizza. Then, setting my phone on the counter, I unstrapped my dagger and took it off, relieved to be done for the day. I headed into the living room afterward, looking forward to some downtime.

While I was waiting for the pepperoni and extra cheese to be delivered, I curled up in the living room to watch TV. It'd been a long time since I had just had an evening to myself, and I decided to catch up on some of my fave programs. I had DVR'd four episodes of *Magic Nights*, a drama about a psychic who solved crimes, and a whole string of various other programs that I had wanted to see. I was ten minutes into *English Gardens Explored* when the doorbell rang.

"Boy, the pizza got here fast," I said to Mr. Rumblebutt, who was sitting on the sofa next to me, licking his paws after a quick bite to eat. I grabbed the twenty that I had set on the foyer console. But as I opened the door, I faced an unwelcome surprise.

There, staring at me with piercing eyes, was my grandfather.

Chapter 18

"WHAT THE *HELL* are you doing here?" I stumbled back, totally surprised. "I told you I never wanted to see you again. What the fuck are you doing at my doorstep?"

Farthing, my grandfather, arched his eyebrows. "I thought you might want to know that your grandmother died." His voice was so cold and collected that it threw a chill into me.

"So, did you kill *her* too?"

He had been responsible for my father's death, and had conspired in my mother's death. He would have had me killed, too, if I had been home—he had admitted that much.

"Is that the best you can come up with?" he said. "Aren't you going to invite me in?"

I sputtered. "You think I would invite you into my house? That I would allow you entry into my life in any way? Didn't Morgana have a little talk with you? She said she was going to."

"Unfortunately, Cernunnos's pussy cat did come knocking at my door, but I have no love for the gods, or for their opinions of me. Now I ask you once again, are you going to let me in?" He leaned against the doorframe as though he owned it, which just infuriated me more.

"I'll let you in my house the day Saílle shows up at my doorstep asking for tea. Get the fuck away from me and stay away." I started to shut the door, but he threw his shoulder against it, slamming it open and knocking me down in the process.

I scrambled to get to my feet, but he was in and had shut the door behind him before I could stand. My shoulder aching, I pulled myself off the floor.

"If you don't leave, I'll kill you. You have ten seconds to get out." I was furious now.

"I'm here to give you one last chance. I know you haven't gone through the Cruharach yet, but rumor has it you're nearing the time. I can make it much easier for you, and as my heir, life will be out lot more pleasant for you in the Dark Court." His eyes were blazing.

"This again?"

He had offered me the chance to go through a ritual that would eradicate my mother's blood from my body, leaving me pure Dark Fae. Then, he told me, he would make me his heir.

"Saílle doesn't believe I know the process. But I do."

"I'll see you in hell before I ever accept your of-fer. Morgana will strike you down for this."

I reached for my phone, intending to call Herne,

but realized I'd left it on the living room coffee table.

Farthing laughed. "I told you, I don't care what the gods say. You would choose to stay a filthy *tralaeth* when you could join forces with me? Your mother's blood diluted you more than I feared."

Before I could react, he whipped out a long knife. The blade gleamed, finely honed, and it was barbed with fine teeth. The metal glinted with an unnatural glow.

"Time to finish what should have been finished years ago."

He leaped toward me, sweeping the knife up in a stab toward my stomach.

I managed to dance out of the way just in time to avoid being gutted. I had taken off my dagger when I got home, and it was on the kitchen table by my phone. Breathing hard, I took a running jump and vaulted the back of the sofa, heading for the kitchen, screaming for Mr. Rumblebutt to get out of the way. He dashed up the stairs.

I entered the kitchen, but I was only a few steps ahead of my grandfather. I spun, grabbing my knife as I did so. Bringing it to bear, I swung a chair between Farthing and me.

"Leave now, and you can leave with your life," I said. "If you choose to pursue this, you aren't walking out of here."

He snorted. "I've fought more battles in the thousand years I've been alive than you can ever dream of. Don't hold much hope of winning this one."

He tossed the chair aside.

I grabbed one of the knives out of the butcher's block. I didn't want to let go of my dagger, but I sent the five-inch-long boning knife flying, managing to peg him in the shoulder. He let out a soft yelp, but merely reached for the hilt and yanked it out, casting it to the side.

"Not a bad throw, Ember, but then you *do* have the Autumn Stalker blood in you. My blood and your grandmother's blood."

I realized that I was caught between the wall of cupboards and the kitchen island. I could climb over it, but I would lose valuable time because it wasn't as easy to vault as the sofa had been. Even though I was adept and trained to fight, Farthing was correct in one thing. He had centuries of treachery behind him. I wasn't sure I could win the fight against him.

The fear reached deep, clenching me in the gut, and I felt something shift. I heard myself snarl and, before I realized what I was doing, I opened my mouth and began to sing. I didn't know *what* I was singing, the language was one I didn't understand, but the melody echoed from my throat, filling the kitchen as it reverberated off the walls to weave a web.

My grandfather froze, staring at me with a terrified look on his face.

I sang as though my life depended on it. As the music swept me up, I lost myself in it, and the ancient words became ones I could understand. I was hearing the song as if it were echoing from the stereo rather than coming from my lips.

You are weary, you are failing. You are thirsty, you are flailing.

You are hungry, you're alone, I hear you crying with a moan.

You are aching, you're in pain. You are drowning in the rain.

Come to me, lonely man. Reach out and take my hand.

I'm your garden, I'm your joy. You are my winning, lovely toy.

Come to me, hear my call. I am your only, one, and all.

I held out my hands, a thirst so deep within me rising up like a light. It surrounded me with a nimbus of blue mist, floating over to surround my grandfather.

He stuttered, looking confused, and dropped the knife that he was carrying. As he reached out, crying, I took hold of his hand and pulled him roughly to me. I leaned down, my lips an inch from his. He stared at me, his eyes filled with fear and wonder.

He opened his mouth and I began to draw his breath and life force into me, breathing deeply, drinking his soul, drinking his life, drinking every drop of his energy and essence. I drained him there, clutching him tighter as he struggled to get away. He screamed, unable to pull out of my embrace. I reveled in the act, feeling my power grow as his fear increased.

I grabbed hold of his ponytail, yanking his hair back as I stared into his eyes. He was still making feeble attempts to get away, but I was stronger than he was, the spell empowering me to hold him in my grasp. I stared into those cold and vicious eyes, and laughed.

"And you thought you could kill me, you petty little man. You thought you could change me. You thought you could control me. How frail you are."

"Ember, let me go—" His voice was faint. There was very little life left in him.

His plea fell like ice, shattering at my feet.

"Let you go? When you came here to destroy me? You think you're ruthless? Look *ruthless* in the face. Welcome it in your own death."

And then, I caught his breath again, draining the last drops of life out of his body. The next moment, he collapsed on the floor. I nudged him with my foot, staring at his lifeless body, sneering at him.

Another moment, and the spell broke.

I was back in control, staring at the corpse of my grandfather.

THE FIRST PERSON I called after Herne was Marilee.

"The Leannan Sidhe side of my bloodline came to the forefront tonight. Can you come over here? I just killed my grandfather."

Marilee knew all about my heritage, and the surrounding factors. "I'll be there in fifteen minutes. Have you called the police?"

"No, I called Herne." I glanced at the body on the floor, my stomach twisting in knots. As much as I hated him, I hadn't planned on revenge.

Marilee hung up, and I forced myself to return to the living room, closing the door so Mr. Rumblebutt couldn't get into the kitchen. I was still carrying my dagger, and I couldn't bring myself to set it down. The doorbell rang and I automatically went to answer it. I peeked around and saw the pizza guy.

"$7.99, please." He held up the pizza box.

Without a word, I quietly set my knife on the table, handed over the twenty, and took the pizza from him, then shut the door before he could hand me the change.

"Ma'am, I've got your change." His voice echoed through the door.

I pressed my forehead against the cool wooden surface.

"It's a tip," I called out.

I locked the door, then picked up my knife again and carried the knife and pizza back to the living room, where I put the pizza on the coffee table. I inched my way toward the kitchen, terrified that if I opened the door, my grandfather would be alive again, waiting for me. Holding my breath, I quietly cracked the door and peeked in. His legs were still sprawled out behind the counter, and I shut the door again.

I didn't know what to do, so I returned to the sofa and curled up in the corner of it, holding my dagger like a shield. Someone pounded on the front door and I jumped. Then Herne's voice echoed from the other side.

"Ember! Open the door and let me in!"

I ran to the door, flipped the latch, and opened it. The moment I saw Herne's face, I fell into his arms, shaking.

"I didn't intend to kill him. I didn't know he was coming over." I stuttered out the words in my haste to explain what had happened.

Herne pushed me back, holding me firmly by the shoulders. "Ember, get hold of yourself. First, are you sure he's dead?"

I nodded, motioning to the kitchen. "He's in there."

Herne walked me to the sofa and sat me down. "You wait here. I'll be right back." He vanished into the kitchen, in a moment later returned, his eyes wide. He sat down beside me and took my hands. "He's dead all right, but there's no blood. What happened?"

I was shivering. Between hiccups, I told him. "I thought he was the pizza guy so I opened the door. He pushed his way in. He demanded that I go through the ritual and when I refused, he pulled a knife on me. He was going to kill me."

The doorbell rang.

Herne looked at me. "Are you expecting anybody else?"

I nodded, clearing my throat. "Marilee."

He answered the door and escorted her in. By then, I had managed to catch my breath. I told them both what had happened.

"I don't know how my Leannan Sidhe side came through, but I knew what to do. I knew exactly what to do. What's going to happen now?"

"What's going to happen is I'm going to call Saílle. And she isn't going to do a damn thing about it. That I will tell you." Herne got up and walked into the foyer.

I turned Marilee. "What should I do?"

"Once you have passed through the Cruharach, *you* will be the one in control. Until then there may be more incidents like this. Your Leannan Sidhe side seems to be your self-defense. She rose up to protect you. You should be thanking her rather than fearing her." Marilee took my hands, gazing into my eyes. "This was an act of self-defense. Your grandfather was trying to kill you. Don't make it out to be anything other than what it was."

I grabbed her hands, holding on like they were lifelines. "What if she comes up when I'm not in danger?"

"I don't think you have to worry about that. And *she* is part of *you*. She's not a separate entity, even though it may feel like it. This is just a part of you that's coming to the surface." Marilee gave me a soft smile. "That's why I doubt this will happen any time other than you trying to protect yourself. It hasn't happened before, but this time you were in a dire situation and your emotions were extremely high. It's no wonder to me that your mother's blood came to the rescue."

At that moment Herne returned. He pocketed his phone, and then sat down on the other side of me.

"I talked to Saílle. She's sending guards out for the body. I have her official word that it will be announced that your grandfather died of a heart attack. There isn't a mark on him, and the only way anybody could find out how he died would be to bring in a Morte Seer. Saílle will have him cremated immediately so that won't happen. She's also decreed that the court will confiscate his possessions. She's sending you a check for the trouble your grandfather caused you. It will be expected that you do not attempt to claim any inheritance."

I stared at him. "I don't want his money. And I don't want blood money from her."

Herne shook his head. "Nope. You can't refuse it. We need these people on our side, so whatever you do with it, is up to you. Just accept it, and let it go."

I hung my head, not wanting to agree, but I knew he was right. "Fine. At least I don't have the Dark Court after me for his death. How do you know she'll keep her word?"

"Because I recorded the conversation and I told her that if she tried to renege, I would take it before a Triamvinate. She knows me well enough to know that I'd do it, and that I'd win. Besides, Saílle was outraged that he defied her. She told him to back off and leave you alone."

"What do you know? I didn't think she would actually care."

I didn't try to fool myself that she cared about my life. No, Saílle had instructed Farthing to leave me be. That he didn't obey her probably came as a slap in the face.

Saílle's guards arrived far sooner than I expected them to. They silently removed the body, handing me an envelope as they finished. They said nothing else, simply left as silently as they had come.

I waited till they were gone, then closed the door and locked it. Carrying the envelope unopened, I returned to Herne and Marilee.

"What is it?" he asked.

I held my breath, opening the envelope. There was a death certificate for Farthing, stating that he had died of a heart attack, and a cashier's check for one hundred thousand dollars. Saílle worked fast, I had to give her that. My grandfather was probably worth ten times that, but it didn't matter to me. I stared at the check for a moment and then silently walked over to my purse, slipping it inside.

"I never in the world thought that this would be the way today ended." I wasn't even sure how I felt. I was still shaking from the adrenaline rush, feeling numb and angry and scared all at the same time. Finally, I turned around and looked at Herne and Marilee.

"It will be all right, love." Herne looked pained, but it wasn't annoyance on his face. Instead, he looked concerned.

Marilee stood and stretched. "I'm going home to mix you up a potion. It will help you sleep tonight, and it will also soothe the Leannan Sidhe side, though I doubt if you will be seeing much of her for the next few days. What you just did was extremely powerful, and will soothe her hunger for quite some time. Your grandfather possessed a lot of energy and she drank him down."

"His...energy...won't taint me, will it?" I had been afraid to ask the question before.

Marilee shook her head. "No. Think of it like fuel."

"True enough, but if you put tainted fuel into a car, it ruins the engine."

"Here's a better analogy. You need so many calories to function. Vitamins, protein, carbs, none of them play into this. Just calories. In that case, it doesn't matter if they come from cookies or ice cream or broccoli or steak. All that matters is that you consume enough calories. That's the way that the Leannan Sidhe work. When they're hungry, it doesn't matter what kind of person they feed from. They have their preferences, yes, but it doesn't matter, as long as it's a person."

That didn't exactly make me feel any better, but it did calm me down.

As Marilee headed out the door, Angel walked in. Rafé wasn't with her, and she looked worried.

"Is your date over?" I asked.

She nodded. "I had a feeling something was wrong, so I took a rain check on the rest of the night. We have a date for Saturday. What's going on?" She glanced at Herne, then back at me. "Why was Marilee here?"

I didn't know if I could explain myself yet again.

Herne turned toward me. "I know it's probably cold by now, but why don't you eat a few pieces of that pizza? Your mother's blood may have gotten its fill of energy, but I think you need more than that. You need actual food. I'll explain what happened to Angel." He stood, motioning for Angel to follow him into the kitchen.

As she followed him, I leaned forward, staring at the pizza box before silently flipping the lid. The pizza was cold, but that never had stopped me before. I wasn't hungry, or at least I didn't think I was, but when I finally picked up a piece and took the first bite, my stomach rumbled and I realized I was starved. As I began to chew, Mr. Rumblebutt came running into the room, giving me a look like, *can I come down now?*

"Come here, you little twerp." Leaning back on the sofa, I polished off first one slice and then a second one, with Mr. Rumblebutt rubbing his head against my leg.

At that moment, Angel and Herne emerged from the kitchen, Angel's expression strained.

"What can I do? Let me go heat this up for you," she said, picking up the pizza box and grabbing the slice out of my hand. As she headed into the kitchen, I glanced at Herne.

"What did she say?"

"She's worried, of course. But she's glad your grandfather's gone. And frankly, so am I. I've already texted my mother." He paused, reaching to brush a stray hair away from my face. "I'm so sorry, love. I feel I should stay here tonight."

"No," I said. "Go home to Danielle. She's only here through Sunday. Angel's home now, and Marilee will be returning with a sleeping draught for me. I'll be all right. My grandfather can't hurt me now. That's the one upshot to this whole horrible experience."

Even as I said it, I wasn't sure. This house had experienced murder before, and had trapped the ghosts within its walls. Part of me was afraid my grandfather might be trapped here, he had so much anger in his heart. But I didn't want to give voice to the thought, because sometimes thoughts created reality.

"I guess I'll be going then. Call me if you need anything—anything at all." He kissed me. As he left, Marilee returned.

She handed me a little bag of powder. "Put this in your tea or milk tonight. It will help you sleep."

Angel returned with the pizza, all warmed up. She also brought me a cup of hot cocoa. As she settled down beside me, she glanced at Marilee.

"Will Ember be okay tonight? Is there anything we have to watch for?"

Marilee shook her head. "I'll sleep on the sofa. That way, if you need me, I'm here. Pour the powder in your cocoa, it won't make it taste bad."

I chugged down the cocoa, and ate a few pieces of pizza. We watched TV for another half hour, and I found myself beginning to yawn. Marilee noticed and motioned for me to go to bed. After bidding her good night, I headed up the stairs to my room while Angel found her a pillow and a blanket. I had been afraid that I would lay awake, reliving the incident over and over, but the moment I slid into bed and my head touched the pillow, I was out like a light. And I slept the entire night without interruptions.

Chapter 19

BY MORNING, I was breathing easier. Marilee left as soon as I woke up.

"Why don't we skip tonight's meeting," she said. "You need to be relaxed for it, and after last night, I think you need a break. I'll see you Saturday."

Relieved, I waved her out. Angel was making breakfast. I looked around the kitchen, trying to erase the memory of my grandfather's body stretched out on the floor, but I kept coming back to the image. To the memory that he had tried to kill me.

There was no sign that he had been there. In fact, the floor looked freshly mopped and I suspected I had Angel to thank for that, but in my mind, I couldn't get away from the picture of him, splayed out after I had siphoned off his life energy.

"How do you deal with the fact that someone who's supposed to love you wants you dead?"

I shook my head. "I don't know how to work through this. I mean, I knew he was behind my father's death, but after confronting him at the Parley, I thought that we were over and done."

"Well, you can be sure it's finished now," Angel said. "He's gone and he's not coming back. I suggest we ask Kipa over to make certain there aren't any lingering wisps of his spirit. He seems pretty good at that sort of thing."

"Yeah, but we ask Herne along with him. When Herne found out that you and I had partied with Kipa, I thought he was going to blow a gasket." I finally let Angel ease me into a chair and picked at the toast she handed me. She was finishing up the bacon and eggs when my work phone rang. I frowned. "It's Herne."

I answered, wondering why he would be calling us when he knew we were coming in, anyway. "Hey, what's up?"

"Ember, I know you're probably still rattled from last night, but we need you and Angel here right away. Can you make it in twenty minutes?" He didn't sound frantic, but he *did* sound worried.

"Sure, we'll be there ASAP." I hung up. "I wonder what's going down now. Breakfast needs to be to-go this morning. Herne asked if we could be there in twenty minutes."

Angel snorted. "Just our luck. Okay, here." She pulled some pita bread out of the refrigerator and filled the pockets with the eggs, bacon, and some cheese, then wrapped them in foil. "We can eat when we get there. Come on. I fed Mr. Rumble-butt, so he's fine."

As we grabbed our jackets and headed toward the door, I wondered what had happened to have Herne so anxious.

WHEN WE ARRIVED at the office, the others were in the break room, waiting. Angel and I slid into our places and unwrapped our pita sandwiches. Angel popped them in the oven to melt the cheese while Herne rapped his fingers on the table. Finally, we were ready.

"What's going on?" I asked.

Herne motioned to Yutani. "Tell them what you figured out."

Yutani gave him a nod. "Right. So, I was looking at the four murders, and at the newest abduction attempt, and the calendar. I noticed that the dead men all went missing about a week before the lunar cycles—the full and the new moon. Our latest abduction attempt on Sunday happened a week before the moon's due to be new. If Lucius is true to his pattern, he'll make another attempt today or tomorrow, and because from this, I surmise that he's sacrificing these men on the days of the new and full moon itself."

"That would correlate with my news," Viktor said. "Erica contacted me. It's too hard to tell with the other three men—they were too far gone—but they estimate that Ulstair died right around the full moon. He was eviscerated. His stomach was splayed open, and they noticed numerous markings that could have been made by bird beaks. My thought is that Lucius is opening them up, then offering them to the Morrígan as a sacrifice."

"But she's not listening to him. She didn't seem to realize that he was doing this," I said.

"The gods aren't omnipotent," Herne said. "She kicked him out of the priesthood, so there would be no reason for her to keep track of him. And he thought he was winning her back."

"Then, to feed his desire to appease her, Lucius will try for another sacrifice." Angel frowned, staring at her notes. "But how easy is it for him to find someone who looks like Garrison? What if he can't find somebody who looks like that? Will he accept a substitute?"

"I don't know," Herne said. "We're dealing with a whack-a-doodle here. He already stepped over the window onto the ledge, so to speak. Who knows if he'll actually jump?"

"We need to stop him before he strikes again," I said. "If he's desperate, he may just kill the next victim on the spot. Do we just go arrest him? How do we approach this?"

Herne leaned back in his chair, considering the question. "Given he's outside the Dark Court's notice—on their 'list'—I think we can safely go in and take him into custody. We'll give him to the Morrígan. She wants us to turn him over to her if we catch him alive."

"We're kind of our own little band of authority, aren't we?" I had gradually come to realize that we had been given a great deal of leeway, as long as we weren't obvious about it.

"We are, at that. But there's a tight line we walk, balanced between the Fae Courts, the police, and the gods. All right, Viktor, Yutani, Ember, you're with me. The Morrígan said that he doesn't use much magic, but so here's hoping we'll be able to take him down." His expression grim, Herne motioned to the rest of us.

We took two cars. Yutani rode with me for a change, while Viktor called shotgun with Herne. I had a feeling that Herne and Yutani's relationship was still strained, and it probably would be for some time, and that was why Yutani was sitting in my passenger seat.

On the way to Lucius's house, I told Yutani what happened the night before.

"He actually came to your house to force an ultimatum? After Saílle told him to leave you alone? He must've been crazed."

I shrugged. "It's going to take me some time to process what happened. There's a part of me—and I don't particularly like that part—who's absolutely thrilled the man is dead. I feel like I've avenged my parents to some degree. There can never be justice for what happened to them, but there's this gleeful little voice inside that is pointing at my grandfather's spirit and laughing, saying, 'You're dead, you're dead, you can't hurt me or anybody else again!' I'm not sure how to cope with those feelings. I'm not a gentle person, in many ways. But I didn't realize I was so vengeful."

And that was the truth. I hadn't considered myself extremely vengeful. Up until I met Farthing, I had been holding out some sort of hope that I had read the situation wrong. That my parents had been killed by strangers. That hope had died when my grandfather had confessed to being part of their deaths, and when he told me that my mother's parents had been part of it as well. There had been no joyful family reunion, nor would there ever be.

"It's never easy to face the past when it's housed in the form of a murderer," Yutani said.

As I wove through the streets, following Herne's car, I debated asking him how he was coping with his own discovery, but I decided to leave it be for now.

"So, do you think we'll catch him today?" Yutani asked.

I shrugged, flipping the turn signal as I merged into the next lane.

"We're facing a psycho. I can't see it being as easy as going up to Lucius's front door and slapping cuffs on him."

"I see what you mean." Yutani paused, then added, "Herne and I had a long talk yesterday. In case you're interested, we came to an understanding. We'll be able to rebuild our friendship, but it's going to take some time. It's not even that I feel he betrayed me by not telling me his suspicions. It's that everybody seemed to be talking behind my back."

I gave him a quick glance. "Yutani, I knew about their suspicions, but trust me, it never seemed to be a subject for gossip. It only came out because he was worried about you. It wasn't like anybody was sitting there, placing bets about when you'd find out."

"Thank you for telling me that. I didn't talk to Herne about that so much. I didn't want him to lie to me to soothe my feelings. But I wondered if I actually had been a regular topic in the office gossip mill."

Herne was pulling into a parking spot up ahead, in front of what looked like a Gothic Victorian mansion. As I eased into a parking spot two cars behind him, I turned off the ignition and turned to Yutani.

"I will tell you one thing and I want you to believe me. *Everybody* in that office has your back. Everyone there considers you part of the family. I'm still an outsider, to a degree, but I've never met a group of people who care more about each other than the Wild Hunt. You and Viktor and Talia took Angel and me in when Herne brought us into the agency. *Nobody's* been bad mouthing you." I glanced ahead. Herne and Viktor were getting out of the car. "We'd better join them. And let's hope this goes easier than my gut says it will."

Yutani reached over, placing his hand on mine and squeezing it gently.

"I know you think that I looked down on you at first, that I didn't think you were up to the job. The truth is, I'm not an easy person to get to know and I'm blunt. And I think you and Angel do a bang-up job. And...thank you for what you said."

And with that, we got out of the car and joined Herne and Viktor.

THE HOUSE WAS both massive and spooky looking. The landscaping around it had been neglected. Patches of knee-high grass filled the front yard, interspersed with blackberry vines and overgrown ferns. The walkway up to the front porch was broken, with weeds poking through the cracks. There was a chain-link fence surrounding the lot, about five feet tall. It was sagging in some areas, and rusting in a few others.

From where I stood, I could count three stories plus what looked like an attic nook on top of the house. It truly was an Addams family special, or worse yet—the Munsters; almost a parody of the Halloween haunted house.

"Either he worked very hard to make his home unapproachable, or he really has ignored any upkeep. It's a wonder the neighbors haven't complained to the city." I glanced around, then realized that the rest of the neighborhood didn't look much better. "Well, even if they did, I don't think they would have a leg to stand on. What the hell kind of neighborhood is this?"

"This is the Bayberry neighborhood, and there's a reason the area looks like this. This was where the Fae courts tried to funnel their poverty-ridden subjects whom they didn't want cluttering up their cities. At one time it was a mishmash of Light and Dark Fae. There were a lot of calls to the police. The Fae eventually wandered off, replaced by equally destitute members of the shifter community. A few humans live here too. Lots of slumlord issues around here. I found that out when I was checking out the place yesterday," Viktor said.

"So basically a trailer trash neighborhood, without the trailers?" Yutani said.

Viktor nodded. "It's not just poverty that runs it down, either. A lot of gang fighting, illegal drug activity, and the occasional pimp's flophouse."

Since prostitution was legal, the only pimps left were ones who trafficked in sex slaves, and sold them cheap. Or ran underaged rings, or fetishes that were so dangerous they were outlawed. They moved from flophouse to flophouse, pulling up stakes every time they thought the cops might be onto them.

I blinked, wondering what had happened to all the *neighborhood renewal* projects that the city government talked about. There had been a big push a few years back to revitalize the poorer areas of the city, but given that the mayor's office was as corrupt as law enforcement, I suspected that the money earmarked for said revitalization had gone straight into the pockets of the vampires who were pulling the strings behind the curtains. Just like the Fae influenced the cops, the vampires influenced the mayor and the city council.

"Are we ready?" I asked.

Herne nodded. "Let's go get our man."

As we headed up the broken walkway, picking our way through the weeds and overgrown tangle that sprawled across the sidewalk, I kept an eye on the windows, but there was no sign of movement, no sign of life. When I reached out attempting to sense any movement or energy, the entire house felt dead. Houses could feel abandoned, and desolate, but they usually had a mournful sense about them. Right now, I sensed only decay and death.

"There's something wrong here," I finally said. "I know he's not supposed to have any magical abilities, but I sense some sort of magic around this yard."

Herne's gaze darted around, and he held up one hand first pause. After a moment, he said, "I understand what you're saying, but this is the only choice we have. If he's not here, were going to set up a stakeout."

"What if he's on the trail, already looking for a new victim?"

"We can't cover the entire beach trail. We don't have enough manpower. If he's not here, we'll decide what move to make next." Herne gave me a shrug, and I realized he was right. There was no way we could cover the entire Beach Trail, so taking it one step at a time was the only thing we could do. The cops weren't going to help us, although realizing they wouldn't hinder us either made me feel better.

As we ascended the porch stairs, they creaked beneath our feet and I saw several broken boards.

"Be careful, there are some rotten planks on this porch, and you don't want to —"

Before I could finish speaking, Viktor suddenly plunged through the floor, the boards splintering as he crashed through a rotten patch. He shouted, disappearing into the hole.

"Viktor!" Herne raced forward, stopping as his

foot began to splinter another board. He backed up quickly, going down on his knees to spread his weight out, much like someone trying to spread their weight out on ice over a pond.

Yutani leapt over the railing into the yard, and I realized he was looking for a way into the crawl-space under the porch. I wasn't sure what to do, but a glance at the door showed no sign that anybody inside had heard us.

"I'm all right, I think," Victor's voice trailed up from below. "But you need to come down here."

"I found a way in," Yutani called.

I glanced at Herne, then at the door. "If Lucius is in there, he's going to hear us. I'm skirting around back to make sure he doesn't escape that way."

"Be careful," Herne said. As I started to head around the side, I saw where Yutani had found the opening into the crawlspace that led to beneath the porch. He was peeking in, and as I passed he motioned for me to join him.

"I was going around back —" I started, but Yutani shook his head and again, beckoned me over with a finger.

"Lucius is probably out, or you can bet we'd have seen him by now. You need to see this. So does Herne."

Herne joined me, and we followed Yutani beneath the porch, brushing away spiderwebs and stray leaves. The smell was dank, and heavy pall of decay hung in the crawlspace. At first I thought it might just be sour earth, but then I recognized that scent. It reminded me of the decay that we had smelled when we found Ulstair's body.

"Crap. That's the smell of death." I saw a flash-light beam flickering ahead from where Viktor was crouching on the ground. Above him, light ema-nated through the hole in the porch. He trained his beam on a patch of earth next to him, and Yutani pulled out his own flashlight, strengthening the light so that we could see easier.

There, next to Viktor, were the skeletal bones of the hand, poking out of the ground.

"Another murder victim?" I asked, thinking no sane person would hide a skeleton beneath their porch. It couldn't be from natural causes, either. *Nobody* dug a hole underneath the porch and lay down in it to die.

"It has to be. But we found all the reports they had of missing men, so *who is this*? The skeleton looks older, like it's been here for some time." Viktor looked up at Herne. "I thought he was dis-missed as a priest just a few months back?"

"That's what the Morrígan said. But then again, remember, he was accused of attacking several members of TirNaNog. What if he's been killing for some time? He could have been targeting an entirely different victim profile before being re-placed by Garrison pushed him over the edge." Herne looked around. "I wonder if there any more bodies buried here."

Viktor flashed his light toward the back of the house. "The crawlspace goes on for quite a ways. I have the feeling that this guy, or woman, isn't alone down here. Let's get inside the house."

We headed out from beneath the crawlspace, and this time we moved around back. The kitchen door led directly into the house, with no porch in between. Two steps led to the door, from a concrete patio that was as cracked as the front sidewalk. The backyard looked as desolate and overgrown as the front, and the trees felt angry to me. I reached out, trying to sense their nature, but pulled away when I sensed how twisted and dark they were. They felt as tainted as the house did.

"This land is saturated with evil energy," I said, not wanting to sound dramatic and yet — it was the truth. "Everything on the lot feels tainted. Whether it's because of what he's been doing, or something else, I don't know."

Herne tried the doorknob, but it was locked. Yutani motioned him aside, and pulled out a set of lock picks. He made quick work of the deadbolt and the door sprang open. As Herne stepped in to what appeared to be the kitchen, I gave one last look to the yard, and followed him. When we were all inside, Viktor shut the door.

We were standing in a large room, a kitchen that looked straight out of the 1930s. A big wood cook-stove stood in one corner of the room, and it was obvious that it had been in use recently because a skillet sat to one side. The stove made me uneasy, there was a lot of cast-iron in it, and I tried to stay away from it.

"How Lucius even uses that, being Fae himself, I don't know. Getting near it makes me queasy."

"Maybe he's got somebody here with him," Herne said, looking around.

The rest of the kitchen seemed just as old, although I knew it couldn't be. The countertops were covered with some sort of linoleum or Formica, and the cupboards had once been white but now were a muddy gray from years of use. Nothing had been updated, it seemed, except for a chest freezer that stood in one corner of the room, near a kitchen table. The table was about the size of a card table, only it was solid wood and had three older chairs with vinyl seat coverings on them.

Something about the freezer caught my attention. I hesitantly walked over to it, not wanting to open it and yet drawn to do so. As I lifted the lid, the room began to spin. I realized I was staring at roughly packed freezer bags filled with hands and feet. I let out a shriek and dropped the lid, stumbling back.

"Crap, I'm sorry."

"I don't think anybody's home," Yutani said. "Or if he *is* home, he's in hiding. We made plenty of noise, so if he has a secret cubbyhole in which to hide, he's probably already there."

"What did you see in there?" Herne asked, crossing to lift the lid. He shut it very quickly, turning around, his face pale. "Well, we have an answer as to whether he's been killing more than just Ulstair and those other men. Apparently he has a taste for flesh."

I let out a soft groan, not wanting to think about the body parts in that freezer. All I wanted to do was to catch Lucius and turn him over to the Morrígan.

There were two doors out of the kitchen. One led to a formal dining room and the other to a back staircase. We began to search through the house, room by room. Like many Victorians, this house was tall and narrow, with only three or four rooms per floor. Other than a powder room and the kitchen, the main floor had a dining room, a parlor, and what looked like a small office. There didn't seem to be a basement, or if there was, the door was hidden. But because so many houses in the Seattle area didn't have basements because of all of the urban flooding, I rather doubted this one did.

We ascended the main staircase to the second floor. There, we found a library and what looked like two bedrooms and another bathroom. One of the bedrooms looked like it was being used, but the other was dusty, filled with cobwebs and dust bunnies, and the comforter on the bed had a half-inch layer of dust on it. We went into the library, poking around. I found a datebook, but it was open to March rather than September, and it seemed like the last appointment entered had been close to the spring equinox. In fact, the last appointment read, "Meeting with the Morrígan" and after that, there were no more entries.

"I think I found the date when the Morrígan kicked him out of the priesthood. The library looks unused otherwise, but could there be a secret entrance to a room in here?"

Yutani closed his eyes. "I don't think so. When I think of the outside and what we're seeing here on the inside, I don't think there's space enough for a secret entrance. Possibly a narrow staircase? But that would have to be it."

We ransacked the rest of the room but found nothing else. As we headed to the third floor, my stomach began to tighten. The energy grew heavier, and once again I felt a feeling of dread. Before I could mention it, though, Viktor spoke up.

"There's something really bad up there," he said. "Even I can feel it."

"That goes for me too," I said.

Herne nodded. "There's heavy magic hanging in the air. If Lucius doesn't use magic, then he's had some help." As he finished speaking, the stairway opened out into what looked like a second parlor. There were three other rooms off of the parlor, and yet another staircase that had to lead to the attic nook. The parlor itself looked relatively benign, furnished with old furniture and heavy draperies, all cloying with a dank smell. But there was something underneath the dampness, another scent that smelled familiar.

"Blood," Yutani said. "I smell old blood."

He gravitated toward one of the doors, and when he approached it, we readied our weapons.

Yutani smashed the door open, but inside was a bathroom. The tub was stained with dried blood, as was the floor. Splatters painted the walls, in a sickening array of designs. On one wall, the rough drawing of a crow with wings spread out was outlined with blood. Runes were etched around the outside, glyphs that I recognized as Turneth, the Dark Fae dialect. I stared at them, able to read them.

"It's a prayer to the Morrígan. It's a prayer begging her to forgive him and take him back."

As we stared at the mess, Yutani cocked his head.

"I hear something upstairs. Come on," he said, heading out of the bathroom and toward the stairway leading up to the attic. We followed, and I wondered if Lucius had holed up there, waiting for us. But as we reached the top of the short staircase and Yutani threw open the door, a flurry of wings rustled, as a flurry of crows came swooping down to attack us.

"Cover your eyes," Herne said, as he raised one hand. I obeyed. A crow landed on my head, trying to pick at my face, and I tried to knock it off while protecting my face. The next moment, there was a brilliant flash that I could see even behind my closed lids, and Herne let out a loud cry. I wasn't sure what spell he cast, but the crow on my head momentarily stopped, and I managed to slam it against the wall. A moment later, I opened my eyes to find a group of stunned crows littering the floor. Yutani quickly shut the door to the attic as we attempted to regroup.

Chapter 20

"**WHAT** DO WE do about these crows before they wake up?"

My face felt wet, and I reached up to wipe a trickle of blood away from my forehead where the crow had managed to wound me. It didn't feel deep, but it was bleeding at a pretty good clip, given head wounds and hands always bled heavier.

"I don't know, but unless he's hiding somewhere, Lucius isn't here." Herne glanced at the crows. "They have been trained to attack. Either that or he has them under some sort of spell. I hate to put them down until we know which it is. For now, move them to one of the bedrooms and close the door."

We quickly shifted all the crows and slammed the door before they could wake up. My cell phone—my work phone—rang. I blinked, I'd forgotten to put it on mute when we entered the house. As I pulled it out, the caller ID read: Angel.

"Yeah? What's up?" I was still breathing heavy, the adrenaline rushing through my veins.

"I think I made a big mistake. Can you put me on speaker?"

Frowning, I motioned Herne. "It's Angel. She wants to be put on speakerphone. She says she made a mistake." I held out my phone, punching the speaker icon.

Angel's voice crackled through. "I'm so sorry, I didn't realize what happened until after she left."

"What happened? Who left?" Herne asked.

"Raven came in to check on our progress. Lucius's file was sitting on my desk. I mentioned that you guys were out hunting for a suspect, but I didn't tell her who. At that moment, Talia needed some help and called me from her office. I told Raven to wait. When I came back, the file was open, and she was gone. The pages were scattered around, but the top one had Lucius's name and address on it."

"Oh crap," I said. "Raven wants revenge, and she's not afraid to go after it. She has no clue who she's dealing with. She has magic and he doesn't, but he's a psycho."

Herne let out an exasperated sigh. "Well, there's nothing we can do to stop her now. We just have to contain the damage. Angel, we'll talk about this later. Meanwhile, Ember, can you call Raven and find out where she is?"

I moved away from the men, putting in a call to Raven. Her phone rang three times, and she finally answered. "Don't try to stop me, Ember."

"Raven? Wait. Can you meet us in ten minutes?"

She hesitated, then said, "I'm not letting him get away with this. Angel told me that you're out looking up a suspect, and I suspect that you're at his house right now. If you had found him, you wouldn't be calling me now. I read through your notes. I think I know where he's hiding."

"You're right," Herne said. He had been listening over my shoulder. "We're at his house and he's not here right now. But you can't take him on alone, Raven. He's done more than kill just a few men. He's a full-blown freak. There are dead bodies everywhere here. He's dangerous."

"I'm not afraid of danger," Raven said. "I want him."

"Then are you afraid of the Morrígan? Because she wants him, too. And she can do more to him than you ever can. Please, tell us where you think he's hiding. Don't try to take him on by yourself. We don't want to see you hurt." Herne was making a good case, but a little extra emphasis couldn't hurt.

I spoke up. "Raven, Herne's telling you the truth. The Morrígan has a special place in hell waiting for him. Let her do what she wants to. At least let us go with you."

There was a pause, and I could practically hear the wheels in her head turning. After a moment, she let out a long sigh.

"Lucius took away the only person I've ever loved. Do you promise me that you're not just going to hand him over to Saílle? Can you promise me that the Morrígan will punish him?"

"Oh, trust me, the Morrígan will make him regret every action. If you kill him, he gets off easy. He won't be punished. The Morrígan isn't the Queen of the Phantoms for nothing. He's done a lot of damage, and the goddess will have her pound of flesh."

Very slowly, Raven answered. "I want your word of honor."

"You have it. If we're able to catch him alive, we turn him over to the Morrígan and she will have her fun."

She paused, then in a rush. "There's a broken-down shack near the drop site where you found Ulstair's body. I know because Ulstair went hiking around the park a lot and he found it one day and told me about it, and showed me a picture he took. My guess is that's where Lucius hangs out. It's close enough to see the running trail through binoculars. He probably sits up there and pinpoints his targets. And if your notes are correct and he's looking for another kill right now, my guess is that's where he's at."

"We're on the way. If you insist on coming, wait in the parking lot for us. Don't try to go in on your own."

As I hung up, Yutani and Viktor were already clattering down the stairs. Herne and I followed, heading to our respective cars. I could only hope and pray that Raven wouldn't endanger herself out of her anger.

I WAS ACTUALLY glad I wasn't in the car with Herne as we drove across the bridge, heading toward UnderLake Park. I didn't want to listen to him bitch about Raven. Obviously, she shouldn't have done what she did, but I understood her motives.

Yutani was quiet as well, so I focused on looking out the window, hoping that we were on the right track. I hated to think that we might be on a wild goose chase, but Raven was intelligent, and I trusted her instincts.

Traffic was light and we arrived to find Raven leaning against her car. As we approached her, I could feel a crackle off of her like sparks off a sparkler. She was upset.

"I'm glad you waited for us," Herne said. "But I tell you now, if you ever steal information from my agency again, I'm dragging your ass in front of Cernunnos and setting him loose on you. Do you understand?" His voice was gruff, that no-nonsense tone which meant he was deadly serious.

She stared back at him, shoulders straight and chin raised. "Son of a god, I hear you. But you would do well to remember that I'm Ante-Fae, and I live by my own rules. That being said, I respect you and I respect your agency. And Ember and Angel are my friends, so I give you my word that I will never steal information from you again. But this monster destroyed my beloved, and others. The Ante-Fae take care of their own problems."

Herne relented a little. "I understand that you want revenge, but this man is psychotic. And far older than you. You may be Ante-Fae but you are young. Even to me you are young. You have powerful magic, Raven BoneTalker, but that does not mean that you can outwit Lucius. Now, if you wish to come with us, you are welcome. But you have to be ready and willing to handle yourself. Can you promise me this?"

She nodded. "I promise, as long as *you* promise that he will either go before the Morrígan or die. I will not leave him alive unless it's to go in front of the Morrígan."

"I think we can all agree on that," Herne said. "All right, since you know where this place is, do you feel comfortable taking the lead? Also, can you make it through the forest in a skirt?"

Raven was wearing a calf-length skirt with a pattern of autumn leaves spread across a field of black. She had on an olive tunic, belted at the waist with a black leather belt. A short capelet in mottled green encircled her shoulders, fastened with a bronze brooch of Celtic knotwork. She was wearing black leather granny boots, laced up the calf.

"I could travel this hill in stilettos, although I usually don't wear them. The Ante-Fae have many talents, and I was born to the earth and born to the woods." She moved to the front, giving me a gentle smile. "Angel told me what happened last night. We'll talk soon."

As we headed up the embankment, I wondered if Lucius had been in the shack before, if he had seen Viktor and me find the bodies. Obviously, he had to know that the police had been there and taken them away, but whether he would alter his

MO because of that was questionable. If he was far enough gone, he might still be tracing his same old routes.

The forest around us was still, the only sounds those of rain dripping from the trees after an early morning storm. The faint sound of insects still trailed in the breeze that gusted past, ruffling the leaves as it sent stragglers into a whirling dance.

We were all quiet. A world of thoughts was running through my head. It was easier dealing with someone who wasn't psychotic because they were more predictable. But Lucius was a loose cannon, already on edge before he ever had been replaced in the priesthood. Now, I suspected he was a raving lunatic.

Raven swung to the right, off the path that Viktor and I had originally taken. We made our way through the undergrowth along the side of the ravine, slipsliding on the wet leaves and detritus that littered the ground. Ten more minutes, and we were headed up the slope again, at a right angle. The hush in the forest seemed to grow stronger, and I found myself breathing shallowly, expecting at any moment for something to jump out from behind the bushes to attack us.

Raven suddenly stopped, and pointed through a thicket of fir trees. "There," she said softly. "Do you see?"

I squinted, shading my eyes and then I saw what she was talking about. There was a lean-to resting against the side of the slope, the roof covered with leaves. It would have been hard to make out if you were just casually scanning the area. But as

I squinted, looking closer, I could see a door on the side, which was closed. There was also a perch on the top of the roof's slope. I had no doubt that from there, Lucius could see through the trees to the Beach Trail.

Herne crouched down, staring at the ground. "Somebody's been through this path today. There are footsteps leading to the shack and they're fresh." He looked up, staring at the lean-to. "He's in there, the trees are telling me that he's there. They don't like him and they don't want him around."

Remembering what Herne had been able to do during our fight with Blackthorn, I looked at him. "Can you send some vines in to catch hold of him?"

He shook his head. "A pity, but no. For one thing, we don't have enough brambles near enough the shack for me to command them. For another thing, we don't know if he's got a victim with him. If he's already captured someone, I could inadvertently hurt them."

He glanced around the clearing that surrounded the lean-to. It wasn't a true clearing—there were still trees and bushes around—but they had been cut back.

"I don't like the feeling that I'm getting," Raven said. "As much as I want to go break in the door, something tells me it's not a good idea."

At that moment, the door to the shack opened.

I stiffened, my shoulders clenching as I grasped the hilt of my dagger. Herne brought up his crossbow, aiming it directly at the door. The others readied their weapons. As we waited, someone tossed a stone out through the opening, then slammed the door again. I frowned, cocking my head, as I stared at the glowing stone. It was gray, yet it seemed to be somewhat translucent.

The next moment, Herne yelled, "Get ready! I know what that is!"

But before he could say more, the gem exploded in a cloud of smoke. The smoke filtered through the area, making me cough, but the explosion produced no fire. Instead, a figure shimmered into view, at least ten feet tall and massively built. It looked like a man made out of rocks.

"Earth elemental," Herne said. "They're freaking powerful. Edged weapons won't work against them and neither will piercing weaponry." He quickly holstered his pistol crossbow, and pushed me to the side. "You and Raven get back. You can't fight this with your dagger, and you don't have the strength to face it."

Viktor wrestled a branch off of a tree trunk. He held it like a club, cautiously waiting as the earth elemental began to move toward us.

Yutani darted around to the side, stripping off his clothes as he ran, changing into his coyote form and vanishing into the undergrowth. I wasn't sure what he was doing, but he obviously had some plan.

I searched for any water elementals, any stream nearby from which I could summon help, but though I could feel the water in the ground and on the trees, there were no water elementals close enough to do any good.

Raven knelt, quickly brushing a patch of ground

clear so that she could see the dirt below. She began to draw symbols in the dirt, whispering under her breath. I wanted to ask what she was doing but didn't want to interrupt her. I watched, trying to guard her, as she pulled a small bag out of her pocket and spilled out a handful of what looked like bones. They actually made me think of vertebrae, but they were tiny, and I realized they weren't from a person. But she planted them in the ground, lining the runes with them.

Viktor raced in, slamming the branch against the side of the earth elemental. He was big enough and heavy enough so that he made an impact, causing the elemental to sway, but the creature lashed out at him, landing a blow to the side of Viktor's head and knocking him to the ground. Viktor rolled out of the way to avoid being trampled.

Herne was over at the base of a small tree whispering to it. I wasn't sure what he was saying, but I tried to keep my focus on Raven, not sure what to do when the elemental headed our way. Raven finished placing the bones on the runes, and she stepped back, motioning for me to move out of the way.

Flesh and bone and bone and flesh, powers rise and powers mesh.

Fight to rise and rise to fight, protect us now with all your might!

With a wave of the hand over the bones, Raven stepped back as a very tall, very large skeleton rose out of the runes. He was easily the height of the earth elemental. He moved forward, lurching toward the elemental.

They clashed, grappling one another. The bones were magically enchanted just like the rocks of the elemental, and they held together even though the elemental tried to break one of the arm bones. The two behemoths locked in combat.

Herne shouted something and I turned to see he was pointing toward the elemental. The tree he had been whispering to was about fifteen feet tall, a slender maple, but it looked like it had beefed up a little. Now, it began to pull itself along the ground, great roots yanking out of the earth, screaming as they pulled free from the soil. The tree lunged forward, its massive trunk splitting into two to form legs. As its branches waved, a low humming filled the air. The humming made me uneasy and I realized it was coming from the tree. It was the sound of anger.

The tree joined the fight, and together with the skeleton, beat back the earth elemental.

At that moment I spied the gem from which the earth elemental had come. It was still lying on the ground, still glowing, and I had a sudden thought.

I darted forward, leaving Raven to fend for herself, and dashed around the edges of the three-way fight. Skidding to my knees, I grabbed the stone. It resonated in my hand. Looking around wildly, I tried to find two larger stones. I caught sight of one beneath one of the fir trees and carried the gem over to it. I set the gem down on it and looked around, trying to find something with which to smash it. Herne happened to be looking my way and I motioned for him to hurry over. He darted around the edges of the conflict, joining me.

"Smash the gem. It will destroy the elemental. I'm sure of it."

He nodded, and a moment later shifted into his silver stag form. He nudged me out of the way, and I stood back as he reared up and brought his front hooves, flaming silver, down against the gem. It cracked, shattering, and as it shattered the earth elemental let out a roar and began to waver. Herne smashed the pieces again, and the elemental began to crumble into dust. The skeleton and tree stopped in their tracks, waiting for orders. Herne turned back into his human form and stared at the broken gem.

"Herne!" The call came from the lean-to.

We all turned to see Lucius standing there, holding onto a leash that he had attached to Yutani. There was a saddlebag across Yutani's back, and I recognized what looked to be plastic explosives taped along the side of the bag.

"Back off, or I push the button and your friend goes sky high." Lucius held up the phone. Herne motioned for us to edge back, and he whispered to the tree and it settled back into its spot and fell asleep again. Raven scattered the runes and the skeleton vanished. We waited, watching as Lucius dragged Yutani away from the shack and tied the leash around a nearby tree.

"I'm going to leave, and you're going to stay here and not follow me. It will take you at least twenty minutes to disarm the explosives, and I have my phone. If I even *suspect* you're on my tail, I'll press the button and the coyote shifter gets it."

Herne raised his hands, nodding. "We hear you."

"You are to wait five minutes before you even begin to move toward your companion." Lucius began to make his way up the ravine.

I couldn't believe we were just letting him go. But if we tried to stop him, he'd blow Yutani up and quite possibly, the rest of us.

My anger swelled, and I could feel the forest responding to me. The birds were starting to grow agitated and I glanced up to see a massive number of crows perched in the trees around the lean-to. But they didn't look like they were targeting us. Instead, I felt a strange affinity with them, and the crow necklace I was wearing began to pulse. It was warm against my throat and I could feel Morgana whispering in my ear. I strained to listen, and realized Cernunnos was there as well. I wasn't sure what they were saying, but I could sense that they were giving me instructions. I dropped my head back as I lowered myself into a trance. Deep within, both the Leannan Sidhe and the Autumn Stalker sides of my nature reared up, watching closely.

Choose your eyes in the forest...

The words echoed in my head, and I wasn't sure who said them but I thought it might be Cernunnos. I didn't know what he meant, but as I glanced around a large crow caught my eye. Crows and ravens were intertwined in their magic. The crow stared at me, its eyes glittering, and I suddenly understood what Cernunnos intended.

I looked at the crow and whispered, "I choose you," and it flew up out of the tree, winging its way up toward the top of the ravine.

I was suddenly seeing through the crow's eyes as it flew, following Lucius. I could see the glint of his phone in his hands, and I felt the crow covet the sparkling object. With a gasp, I realized there *was* something I could do.

Grab his phone...

The moment the words formed in my head the crow spiraled down, flapping its wings in his face. As he jerked back, Lucius dropped his phone and the crow snatched it up and flew away, heading back toward me.

Herne and Viktor raced toward Yutani as the crow flew overhead, spiraling down to drop the phone at my feet. I cautiously picked it up, staring at the app that was open. I wasn't sure how to work it, but as long as I held that phone in my hand, Yutani would be safe.

"He's coming back," Raven said, pointing toward Lucius, who had turned to race back down the ravine.

Herne and Viktor worked frantically, stripping the vest off of Yutani. I glanced at the timer on the app and saw that it had started to move again. Damn it! How was Lucius doing that?

"Get rid of that vest! The app is still functioning and it seems to be counting down."

As I yelled at Herne, he hurled the vest at the lean-to. Then, with Viktor and Yutani on his heels he barreled toward Raven and me.

"Run!"

Raven and I turned and started to race down the path. It was tricky, and the vines and undergrowth were hard to navigate, but we flew as fast as we could.

Something goading me, I suddenly turned, just in time to see Lucius reach the shack. I caught my breath, staring at him as he leaned over to pick up the vest. Beside me, Raven whirled and grabbed the phone out of my hand. Before I could stop her, she scanned the timer, and punched at a button.

The explosion rocked the park, sending a slide of debris down the hill. Luckily, we weren't in its path, but the force of the blast knocked us off our feet. I hugged the ground, hoping that there wouldn't be another landslide.

Herne was on his feet first and he grabbed my hand, yanking me up to his side. Viktor practically lifted Raven into his arms.

"We have to get out of here," Herne said.

I struggled to pull away from him. "Not before I summon some rain. There's a fire going like crazy over there and I can't leave it." I reached out into the air, trying to summon all the condensation and humidity that I could feel. I called again, focused on drenching the shack, and the already heavy skies suddenly cracked open, drenching us within seconds. The flames flickering on the lean-to began to sputter and die, and a few moments later, with the rain still pounding, the fire vanished into a wisp of smoke.

Panting, soaking wet, I leaned over, pressing my hands on my knees to try and catch my breath. I wasn't sure if I had caused the storm or if it had just been coincidence, but either way, at least the forest was safe.

Herne turned to Raven. "Why?"

She straightened her shoulders, ignoring the drenching rain. "He could have gotten away. He could have made it to safety. I promised I wouldn't do anything as long as we caught him, but we hadn't done that, had we? And he was in possession of the explosives again. I wonder where he got them in the first place."

"We may never know. But I'm pretty sure when we search his house, we'll find more. As well as more bodies." Herne let out a long sigh, shaking his head. "You're a bit of a loose cannon, Raven."

She shrugged. "Yes, but the job is done. Ulstair's death is avenged. And there won't be any more victims, at least from Lucius. One last psycho in the world to worry about." And with that, she turned and started walking back down the path, toward the parking lot.

Chapter 21

THE MORRÍGAN WAS none too happy when she found out that Lucius was dead, but she sent in her own people to search through his house. Apparently, it truly was a chamber of horrors. They found fifteen other bodies buried beneath the house, and parts of four more in the freezer. There was a debate raging whether he was using them to feed his birds or himself, but nobody really wanted to know. The Morrígan took the crows and ravens home, determined to free them from their enchantment.

We notified Saílle about Lucius and his activities, and she agreed to talk to the authorities and work something out with them to explain what had happened. I didn't want to admit it, but she did have a way of making things happen. She reminded me to cash the check before I lost it, and she also said she was sending me a few things from my grandfather's place. I started to tell her I didn't want them, but she hushed me up and said that I would change my mind when I saw them.

The next two days were a blur of paperwork as we wrapped up the case. By Friday afternoon, we were all exhausted, and I was looking forward to the weekend, which Herne had promised would be drama free.

Angel and I were sitting in the waiting room, waiting for the others, when Herne came out of his office followed by Raven. I blinked, wondering what *that* meeting had been about.

Raven wandered over, sitting on the sofa next to me. She crossed one leg over the other, and grinned at Herne, who stopped in front of us.

"Are you sure you won't change your mind? I'd rather have you where I can keep an eye on you. My father strongly suggested that it be a good idea if you take us up on our offer."

I glanced at Raven. "What offer? What's going on?"

Herne cleared his throat. "I offered Raven a position with the Wild Hunt. I think she'd make an excellent addition to our team, except she turned me down."

Angel and I immediately perked up.

"Oh take the job, please! We'd love to have you work here," I said.

"What she said!" Angel joined in.

But Raven shook her head. "I love hanging out with you guys. I enjoy your company and I'm grateful for all that you've done. But I don't play well with others. I run with scissors, I kick sand in people's faces, and there's a whole lot about me that you don't know."

Herne laughed. "My father seems to know quite a bit about you."

She glared at him. "I sincerely doubt whether he's told you half of what he found out. Anyway, again, thanks for the offer, but no thanks. However, maybe we can consult with each other on occasion. I've had times where I've needed an investigator, but didn't know who to call."

"Are you sure?" I asked, disappointed.

Raven shook her head, smiling. "Yeah, I'm sure. But as I said, I wouldn't mind some cross consultations at times. Meanwhile, why don't you and Angel come over to dinner Sunday night? I can invite Rafé as well." Her grin widened as Angel blushed. "He's really smitten with you, and that makes me happy. Rafé deserves someone in his life."

Angel and I agreed, then waved as Raven took off. Herne tapped me on the shoulder.

"Come here for a minute, please? It won't take long."

I followed him into his office, where he shut the door and then immediately pulled me into his arms, kissing me so deeply that I could barely catch my breath. The feel of his hands on my back made me shiver.

"I'm tired," he said. "But I needed to kiss you. Tomorrow will be my last day with Danielle before I sent her off to the island of the Amazons. But Sunday night, when I come home, will you come over and spend the night?"

I nodded. "Yes, I want that. I want you. I need

you." As he wrapped me in his arms again, I closed my eyes and let myself drift in the comfort and safety of his embrace.

We were standing there like that when someone tapped on the door. Talia's voice echoed from outside. "We're ready if you are!"

Herne kissed me again, then gently let me go and we joined the others in the waiting room. Angel was holding a box.

"While you were in there, someone dropped this off. It's from Saílle. It's for you."

I sat down beside her. Taking the box, I gently lifted the lid. Inside were three items. One was a picture of my father when he was young. I held it, looking into those youthful eyes, wondering if he knew even back then how his life would turn out.

I slowly replaced it in the box and picked up the second item. It was a ring box, and I opened it to find an absolutely stunning sapphire ring. A note attached to the box said that it had been my grandmother's, and she had asked that it be sent to me after her death, but that Farthing hadn't obeyed her wishes. I stared at it for a moment, wondering why she wanted me to have it. But as I lifted it out of the box all I could feel was warmth and contentment.

The third item was a beautiful dagger, which looked a lot like the one tattooed on my arm. Each one of us who belonged to the Wild Hunt Agency had the tattoo of a dagger on our left forearm, surrounded by vines. As I held the dagger, there was something familiar about it, but I couldn't put my finger on it. It wasn't the one my grandfather had waved at me, I knew that much.

"Does anyone know what this is?" I asked holding it up. "And don't say a dagger."

They all laughed, but Herne was the one who answered.

"Yes, I know that style of blade. It's a dagger from the Autumn's Bane. It probably belonged to one of your grandfather's ancestors. Hold off on using it until we can tell if it's cursed or magical."

I slowly replaced the blade in the sheath and put it back in the box, then closed the lid. Saílle was right. Even though I had wanted nothing to do with my grandfather, these items meant a great deal to me and I wasn't even sure why.

As we headed out into the night, I thought about how much everyone in the Wild Hunt had come to mean to me. They were my family. For so long I had only had Angel, and before that only Angel and my parents. But now I had brothers and sisters, as well as a lover. As Angel and I fastened our seat belts and she pulled out from the parking garage, I set the box on my lap.

Sometimes family meant genetic ties. And sometimes family came from the heart rather than from the blood. But always, I felt that true family should mean love and loyalty.

We rode in silence. As we arrived home and I stepped out of the car, there was a crow perched on the fence post, watching me. I wasn't sure if it was the same one I had met in the forest, but it looked familiar.

In less than six weeks I would enter the Cruharach and come through the other side, hopefully transformed and safe. I wasn't sure who I was becoming, but I knew that wherever the road led me, and whatever transformations awaited, I was ready to meet them.

And I wouldn't meet them alone. I would have Angel and Herne by my side, and Marilee, and Morgana and Cernunnos waiting to help me. I'd have Yutani and Viktor and Talia...and Raven. Yes, whatever happened, I had allies whom I could rely on.

As we entered the house and flipped on the lights, Mr. Rumblebutt came running up to leap in my arms. I buried my face in his fur as he started to purr, and whispered, "It's good to be home." And I meant every word.

If you enjoyed this book and haven't read the first three, check out THE SILVER STAG, OAK & THORNS, and IRON BONES. Book 5—THE HALLOWED HUNT—will be within a couple of months and plenty more to come after that.

Meanwhile, I invite you to visit Fury's world. Bound to Hecate, Fury is a minor goddess, taking care of the Abominations who come off the World Tree. Books 1–5 are available now in the Fury Unbound Series: FURY RISING, FURY'S MAGIC, FURY AWAKENED, FURY CALLING, and FURY'S MANTLE.

For a dark, gritty, steamy series, try my world of the Indigo Court, where the long winter has come, and the Vampiric Fae are on the rise. NIGHT MYST, NIGHT

VEIL, NIGHT SEEKER, NIGHT VISION, NIGHT'S END, and NIGHT SHIVERS are all available now.

If you prefer a lighter-hearted paranormal romance, meet the wild and magical residents of Bedlam in my Bewitching Bedlam Series. Fun-loving witch Maddy Gallowglass, her smoking-hot vampire lover Aegis, and their crazed cjinn Bubba (part djinn, all cat) rock it out in Bedlam, a magical town on a magical island. BLOOD MUSIC, BEWITCHING BEDLAM, MAUDLIN'S MAYHEM, SIREN'S SONG, WITCHES WILD, CASTING CURSES, BLOOD VENGEANCE, TIGER TAILS, and Bubba's origin story—THE WISH FACTOR—are available.

If you like cozies with an edge, try my Chintz 'n China paranormal mysteries. The series is complete with: GHOST OF A CHANCE, LEGEND OF THE JADE DRAGON, MURDER UNDER A MYSTIC MOON, A HARVEST OF BONES, ONE HEX OF A WEDDING, and a wrap-up novella: HOLIDAY SPIRITS.

The newest Otherworld book—HARVEST SONG—is available now, and the final book in the series, BLOOD BONDS, will be available in April 2019.

For all of my work, both published and upcoming releases, see the Bibliography at the end of this book, or check out my website at Galenorn.com and be sure to sign up for my newsletter to receive news about all my new releases.

Cast of Characters

THE WILD HUNT & FAMILY

Angel Jackson: Ember's best friend, a human empath, Angel is the newest member of the Wild Hunt. A whiz in both the office and the kitchen, and loyal to the core, Angel is an integral part of Ember's life, and a vital member of the team.

Charlie Darren: A vampire who was turned at 19. Math major, baker, and all-around gofer.

Ember Kearney: Caught between the world of Light and Dark Fae, and pledged to Morgana, goddess of the Fae and the Sea, Ember Kearney was born with the mark of the Silver Stag. Rejected by both her bloodlines, she now works for the Wild Hunt as an investigator.

Herne the Hunter: Herne is the son of the Lord of the Hunt, Cernunnos, and Morgana, goddess of the Fae and the Sea. A demigod—given his mother's mortal beginnings—he's a lusty, protective god and one hell of a good boss. Owner of the Wild Hunt Agency, he helps keep the squabbles between the world of Light and Dark Fae from spilling over into the mortal realms.

Talia: A harpy who long ago lost her powers, Talia is a top-notch researcher for the agency, and a longtime friend of Herne's.

Viktor: Viktor is half-ogre, half-human. Rejected by his father's people (the ogres), he came to work for Herne some decades back.

Yutani: A coyote shifter who is dogged by the Great Coyote, Yutani was driven out of his village over two hundred years before. He walks in the shadow of the trickster, and is the IT specialist for the company.

THE GODS, THE ELEMENTAL SPIRITS, & THEIR COURTS

Cerridwen: Goddess of the Cauldron of Rebirth. Dark harvest mother goddess.

Cernunnos: Lord of the Hunt, god of the Forest and King Stag of the Woods. Together with Morgana, Cernunnos originated the Wild Hunt and negotiated the covenant treaty with both the Light and the Dark Fae. Herne's father.

Coyote (also: Great Coyote): Native American trickster spirit/god.

Danu: Mother of the Pantheon. Leader of the Tuatha de Danann.

Ferosyn: Chief healer in Cernunnos's Court

Herne: (see The Wild Hunt)

Kuippana (also: Kipa): Lord of the Wolves. Elemental forest spirit; Herne's distant cousin. Trickster.

Morgana: Goddess of the Fae and the Sea, she was originally human but Cernunnos lifted her to deityhood. She agreed to watch over the Fae who did not return across the Great Sea. Torn by her loyalty to her people, and her loyalty to Cernunnos, she at times finds herself conflicted about the Wild Hunt. Herne's mother.

The Morrígan: Goddess of Death and Phantoms. Goddess of the battlefield.

THE FAE COURTS

Navane: The court of the Light Fae, both across the Great Sea and on the eastside of Seattle, the latter ruled by Névé.

TirNaNog: The court of the Dark Fae, both across the Great Sea and on the eastside of Seattle, the latter ruled by Saílle.

THE ANTE-FAE

Creatures predating the Fae. The wellspring from which all Fae descended. Unique beings who rule their own realms. All Ante-Fae are dangerous, but some are more deadly than others.

Blackthorn, the King of Thorns: Ruler of the blackthorn trees and all thorn-bearing plants. Cunning and wily, he feeds on pain and desire.

Raven, the Daughter of Bones: (also: Raven BoneTalker) A bone witch, Raven is young, as far as the Ante-Fae go, and she works with the dead. She's also a fortune teller, and a necromancer.

Straff: Blackthorn's son, who suffers from a wasting disease requiring him to feed off others' life energies and blood.

THE FORCE MAJEURE

A group of legendary magicians, sorcerers, and witches. They are not human, but magic born. There are twenty-one at any given time and the only way into the group is to be hand chosen, and the only exit from the group is death.

Merlin: Morgana's father. Magician of ancient Celtic fame.

Taliesin: The first Celtic bard. Son of Cerridwen, originally a servant who underwent magical transformation and finally was reborn through Cerridwen as the first bard.

Ranna: Powerful sorceress. Elatha's mistress.

Rasputin: The Russian sorcerer and mystic.

Väinämöinen: The most famous Finnish bard.

FRIENDS, FAMILY, & ENEMIES

Aoife: A priestess of Morgana who guards the Seattle portal to the goddess's realm.

Celia: Yutani's aunt.

Danielle: Herne's daughter, born to an Amazon named Myrna.

DJ Jackson: Angel's little stepbrother, DJ is half Wulfine—wolf shifter. He now lives with a foster family for his own protection.

Erica: A Dark Fae police officer, friend of Viktor's.

Elatha: Fomorian King; enemy of the Fae race.

Marilee: A priestess of Morgana, Ember's mentor. Possibly Human—unknown.

Myrna: An Amazon who had a fling with Herne

many years back, which resulted in their daughter
Danielle.

Playlist

I often write to music, and A SHADOW OF CROWS was no exception. Here's the playlist I used for this book.

AJ Roach: Devil May Dance
Air: Napalm Love; Playground Love
Android Lust: Here and Now; Saint Over
Arch Leaves: Nowhere to Go
AWOLnation: Sail
Band of Skulls: I Know What I Am
The Black Angels: Currency; Half Believing; Comanche Moon; Hunt Me Down; Grab as Much (As You Can); I Dreamt; Death March; Holland; Young Men Dead
Black Mountain: Queens Will Play
Black Rebel Motorcycle Club: Feel It Now; Fault Line
Broken Bells: The Ghost Inside
Camouflage Nights: (It Could Be) Love
Chester Bennington: System
Clannad: Newgrange
Cobra Verde: Play with Fire
Colin Foulke: Emergence
Crazy Town: Butterfly
Creedence Clearwater Revival: Green River; Run Through the Jungle; Born on the Bayou; Susie-Q

Damh the Bard: Spirit of Albion; Land, Sky and Sea; The Cauldron Born; Obsession; Cloak of Feathers; Morrígan; The Wicker Man

Dead Can Dance: Yulunga; Indus

Deftones: Change (In the House of Flies)

Dizzi: Dizzi Jig; Dance of the Unicorns

Eastern Sun: Beautiful Being (Original Edit)

Eivør: Trøllbundin

Faun: Hymn to Pan

FC Kahuna: Hayling

Gabrielle Roth: The Calling; Raven; Mother Night; Rest Your Tears Here

Gary Numan: Ghost Nation; My Name is Ruin; The Angel Wars; Hybrid; Petals; I Am Dust

The Gospel Whiskey Runners: Muddy Waters

Gypsy Soul: Who?

The Hang Drum Project: Sukram; Shaken Oak; St.Chartier

Jay Gordon: Slept So Long

John Fogerty: The Old Man Down the Road

The Kills: Nail in My Coffin; You Don't Own The Road; Dead Road 7

King Black Acid: Rolling Under

Led Zeppelin: Ramble On

Lorde: Yellow Flicker Beat; Royals

Low with Tom and Andy: Half Light

Marconi Union: First Light; Alone Together; Flying (In Crimson Skies); Time Lapse; On Reflection; Broken Colours; We Travel; Weightless; Weightless, Pt. 2; Weightless, Pt. 3; Weightless, Pt. 4; Weightless, Pt. 5; Weightless, Pt. 6

Nirvana: You Know You're Right; Come As You

Are; Lake of Fire; Something in the Way; Heart Shaped Box; Plateau

The Notwist: Hands on Us

Orgy: Social Enemies; Blue Monday

A Pale Horse Named Death: Meet the Wolf

S. J. Tucker: Hymn to Herne

Saliva: Ladies and Gentlemen

Seether: Remedy

Sharon Knight: Ravaged Ruins; Bewitched; 13 Knots; Let the Waters Rise; Star of the Sea; Siren Moon

Shriekback: Over the Wire; Night Town; Dust and a Shadow; Underwaterboys; This Big Hush; Now These Days Are Gone; The King in the Tree; And the Rain; Shovelheads; Wriggle and Drone

Spiral Dance: Boys of Bedlam; Burning Times; Rise Up

Stellamara: Aman Doktor; Seven Valleys; Firtina

Toadies: Possum Kingdom

Tom Petty: Mary Jane's Last Dance

Tori Amos: Caught a Lite Sneeze; Blood Roses; Mohammad My Friend

Traffic: Rainmaker; The Low Spark of High Heeled Boys

Tuatha Dea: The Landing/Tuatha De Danaan; Wisp of A Thing (Part 1); The Hum and the Shiver; Long Black Curl

Wayne Static: Not Meant For Me

Wendy Rule: Let the Wind Blow; Elemental Chant; The Circle Song

Woodland: Blood of the Moon; The Grove; Witch's Cross; First Melt; The Dragon; Secrets Told

Zero 7: In the Waiting Line

Biography

New York Times, *Publishers Weekly*, and *USA Today* bestselling author Yasmine Galenorn writes urban fantasy and paranormal romance, and is the author of over sixty books, including the Wild Hunt Series, the Fury Unbound Series, the Bewitching Bedlam Series, the Indigo Court Series, and the Otherworld Series, among others. She's also written nonfiction metaphysical books. She is the 2011 Career Achievement Award Winner in Urban Fantasy, given by RT Magazine. Yasmine has been in the Craft since 1980, is a shamanic witch and High Priestess. She describes her life as a blend of teacups and tattoos. She lives in Kirkland, WA, with her husband Samwise and their cats. Yasmine can be reached via her website at Galenorn.com.

Indie Releases Currently Available:

The Wild Hunt Series:
The Silver Stag
Oak & Thorns
Iron Bones
A Shadow of Crows
The Hallowed Hunt

Bewitching Bedlam Series:
Bewitching Bedlam
Maudlin's Mayhem

Siren's Song
Witches Wild
Casting Curses
Blood Music
Blood Vengeance
Tiger Tails
The Wish Factor

Fury Unbound Series:
Fury Rising
Fury's Magic
Fury Awakened
Fury Calling
Fury's Mantle

Indigo Court Series:
Night Myst
Night Veil
Night Seeker
Night Vision
Night's End
Night Shivers

Otherworld Series:
Moon Shimmers
Harvest Song
Earthbound
Knight Magic
Otherworld Tales: Volume One
Tales From Otherworld: Collection One
Men of Otherworld: Collection One
Men of Otherworld: Collection Two
Moon Swept: Otherworld Tales of First Love
For the rest of the Otherworld Series, see Website

Chintz 'n China Series:
Ghost of a Chance
Legend of the Jade Dragon
Murder Under a Mystic Moon
A Harvest of Bones
One Hex of a Wedding
Holiday Spirits

Bath and Body Series (originally under the name India Ink):
Scent to Her Grave
A Blush With Death
Glossed and Found

Misc. Short Stories/Anthologies:
The Longest Night: A Starwood Novella
Mist and Shadows: Short Tales From Dark Haunts
Once Upon a Kiss (short story: Princess Charming)
Once Upon a Curse (short story: Bones)

Magickal Nonfiction:
Embracing the Moon
Tarot Journeys

For all other series, as well as upcoming work, see Website

CPSIA information can be obtained
at www.ICGtesting.com
Printed in the USA
LVHW041550270619
622553LV00004B/580